AN ACT OF VENGEANCE

A.J. MCCONNELL

PART ONE

The Killing

CHAPTER 1

"Jesus, that was close." Sergeant Dave Edwards shouted to himself.

The mortar had exploded only ten feet from the position 4 Platoon had taken behind an old, badly constructed stone and mud wall. Not much protection but it was the best they could find under the circumstances. A barrage of bullets followed, ricocheting off the ground with the familiar whizzing only a soldier would recognize before silence descended once more. The enemy moved and jostled for position in readiness to launch another salvo once they were more confident about hitting their targets. They had the upper hand. The ability to run away and merge into the crowd of civilians was a tactic widely used and one which the coalition forces had no defense against.

"Where in Christ's name is it coming from?" Was the shout over the radio.

"I'm not too sure Sarge," came the reply, "but I would guess they're holed up to the right of the cattle shed."

The cattle shed in question was a dilapidated shack that looked like it hadn't housed any kind of animal for about thirty years. It was no more than a ramshackle lean-to but it was enough to give one or two of the enemy enough cover to get off a couple of rounds before retreating to town and mingling into the crowd, never to be seen again; or at least not until the next time. The silence continued. What seemed like an eternity passed but was no more than two or three minutes. A lifetime when you're under fire. 'Now is the time' Dave thought to himself. Just have a quick look.

Sgt. Dave Edwards was an excellent soldier. He had been a boy entrant, always wanting to be in uniform and in the Kings Regiment, his local Infantry unit. He excelled at everything he put his mind to, not only a good fighter but also a good leader to his lads. He was twenty-nine and only ten years older than the youngest member of the team but he had a wise head on young shoulders. A staunch believer in 'don't ask others to do what you are not prepared to do yourself' he was always the first in and the last out in any contact situation. This time was no exception. As he prepared to peek around the corner of the wall, he noticed his Platoon Commander, Nolan, give a slight nod in his general direction. Dave took this as a message of 'All Clear.' As he looked at Nolan one last time he seemed to look away at the last moment as if he was trying to hide his eyes away from what was about to happen next. Dave peered around the corner and could see movement up ahead in the area they thought the rounds and mortars had been coming from. He balanced tentatively on his haunches and readied himself for another look. Suddenly he felt a firm push at the base of his back. It all happened in slow motion. His Corporal, Squires, had slipped and fallen into Dave and, as he fell from behind his only source of protection, a single shot rang out from the sniper rifle some 200 meters across the sandy no-man's land.

The shot hit Dave square in the chest with such intensity that parts of his body armor had been forced into the cavity. His body slumped backwards onto the ground as if someone had just turned off the switch that controlled his limbs. He was exposed. The shooter would take another shot at his unmoving torso if given the opportunity but Dave's team behind him quickly gathered their thoughts and emotions and pulled him back behind the wall.

"MEDIC... where's the medic... MEDIC!?" Screamed one of the platoon.

Scrambling along the line, racing as fast as he could Andy Trotter raced towards his fallen friend. An incredibly capable medic, Andy was a Royal Medical Corps member attached to the Kings, and the platoon were glad they had him. He was known as Rodders to his mates after the hapless character from 'Only Fools and Horses', despite being one of the most switched-on people ever to grace the ranks of 4 Platoon. He was as steady as the rock of Gibraltar and incredibly calm under pressure. He arrived, out of breath but unwavering. He quickly moved Dave onto his side to inspect the damage to his back. There was no exit wound meaning the round was still lodged inside Dave's body along with any other crap blown into him by the sniper round.

Rodders gave orders with pinpoint accuracy. "Get on the radio now. Call the camp and tell them we need a CASEVAC asap. One down, gunshot wound to chest." As he barked out the orders Dave could see and hear him through pinhole eyes and muffled ears. He blinked and noticed the view go ever so slightly pink. The more he blinked the deeper the shade of pink became, before it turned red and then he couldn't see anything from the blood that filled his eyes. He could feel pain and knew his shallow breaths were mostly dust and sand but none of that mattered right now. The warm air that filled his perforated chest was eerily pleasing and made him want to close his eyes and sleep, but Rodders wouldn't allow that to happen.

"Dave... Dave, come on mate stay with me. C'mon son, stay with me." Rodders spoke calmly but inside his brain was working overtime to assess the situation and administer what life saving treatment he could as his friend lay dying in front of him. "Don't you dare die on me you dick. Danny, get me another field dressing and hold it there as hard as you can." Rodders instructed one of the younger guys from the platoon who stared, scared at the sight of a man dying in front of him for the first time. "DANNY!" Shouted Rodders. The kid snapped out of it, so Rodders' tone became softer and more sympathetic. "Get me another dressing mate and hold it there as tight as you can. Can you do that Danny?"

"Yes Corporal," Danny sprang into action, albeit ten seconds late. Rodders worked quickly in an attempt to stabilize the Sergeant, running in an IV line as soon as he could find a suitable vein. In the background Dave could hear the relentless cracks of rounds going off as the platoon suppressed fire without a clear indication of who and where they were aiming at.

Dave listened to the melee going on around him and in his mind, he knew he had been hit: badly. The blood started to fill his lungs and breathing became difficult. He slightly tugged at Rodders' jacket and tried to speak. At first Rodders ignored the pulling of his uniform, busy with the matters at hand but Dave gathered his strength and pulled harder. As Rodders leaned towards his mate he could smell the sweet sticky blood on his breath as he uttered the words, "Jenny... tell Jenny ... I..." At that moment a spurt of red spewed from Dave's mouth and covered Rodders' face. Unfazed he drew closer to Dave who whispered quietly. "Tell her I love her." Rodders looked at him and steely faced answered.

"I will mate, don't worry. Though you can tell her yourself when we get home."

Dave looked at him and gave a wry smile as if to say, 'You lying bastard.'

Rodders frantically tried to stem the blood from the hole in Dave's body, but it kept coming, unstoppable, no matter how much pressure they placed on the gaping wound. Rivulets started appearing everywhere and even Rodders didn't know where it was all coming from. Pools started forming in the red sand around them. *This isn't like the movies*, thought Danny, the young soldier tasked with helping Rodders. Bruce Willis and Stallone get shot and wrap a dirty old rag around it and march on bravely to save the day. What Danny saw was carnage. The damage was unbearable to look at. A hole blown into the front of his Sergeant and bits of flesh that Danny didn't recognize scattered around them. Danny was overwhelmed and turned around on his knees and threw up into the bloodied dust behind him. On another day, Rodders would have sympathized with the young lad. After all, it was the same reaction he had in the same situation a couple of years before. But today every second counted.

"Get a grip on your shit son. Hand me those scissors and stay switched on." That was Danny's initiation into the horror of war and the duty of the Combat Medic.

"Where's the chopper!?" Rodders yelled above orders being shouted and men still attempting to find the shooter. Everything seemed to stretch out for hours although no more than fifteen minutes had passed since the incident. In the distance the familiar sound of the Chinook rumbled in the sky as the MEDEVAC team arrived to take Dave and the rest of the team back to base.

As the giant helicopter landed, it stirred up a whirling tornado of hot sand and dust which was almost impossible to see through. The noise and the heat were unbearable and the sun only just penetrated the cloud. Once the haze had settled and initial disorientation had passed, the outline of the aircraft became apparent. Only then did the group begin to move.

"Move, move, move!" Rodders shouted to the stretcher team who lifted Dave in near perfect time. "Get him on, c'mon move your arses." Rodders went straight to the CASEVAC Doctor and started to brief him on Dave's condition. Nods from the Doctor and medics gave Rodders satisfaction, he knew these guys were the best in the business and would do everything humanly possible in the fight to keep Dave alive.

As the team loaded the last man onto the chopper, Rodders stared out just as the Captain, the last man on the ground, was about to board and noticed something quite unusual. The Captain had given a sly but noticeable hand gesture. A clenched fist by his side followed by a flat hand, palm down in a no-go motion. Rodders squinted to see if he could see anyone around but there was nobody about.

As the chopper lifted and the dust was left below them, Rodders looked out of the back of the open ramp of the flying beast. In the area they were shooting towards he thought he could see one man with what appeared to be a rifle uncovering himself from some sandy camouflage. Rodders took a second to look away and back again just to clear his eyes. He could definitely see movement. He was certain it was a man with a gun. As the helicopter tipped forward slightly, the vision disappeared over the end of the ramp and the aircraft lurched forward.

Thoughts of Dave instantly re-entered Rodders mind and he turned and walked towards the medics treating him.

The Doctor looked at Rodders with an expression he dreaded. The stare and the gentle shake of the head to signal that Dave was not going to make it back alive. Disappointment filled him in an instant. Rodders went over and took Dave's hand, expecting a feeble grip but in a moment of perfect clarity Dave opened his eyes, looked at Rodders and pulled him towards his mouth. The words seemed to go on forever and Rodders wasn't too sure if what he was hearing was correct. He frowned and looked at Dave. To Rodders the world went quiet, like he was caught in time as he tried to grasp the gravity of what he was hearing. And then, within a split second he was back amid the roaring bedlam unfolding around him. Dave looked at him and one more time said the words that would stick with Rodders his entire life. He felt sick to the stomach at Dave's revelation but kept his nerve and showed no emotion. To show any reaction would put him in certain danger.

Dave's grip began to loosen and Rodders knew he was slipping under for the last time. As his hand went limp the CASEVAC Doctor who had been working on Dave the whole time took over in a last-ditch attempt to save his life. It was futile and Rodders knew it. Two minutes later, the mate he had known in life and in the heat of battle died right there in front of him on a gurney, in a chopper two thousand feet above the arid Afghani desert.

CHAPTER 2

No matter how long you're in the military you never, ever get over the death of a friend.

By the time the chopper landed in Bagram, Rodders was physically and emotionally drained. The sweat and blood from his friend had clogged and matted the hair on his head and face and was beginning to smell under the hot sun. No matter how many times he showered he would remember that smell, a reminder of his failure to save his Sergeant's life. 4 Platoon walked slowly away from the helicopter as the blades wound down and eventually came to a slow, whining stop. Once away from on the landing pad they slumped to the ground in exhaustion, rifles in hand, kit covered in desert sand.

Rodders sat slightly away from the main group, consumed by what Dave had said to him on his death bed. As he sat, dejected and worn out, the Platoon Commander made a beeline for him. Rodders wasn't in the mood for a pep talk but it was standard practice for the medic to report after any situation involving casualties. This one was different, and they both knew it. Nolan had lost his best NCO and Rodders had lost one of his best friends. Words were coming. Rodders knew he meant well but eyed him with caution as he approached.

"Corporal Trotter. Are you ok?" said Nolan, succinct and to the point.

"Yes Sir." Rodders answered, lying through his teeth. "I just need to get my head around this for a bit. Let it sink in, you know?"

"I do know Rodders," Nolan nodded. "I know exactly how you feel. A few years ago, I lost six guys in one contact. *Six.* What a kick in the bollocks that was I can tell you, but you know it's all part of the job, part of being a soldier. Nothing will make it better. I can almost guarantee you're wondering if you could have done something different, but you did everything you could. I know that. I saw you working on him. You did a great job so don't beat yourself up about it".

Rodders knew he was right. He didn't know Nolan that well; he had only been with the platoon for about eight or so months. Normally the Platoon Commander would be a Lieutenant and the Captain would be a Company Commander but due to losses, Nolan had been tasked with 4 platoon. Nobody knew where he came from. Some speculated he had been on an Intelligence tour for eighteen months or so, but it was only a rumor. The Kings was a big regiment and Rodders was sure over the coming months more information about him would filter through.

"I saw you chatting to him." Nolan looked at the ground and kicked the dirt with his right foot.

Rodders instantly switched on. He was looking away from Nolan when he said it and quickly composed himself before turning to face him.

"Yes sir. He asked me to tell Jenny, his wife, that he loved her." Rodders turned away again wondering what was coming next.

"Yes, but what was he *shouting* to you in the chopper Corporal?" Nolan's tone had changed and Rodders could feel the tension growing between them. The friendly chat had now turned into something more official. He was no longer 'Rodders', he was 'Corporal.'.

"What do you mean, Sir? I couldn't hear any shouting over the noise of the chopper." Rodders lied. "But if he was, I'm guessing he was just making sure I knew what to say to Jenny."

Nolan looked directly at Rodders, his face as straight as a die. "Are you sure Corporal? You looked like you were listening intently to something."

"No Sir. To be honest I can't remember, I had a lot going through my head at the time. I only remember him telling me about Jenny and me saying I would tell her he loved her. Like I say Sir, the noise just blocked everything out."

The boss looked at Rodders, trying to figure out if he was lying or telling the truth and after ten or so seconds, his expression softened and he backed down.

"I'm sorry Corporal." Nolan eased off. "I didn't mean to sound rude or abrupt. I'm only thinking that he may have said something to you that I might be able to use in a letter to his family. It's going to be tough. Sgt Edwards and I never really spoke much outside of military channels. I haven't been here long and it's been bloody hectic in that time. You knew him best, I understand he was one of your best mates, can you help me compile something to his wife?"

"Of course, Sir." Rodders knew the boss was talking bullshit. He could see it in his face.

"If you can remember anything he said to you, and I mean *anything*, let me know would you? It could be very helpful."

"I will Sir."

"Good man. Now listen, you've had it rougher than most today so clean your weapon and kit tomorrow and try to get a hot shower, some food, and a decent sleep before we get debriefed tomorrow, OK? Let's speak again in the morning and see if we can decipher what the Sgt was so intent on telling you earlier."

"Yes Sir, I'll speak to you tomorrow." Rodders said through gritted teeth.

Nolan wandered off towards the rest of the platoon, looking over his shoulder once to catch Rodders' eye one more time before stopping and chatting to five of the platoon who were huddled together in a tight group smoking. Their voices were hushed but Rodders knew they were talking about him. Two of them looked over briefly and in that exact moment Rodders has a sinking feeling.

He sat, staring at the ground for a minute or two, in a trance trying not to jump to any conclusions.

Rodders heaved himself up, picked up his weapon and kit and walked off in the direction of his accommodation: a large canvas tent he shared with seven other men. The flimsy wooden screen door was pushed open by Rodders' shoulder and quickly swung closed behind him with a dull slam. It was a depressing sight to behold. Eight military grade camp beds lined up, four on one side and the other four a mirror image on the other. Although the conditions were harsh and the desert blew in sand daily, the men were meticulous about tidiness and hygiene. The beds were made, some with sleeping bags and some with a single blanket. The desert may be hot during the day, but it can be intensely cold at night, sometimes with a light frost covering surfaces in the morning. In the center of the room was a wooden six-legged table splattered with stains from coffee and tea mugs being placed upon it. Beside each bed space stood a metal locker. This is where the men kept most of their uniform and next to that a footlocker for personal possessions and other pieces of military equipment.

As Rodders looked around the empty room he became heavy inside. He missed home. He missed his family and he missed Dave already. A hopelessness fell upon him as he slumped onto his bed and screamed at the top of his voice, "JESUS CHRIST!" A tear welled up in his eyes and he looked around just be certain he was alone. He lay on his back, stared at the canvas roof and cried, silently at first before sobbing with raw emotion. His shoulders rose and stooped as the anger, fear and adrenalin drained from his body. He stopped suddenly when he heard voices outside. As he wiped his cheeks dry, he turned over onto his side, closed his eyes and quickly drifted off to sleep.

He awoke suddenly with a start. He sat bolt upright, eyes wide and alert. The others were sitting talking quietly around the table when he sprung up from his sleep.

"Are you alright Rodders?" Deano was one of the room's more vocal occupants. "You look like crap mate, keep your head down for a while longer and get some more kip." Rodders looked at him for a second, his eyes adjusting to the light from the bulb hovering above their room.

"I'm ok Deano, thanks. I've slept too long as it is. What time is it, how long have I been out?"

"It's just before nine o'clock bud, you came into the tent at three, so you've been on your back for six hours. Not that you don't need it, you've had a horrendous day and you must be knackered. You sure you're ok?" Deano reiterated.

Rodders rubbed his face with his hands and then ran his fingers through his matted and dusty hair. "I'm fine Deano. I need a shower though. Is there any hot water left do you know?"

"None of us have been in yet mate so should be loads. You go, we'll get in after you."

"Cheers lads." Rodders picked up his towel, shower gel and razor and headed off towards the shower block.

The shower block was a modified twenty-foot steel shipping container, fitted out with sinks and mirrors for shaving. At least a proper, hot shower at the end of a long, hot day patrolling the surrounding area was on offer.

Rodders looked back at his reflection in the mirror. As Deano had kindly pointed out earlier, he did look like crap.

More than he had twenty-four hours earlier, that was for sure. The pores in his skin were blocked with fine powdery dust mixed with the sand. He had chapped lips from the sun and no matter how much Vaseline he put on, they would never stop cracking under the sheer heat of the day and the wind at night. His hair was longer than usual and looked like he had been dragged down the road behind a cart horse. His face sported a stubble of three days and as he looked closely, he spotted two short grey hairs on his chin amongst the brown and ginger poking through. *Christ*, he thought to himself. *I'm only 31.*

As he filled the sink up to shave, the mirror steamed over and he wiped away the condensation with his hand. He lifted his head to put some shaving foam to his face when Dave's words came into his head again.

"It was Nolan and Squires."

He gazed into the mirror and started scraping the stubble from his skin. "It was Nolan and Squires." He continued to shave but the words kept repeating in his head. He was totally oblivious to the fact he was pressing the razor so hard to his face it started to bleed from the pressure.

"Rodders!" Deano shouted from behind. "What are you doing mate? Look at yourself." Startled, Rodders looked at his reflection and saw blood gushing from a thin gash on his face. "Shit!"

"Finish up your shave and shower, we've got something for you, hurry up or it'll be gone." Deano said excitedly. Rodders knew what it was. The lads had been making spirits on the sly and it was ready to drink. He knew they were trying to make him feel better and although he really wasn't in the mood there wasn't any real way to avoid the situation in an eight-man room. He dragged out the shave and shower, hoping that it *was* gone by the time he got back to the room.

The lads had already made a dent in the bottles by the time he arrived back to the tent.

They were unusually quiet, partly because they didn't want to get caught but mostly because of in the events of the day. The mood was somber. Rodders sat at the table and took a shot glass, filled it with some strange looking alcoholic spirit and downed it in one. It burned his lips as it touched them and then his throat on the way down.

"Jesus Christ. What the hell is that?" He exclaimed.

"It's the good stuff." Replied Deano. "For the Sarge." They raised the glasses and toasted.

"The Sarge." They said quietly.

"To Dave." Said Rodders.

Davis, the youngest member of the group caught his eye whilst making the toast and Rodders assumed he had something to say. Instead he simply raised his glass, looked him straight in the eye and nodded his head in appreciation of the toast. Rodders stared at the floor momentarily and considered approaching the lad but decided it was not the time. What he had to say could wait.

About twenty minutes later the door flew open and Squires came into the tent. "I see it's ready then." He said, looking at the half empty bottles.

"Yes mate," Deano nodded. "It's ace as well. Here, have a shot." Rodders eyed Squires with quiet contempt but didn't openly show it.

"How are you holding up Rodders? Are you ok? I know you and the Sarge were mates and all," said Squires, not really caring.

"So, so Squires, you know how it is, you've been there and seen it all before," came Rodders reply.

"Aye, it's a pisser like, but it's the job eh?"

"Funnily enough, the boss said exactly the same thing earlier today", said Rodders with a sarcastic tone. It wasn't lost on Squires who flinched almost imperceptibly.

"Let's have a toast to the Sarge." Squires was trying to diffuse a potentially explosive situation. Rodders could sense there was something brewing and didn't want confrontation, at least not here and now.

"You're a bit late for that," said Rodders staring straight into Squires eyes. "Anyway, I need a pee. Line them up Deano, I'll be back in two shakes of a lamb's tail."

He rose from the table and took a deliberate step backward to feign being tipsy, before walking out of the door in the direction of the toilet block. Just before entering, he glanced behind him. There was no one to be seen so he quickly entered and went straight to a cubicle.

Once inside he locked the door, got onto his knees, and rammed his fingers down his throat to make himself vomit. He did so instantly. Not a lot, but the concoction he had been downing came out with force. He did this until he was satisfied he was ok to carry on drinking. He staggered back to the impromptu party and sat back down at the table.

Squires poured him another drink. This time it was a double, which Rodders put into his mouth and spat straight back out again on purpose. Rodders knew they wanted to get him drunk and find out what Dave said as he lay dying.

"Is that the same stuff?" He shouted.

"Of course, it is." Squires didn't realise that Rodders was wasting it on purpose but he couldn't risk them getting suspicious. *Think fast. Go on the offence,* he decided.

"Sorry, I wasted that," he said. "Let's have another." Some of the guys were oblivious to what Squires was up to but not all of them. Some enjoyed their drink while others watched as Rodders *appeared* to get drunk in front of them.

"Let's get another bottle." Squires' words were met with muffled cheers and giggles from the other blokes who were having nothing but a good time. They all nodded in agreement.

Rodders plan was working. In between the drinks he had to swallow to make his charade look genuine, he spilled, spat out and knocked over the rest. In reality he probably only consumed a couple of shots but gave the illusion he was well on his way to getting inebriated.

"Ah mate," said Squires, eventually making his move. "The Sarge was a good guy, wasn't he? Did he say anything before he passed away Rodders? He must have said something, poor bloke, knowing it was all going to end."

Rodders was seething inside at this low life. He knew what he was up to but wasn't too sure where it would lead. He played it calm.

"What do you mean?" He slurred, "did he say anything? Of course, he did, the poor bastard was dying wasn't he. He said he... erm... hang on. He said he wanted me to love his wife. No, that's wrong sorry. He wanted to say *he* loved his wife." The act was Oscar worthy but the performance wasn't over yet.

"Surely, he said more than that Rodders? The boss saw him shouting at you in the chopper. What was that all about?" Squires was pressing.

"What chopper? Oh, the one earlier, Jesus, I must be bladdered if I can't remember that. Er, he said he loved his wife and er..."

"We know that mate," Squires tone was getting impatient, "What else did he say?"

Rodders was alert and on his guard but still improvised his drunkenness. "Why? Why do you want to know?" Came the direct question.

Squires took a step back and thought for a second. "I'm just interested Rodders. He was my friend as well, I just thought it might be something to do with the lads, you know?"

Rodders hated him. Doing Nolan's dirty work and making it look like he was interested in the Sarge. He needed to keep his cool.

"I'll tell you what... he did actually say something else. He said, 'Tell Deano he still owes me 120 quid for the Play Station games I sold him.'"

Deano's head raised quickly as he looked around the room, first at Squires and then to Rodders.

"Shit," he said with a start. "I forgot about that, I did as well."

"I didn't want to say it to the boss because, to be honest I thought it was funny and just the kind of thing Dave would say just to get a final laugh. The boss might have taken it the wrong way, like I wasn't being serious. Thought he'd give me a bollocking so I lied and said he told me nothing. But God's truth that's what he said. Even when he was all shot up, he was trying to make me laugh."

The tent fell silent. They all looked at each other until a snort of amusement came from Squires and they all broke into fits of laughter.

"Jesus." Squires scoffed. "All that secrecy for that? Typical Sarge, eh?"

"You know what he was like," said Rodders. "He was always a wind-up merchant. He had the last laugh... as always. Right, I need to get to bed." Rodders stood up, wobbled, and walked the ten feet to his cot. He put on his sunglasses and loosely slid in some sponge ear plugs, sat upright and pretended to doze off.

Twenty minutes passed and as Rodders expected, Nolan walked into the tent and approached Squires. They whispered something to each other and then he heard Deano call out his name to check if he was sleeping. When Rodders didn't reply, he tip-toed over to see if he was awake and signaled back to the boss to confirm he was asleep and also wearing ear plugs. Once Deano had returned to his place by the table, Rodders slowly opened his eyes behind his dark sunglasses. He could see them quite clearly. The boss was whispering something to Squires and as he looked around the room one more time to check on Rodders he handed him a package wrapped in brown sellotape. Squires gave it to Deano who slipped it into an ammunition pouch and into the locker beside his bed. The boss gestured his head to the pair to follow him outside. As they did so, Rodders closed his eyes until they were clear of his space. They stood just outside the door and Rodders could hear the conversation better.

"Well?" Nolan asked.

"He knows nothing, Sir. Some rubbish about Deano owing him money, which incidentally he did. I wouldn't put it past him to say something like that to be honest. He was a funny guy who kept everyone's spirits up. Rodders would have told us, he's absolutely wasted and couldn't keep lying to us even if he tried his very best. I think he's telling the truth."

"Keep an eye on him anyway," said the Boss. "We can't have any more screw ups." He was edgy, especially as he was hanging around the enlisted men's quarters. That in itself would raise eyebrows. Officers tended not to mix with the plebs much, even in this modern army as the TV adverts liked to claim.

"Did anyone see you push him?" Nolan fired the question at Squires.

"No, if anyone did see anything it would have looked like a slip. Everyone thinks he fell over into sniper view. Were all clear on this one."

Rodders eyes opened wide when he heard the revelation. He clenched his fists but didn't move from his position. He thought about the weapon at the side of the bed but regretted the thought instantly. He shook inside. What was he hearing? The company commander and Corporal Squires had conspired to kill the Sarge. Why? How many others were involved? Deano was, that's for sure. Thoughts raced through his head that he couldn't control but he knew he had to so as to maintain his cover story of being drunk and incapacitated. The package. It must be something to do with the package.

"Keep it safe." Nolan instructed.. "I've spoken to the Leader. There's another load coming soon. This is only a taster of what we can do here so keep it tight and we will be laughing, OK?"

"OK Boss," said Squires.

"And keep an eye on that one. I still don't trust him, but I don't want more blood on my hands after today so make sure he's watched."

"Yes, Sir." Deano and Squires said in unison. With that Rodders could hear the boss walking away as the other two reentered the tent, back to sleep next to Rodders who no longer felt safe.

CHAPTER 3

Rodders endured a sleepless night. Tossing and turning in his cot trying to shake off the thoughts of last night and the repercussions it could have on him. He could see Dave's face clearly: blood-stained teeth and eyes filled with dread and fear. The grip he had on his hand felt real enough but even in a state of semi-consciousness he knew it wasn't really there. He could feel the heat on his neck and the sand on his skin. The whirling of the wind exacerbated by the whipping of the chopper rotors was playing tricks with his mind but still, he couldn't shut it out. Then, when he opened his eyes, it all stopped. Instantly.

He stared at the canvas roof of his makeshift home and sighed. He knew some serious stuff now and if they found out he knew, he too would be dead. He waited for ten minutes and saw that Squires and Deano were already awake and sitting at the table drinking tea out of a plastic mug. He had to formulate a plan and quick. He had an idea. It was simple but needed to be played out just right or he would be rumbled and in deep trouble. He sat up and spoke with a false, grainy voice.

"Alright boys. What the hell were we drinking last night, petrol? It was rotten. Did I throw up on anyone?"

"Can't you remember?" Chimed in Deano.

"The last thing I remember was having a laugh about some PlayStation games or something like that. Then I had a cup of tea.... Did I have a cup of tea, or have I just dreamt that? Anyway, I remember hearing Shiny Happy People by REM and then nothing after that. Am I close at least?"

"Yeah, that'll do. You're not far off but don't you remember getting your knob out and waving it around like a Light Sabre?" Squires was smirking.

"Christ, I didn't did I?" Rodders knew full well it was a wind up.

"Nah," said Deano. "You bailed out legless and went to sleep and that was it mate. Goodnight Vienna you lightweight." They all laughed but there was an edge in the air.

Rodders sat on the edge of his cot, rubbed the sleep from his eyes and decided to stand. He walked over and sat at the table and asked one of the boys to pour him a brew, he was a Corporal after all, and rank still had its privileges.

After the usual chit chat Squires announced to the room that there would be a debriefing at 09:00 in the Operations Room. An hour away, thought Rodders. Enough time to wash and get his story straight in his head for the barrage of questions he would get about the shooting of the Sarge the previous day.

The whole platoon was crammed into the Ops Room by 08:45 ready for debriefing. The usual whispers and laughs when they were all together occurred until 09:00 sharp when the main door to the room swung open and in marched Nolan with the Battalion Commanding Officer, Lieutenant Colonel Marsh. Accompanying both men was the Chaplain, Major Low, a well-respected man who was liked by everyone who knew him.

The company Sgt major gave a loud "ATTENTION," and everyone braced but did not leave their seats.

Captain Nolan spoke first, after the nod from the Colonel.

"Thank you, Sgt Major. At ease gentlemen. Gents, we all know why we are here so let's get on with it and get our heads around yesterday's tragic events where you all know, we lost a dear friend and excellent soldier, Sgt Edwards. His death is a great loss, not only to the Regiment but also to all of us who knew him personally. He was a rising star of the unit: a Sergeant at 27 and on the ladder to a superb career, cut short by yesterday's events. I can tell you all now, his wife has been informed and arrangements are being made to repatriate Sgt Edwards back home to Blighty. This is a huge shock to us all, but we must remember, we are all professional soldiers, and we must carry on with the mission at hand and that is to patrol and weed out the terrorist element and protect the civilian population. We are only one month into this four-month tour and already we've been hit by tragedy. Now gents, the CO would like to have a short chat with you before we fall out and go about our duties. Corporal Trotter, could you come with me outside for a moment while the CO addresses the platoon?" Nolan stood and left the room via the door he entered.

Here we go, thought Rodders. All he had to do was keep his nerve, stand his ground, and not screw up. Simple.

They met outside where the smell of stale cigarette ends baking in the sun made Rodders baulk, but he stood and waited for the boss to arrive, like a good obedient soldier. If he wasn't an officer, he would have ripped his head off by now, but he was so that was the end of it.

"So, Corporal Trotter, have you remembered anything about yesterday's events, you know what the Sgt was screaming at you in the chopper?" Nolan was probing.

"To be honest Sir, I knew yesterday but I felt a bit embarrassed about telling you in case you though I was making light of a terrible situation," he replied. He proceeded to tell the boss the elaborate story regarding money and PlayStation games, looking directly into Nolan's eyes as he spoke.

"I understand," said the boss. "Nothing else?"

"No sir," he lied. "That's all I can think of. If there was anything I would have told you. Like I said Sir, I only kept quiet in case you thought I was making light of the situation. I feel stupid now."

"Well," said the boss, "It sounds like something Sgt Edwards would say. Let's leave it there. Oh. By the way you have to be interviewed by the Head Med. Nothing untoward, just a chat about techniques you used and how they can improve things."

"Yes Sir," said Rodders. "I've done one before, on several occasions actually".

"Of course," he replied, "of course. Right then Corporal, you can run along and see the Head Med now." At that Rodders knew he was being dismissed like a school child. Who tells a grown man to run along? He stood to attention and saluted the person who had organized and carried out the murder of one of his best friends. He hated every second of it, but he was playing the game and was determined to get to the bottom of it.

As he marched away to be interviewed he realised that everyone else was being given a pep talk by the CO and this was the perfect time to go the tent and check out what Deano had hidden the night before. It would be dangerous and time was tight but this would be his only chance to get in and out. He picked up his pace and set off on a steady jog. It was only two minutes but the sweat was running down his back and into his pants. He was wet through and knew he would need an excuse to go back to the tent and this was as good as any.

He entered the darkened tent cautiously. He had a quick scan just to be sure no one was present and headed for Deano's bedside locker. It was locked, of course it was, whose wasn't? But Deano's lock was cheap. He never really bought anything decent, except for clothes. He was always smartly dressed when at base in the UK, but he didn't own a car, or jewelery or anything expensive. Rodders pulled the lock and gave it a firm twist. The mechanism gave way and the lock popped open. Easy. He opened the locker with haste, the ammunition pouch still there with the sellotaped packed stuffed into it. He didn't remove the package in case a tell-tale had been placed on it. A hair or a pen mark to show if anyone had moved it without Deano's knowledge, so he inspected it in situ. It was soft inside, maybe some kind of explosive? There was residue on the sellotape where whoever had packed it hadn't quite done a top-notch job. Rodders rubbed the powder, sniffed it, and instantly knew what it was. Opium. He quickly and purposely wiped his fingertip onto the cuff of his jacket and started packing the locker exactly as he found it. That's when he heard the voices approaching the tent.

"Bollocks," he whispered to himself, frantically trying to reattach the lock and twist it back into shape before the door inevitably swung open and he was discovered. The ammo pouch was placed exactly where he found it and the lid to the locker closed, but where was the lock? He swept the area with his eyes, scanning the floor for the lock. He knew he put it down here. He looked at where his brain told him it was, but it wasn't there. What had he done with the bloody lock? He was starting to get scared now. He could hear the voices getting closer and he recognized Squires' laugh. Then it clicked. He opened the locker and there was the lock sitting on top of the ammo pouch. He swiftly closed the lid, threaded the lock through the clasp, closed the mechanism and twisted it slightly in the opposite direction. The lock snapped closed. He pulled it just to make sure it had engaged properly and it had. Deano would never know.

He leapt up and over to his bed space and removed his shirt just as the door opened and Squires came in followed by Deano.

Deano instantly looked at his footlocker. He could see the lock was on but walked over to check anyway. He pulled out a crappy looking key from his wallet and opened the sturdy box. His movements were watched by Squires as he made his way across the tent.

"What are you doing here?" Said Squires nosily. "I thought you had an interview with the Head Med?"

"I do," said Rodders, feigning breathlessness. "But I'm wet through from the heat and I can't go and see the Doctor soaked to the skin, can I? I'm going to get right in the crap, so I've had to come back for a new shirt and some spray on. By the way I'm out, does anyone have some deodorant I can borrow?" He acted casually. Something he was becoming quite adept at. He could sit and think about how he nearly got caught later but he had to stay collected for now.

Deano surveyed his locker and appeared confident everything was in order by giving Squires a sly nod.

With this confirmation Squires' tone changed and relaxed. "There's some in my locker but you had better get a wriggle on as you're due to see him soon, aren't you?"

Rodders opened up Squires' locker, took out some cheap and nasty deodorant and liberally sprayed himself with it.

He pulled on his beret, smartened himself up in the mirror on his locker door and started walking out of the tent. As he passed Davis's bunk he sat up in bed, the bunk directly opposite Deano's rubbing his eyes as though he had just woken up. He had been there all along, under the covers and Rodders hadn't noticed. Had he seen him rifling through the locker? There was no way he could have missed it, surely? He caught Davis' stare and watched as he slowly and silently shook his head ever so gently from side to side acknowledging that he had seen him but wouldn't say anything. Rodders surreptitiously nodded in return and then continued with what he was doing.

The station hospital was a brisk ten-minute walk away from the tent but Rodders didn't want to get soaking again so he took his time. During his walk he wondered why Davis was staying silent and why he was in the tent in the first place instead of being on duty. Questions that needed answering but could wait for now. Then he remembered, he had left his jacket hanging in his locker. He was going to do a simple narcotic test on the residue to confirm the substance was opium. Not to worry, he could still pick up a test from one of the girls in the pharmacy and carry it out at a time of his choosing.

He arrived at the hospital with five minutes to spare. He entered the air-conditioned building which was instant respite from the heat of the morning sun. Rodders stood in the doorway for a moment to soak up the chilled air as if it was the last time he would ever experience it.

"Ahem." The Lance Corporal behind the counter politely cleared her throat. "Morning" she said in a soft but quiet northern accent. "Can I help you at all?"

"Hi. Yes, you can. I'm Corporal Trotter. I have an interview with the Head Med.... sorry the CO in regard to the contact situation with 4 Platoon yesterday."

"One moment," she replied. "What time is your appointment?"

"10:00 o'clock." She scanned the appointments book. Then she flipped the page. "Ah yes. Corporal Trotter. You're a bit early," she said.

"I was told 10:00 by my boss."

"It is 10:00 but you're a day early. It's 10:00 tomorrow, not today." She gave a shy giggle to lighten the situation and Rodders responded with the same. He gave her the 'Doh! Silly me' expression and then it dawned on him. He had been set up. The boss *never* got his timings or dates wrong. This was a ruse to get him out of the tent and go through his locker. The jacket. It had the evidence on it.

He turned and started walking as fast as he could without drawing attention to himself. He followed the path of least resistance and took a short cut through one of the admin buildings. After exiting and throwing up a few salutes he arrived back at the accommodation. He took a moment to get his breath and compose himself. He puffed out his chest, got his story straight and entered the tent.

As soon as he walked in, he instinctively knew something wasn't right. Everyone had returned and they were now milling around, not actually doing anything but trying their utmost to look busy. It appeared false and it was. He caught the eyes of a couple of the guys but they quickly turned away.

He went to his locker. He had hung the jacket over the corner of the open door but it wasn't there. As he opened the door, he saw the garment hung up on a wooden hanger, brushed clean of any dust and more importantly, any evidence. The cuff was clean. The opium residue had been removed, either on purpose, and in which case he had been rumbled, or by accident as the jacket had been hung up. Either way, Rodders didn't feel comfortable.

"Young Davis here hung your jacket up for you Rodders," said Squires. "You know how the boss likes things squared away, all neat and tidy like. Who knows, he could pop by at any time and if he saw it, we would all be in trouble." Rodders noticed the cockiness in his voice. "Ah, thanks Davis," Rodders forced a smile onto his face. "I forgot about that. Sorry lads, my mistake. Good job he didn't come by."

"He did but he didn't see the jacket." Deano instantly knew he had said the wrong thing but couldn't work out how to back pedal his way out of the sticky situation he had landed everyone in. Squires gave him a "Shut the hell up" look before trying to salvage things.

"Erm, yeah, I forgot to mention it. He did swing past while you were at the Med Centre. I think he came to tell you he had his days mixed up and the interview with the Head Med wasn't until tomorrow."

"Oh right," said Rodders. "But surely, he knew that I would have already left to go over to the Med Centre when he came to the tent. Why didn't he just head over there and catch me before I went in?"

"I don't know do I?" Squires' tone was hostile. "I'm not his personal assistant, am I? Maybe he couldn't be arsed, maybe he didn't give a shit? He's an officer, he doesn't run around after the pond life like us does he? I'm only the messenger."

"Ok, for Christ's sake, I'm just saying, no need to have a hissy fit. Calm down you dick!" Rodders fronted and Squires hunched his shoulders and turned away.

Rodders turned his attention back to the locker. Apart from the residue being wiped from the jacket, things had moved on the shelves. Nothing tipped over or broken but things had been rearranged, ever so slightly in the hope he wouldn't notice upon his return. The empty deodorant can was on the wrong shelf and a book he was reading had been moved, someone probably looking for some kind of evidence between the pages. A magazine that revolved around the latest cinema releases had been taken out completely and as he searched for it, he saw it lying on the table in the center of the room.

When Squires saw him perusing the table, he made his move.

"I forgot to tell you. When Davis was putting your jacket away your magazine fell out onto the floor. This was inside it." He handed Rodders a note, his name was emblazoned across the front. It was handwritten and he recognized the writing as Dave's. He had never seen it before and was at a loss to its origin. He wasn't sure how to react. He picked up the note, which had been folded in half and began to read.

Rodders you slacker. Just a quickie as were due on patrol soon. I've been thinking about getting out of the Army and I've thought of a great idea for a small business but I can't do it on my own. I need a good medic to make it work. If you fancy it, I'll fill you in when we get back.

I'm only writing this note as things are hotting up with the locals and you never know, I might get popped or stand on a mine in the next 72 hours. Ha ha. If I do though remember to tell Jenny I love her and don't forget, keep your feet on the ground and keep writing about that car you're always talking about. Later bud. Dave

Rodders recognized the humor as Dave's but had no idea what he was talking about in relation to leaving the Army. Dave *loved* the military, and a bunch of wild horses couldn't pull him away from the lifestyle he enjoyed so much. He was going to be a Warrant Officer one day and then probably earn a commission after that. He was a grafter and although he hated being away from home, he craved the adrenalin he got from the excitement of action. The next bit was a bit cryptic though. He did have a car. It was a total heap of junk, a 1993 Vauxhall Astra. He spent most of his life on detachment so the idea of owning an expensive car to just sit and rust back in the UK was foolish to him. He wasn't even into cars, truth be told. It was a means of getting from A to B for him. What point was Dave trying to make? *Keep your feet on the ground and keep writing about that car you're always talking about.* He could see Dave's face mouthing the words to him but was clueless as to what they meant. He was pulled back into the room abruptly by Squires chiming in.

"So, what is it Rodders?" he said. "His last will and testament or something? I didn't know you had a car. I've never seen you driving it about back at base. You could have given us all a lift the pub. Was he thinking about jacking? He never mentioned it to me."

"You read it then?" Rodders said angrily.

Squires froze. "Well yeah, by accident like. It fell open onto the floor, so it was pretty hard not to see what was inside."

"That still doesn't mean you read someone else's letters does it? And for your information he didn't tell you *anything* because he didn't *like* you, that's why. And while we're at it, yes, he was talking about quitting because he was fed up with being stuck in this dump with a bunch of dickheads like you lot, so wind your necks in, sit down and shut the fuck up!"

He wasn't that upset but had to act as though he was just to get them off his back. He needed a reason to storm out of the tent and get some personal space to think things through and this was perfect. He knew they would leave him be for a while. He stared at them all and slammed his locker door and left the tent.

Once outside, he headed to the toilet block to re-read the note. He pored over the writing. He racked his brains as to what Dave was trying to say, but nothing would click and Rodders started to lose his temper with himself.

He thought about the opium. There must have been a kilogram in the ammo pouch. That's what druggies deal in isn't it, kilograms? If there's more coming in how much they have already sent out and more importantly how? Then he shuddered. Dave wasn't involved in it, was he? Who was? Nolan was obviously leading the group, although he did mention another leader when he was chatting to Squires. Put that on the back burner. Nolan, Squires, and Deano for sure. But they spoke openly in front of the rest of the tent about the situation when they thought he was asleep, so he had to assume everyone in the billet knew or was involved at some level. Christ! Who *wasn't* involved?

He could understand Squires being up to his eyes in it. He wasn't well-liked and was a bit of a bully. Not a physical bully, more the kind that used intimidation, one who harped on and on about something until you walked away from it and he and his minions would laugh at you behind your back. The only reason he didn't get a slap was because he was a Corporal. He was also skint. It was well known he liked to gamble on anything from horses to which cockroach would climb the wall of the tent quickest. He owed thousands, to the point where the company clerk had been given instructions to take control of his wages and limit the amount he was given in a vain attempt to pay off his debts. It didn't work. He still managed to gamble away his monthly ration of cash and his biggest downfall was cards. He didn't need a mobile phone or internet connection to win or lose at cards. Every tent had a set to while away the hours and he used them to his advantage by cheating and fleecing the younger members of the platoon.

He was a self-centered and downright nasty individual who didn't care about anyone but himself and Rodders viewed him as the last person he would ever trust to have has back in battle. He would be the first to surrender, run away or as was now the case, throw his Sgt to the wolves and push him into the line of fire. He was *the* perfect candidate to be coerced into any criminal act where money was involved. Rodders concluded that Squires was the boss' right hand man.

He sat deep in thought for a minute and wondered why Deano had been drawn into this racket. He was a good guy. A bit of a fool and, in reality, not the sharpest tool in the box but he knew he knew his limitations and never attempted to go beyond them. He was a private soldier but would, if he ever made Lance Corporal never go above that rank.

He liked a drink did Deano. He wasn't an alcoholic, but he was a large guy and he enjoyed a good session whenever he could get one in. He wasn't a bully in the natural sense either. All bullies are cowards and the lowest of the low, but Deano was different. He would be mortified if he actually knew some of the younger lads were quite scared of him, but he never really picked up the signals, due to the fact he was either drunk or too stupid to see them. He didn't fight or seek out trouble even though Rodders was sure he could handle himself quite admirably in a scrap. Why was he involved? Rodders struggled to find the connection to Deano and the reasons to get into the smuggling game. There were of course two strong possibilities. He didn't know the full story and what was occurring in the background, or he was being blackmailed into crime by one or more of the others involved. Deano had a good relationship with the Sarge as well. He was the kind of guy who would use up his free time to help you move house or run you into town if you needed a lift. Most of all he was popular. The women on camp saw him as harmless and soft and he was never intimidating, even though he towered above most other people. The chances of him knowing about Squires pushing the Sarge were slim to none. Rodders didn't see him as a threat.

He scribbled down the names of the men in the tent and stared at it, trying to ascertain the personality of each man as he went. Bairdy, Stevens and Davis all seemed to be spot on. He was no different to most of these blokes, maybe a bit more switched on and mature due to his rank but essentially, he was the same, apart from Hays. He didn't like Hays and he, like Squires was a bully. He didn't actually know the guy that well, because he tried to avoid him whenever he came onto the scene.

He looked at the ceiling for a moment and thought about home. He himself had come from humble beginnings. His father worked as a joiner, his mother a school dinner lady. Rodders had always yearned for a bit of adventure. When he was younger, he took every opportunity to camp outside with his friends and had envisioned himself as an outdoor pursuits in instructor of some kind. The Bear Grylls type, or so he thought, but once he discovered pubs, girls, and late nights it all came crashing down around him. The plans of his youth soon dissipated and he ended up working shifts in a call center, a job he hated but which paid a half decent wage to fund his party lifestyle. Then one day he saw a TV advertisement for the Army and a life of low wages, servitude and ill-fitting uniform took over as the daily norm. Thinking back, he smiled to himself. For all its bad points the good points far outweighed them. He loved being a medic and helping those in need and he knew that one day the training would stand him in good stead in civvy street when it came to getting a job. All of that seemed so distant as he stared at the list of names he had created.

Why or what had turned these ordinary young soldiers into a mob of criminals? He was convinced they didn't all know about Dave's death, but he needed to find out which members of the gang did. His mind raced with so many thoughts that he began to get a headache.

When he felt the pins and needles in his backside, he scanned his watch for the time. Jesus, he had been sat on the pan for over an hour. Hopefully the lads would think he was just getting to grips with the death of the Sarge and no questions would be asked.

He slipped the note back into his pocked, flushed the toilet even though the bowl was empty and returned to his accommodation.

As he entered the tent, he could hear the laughter of the guys who, as he saw when he entered, were playing cards and drinking tea until their next batch of firewater was ready. As usual, Squires was holding court and dealing, a position he used to control the game on his terms. Rodders slid over to the table mostly unnoticed and watched as the younger men stared at their cards intently, trying to figure out their next moves.

Phil Lewis, one of the platoon Lance Corporals was biting his lip and deep in thought when he eventually decided to twist. The seven of hearts put him on nineteen.

"I'll stick." he announced. Squires eyed him up momentarily and turned over his own cards. Twenty-one and another win. The table erupted with laughter as Phil, defeated for the fifth time in a row lifted himself from his seat and walked away, not really knowing what had just happened. Rodders, recognizing an opportunity went over to his bed space to try to cheer him up.

"You ok fella?" He asked. Lewis looked up at him with sad eyes. He drew a deep prolonged breath and let it out slowly.

"Yeah, I suppose. I've never known a bloke with as much luck as Squires. Do you reckon he cheats?" Rodders didn't know whether to laugh or cry at the naivety of the question. He shrugged his shoulders and decided not to advance on it. He peered over at Squires who showed no remorse over fleecing a member of his own squad, sitting gloating whilst counting his ill-gotten gains.

"You seem down Phil. Is everything alright?" Lewis stared at the ground for a moment.

"Not really mate," he replied. "I'm in a bit of trouble to be honest." Rodders sat on the camp bed beside Lewis. He didn't ask him to talk, the gesture of sitting down was the signal to chat but only if he wanted to.

"What do you mean?" Rodders pushed.

"Well, you know I've got a bird back home and we're looking at getting engaged and all that?" Rodders nodded.

"She told me she's eight weeks pregnant. I love her to bits but she doesn't know I've got another kid to a girl I met in Lanzarote a couple of years ago. A little girl called Leah. I only see her a couple of times a year as her mother doesn't want me to be too involved but how can I pay for all of this with one kid, one on the way and a wedding and everything else that goes with it on my wages?" He stared at Rodders, eagerly awaiting some fatherly advice that would ease his problems. Rodders thought for a moment. He wanted to help Lewis and as an NCO it was his duty to aid his subordinates, but he had to be cautious in his approach. He wanted to probe a bit more to see if Lewis would divulge some information about Dave's death. He knew that he was at a vulnerable stage and although he did feel a pang of guilt taking advantage of the situation, he needed to know more about what was going on behind the scenes. This chance wouldn't happen again. He decided to open with a simple query.

"Have you thought about stopping gambling?" He replied. "I mean where do you get the money to do that for starters?" Lewis shook his head, still thinking caught up in his problems and not really listening to the question. His breathing became shallow and Rodders thought he was going to break into tears, but he regained his composure and looked him straight in the eye.

"I'm trying to win back what I lost last week, mostly to that lucky sod," he flicked his head towards Squires, still sitting at the table in the center of the room. "He's taken over two hundred quid off me in three days. I'm sure he's up to something." He seethed quietly. He removed a wallet from the left breast pocket of his camouflage jacket and thumbed through the receipts and loose pieces of paper that filled the spaces to try and find some forgotten cash. Rodders studied his actions and decided to cut the chit chat and go straight for the jugular, in as subtle a way as possible.

"Trying to gamble it back is not the way to go mate. Have you got some other means of getting hold of some cash"? It was a loaded question aimed at making Lewis talk.

"As it happens me and a few of the guys have something on the go which will pay well if we ever get what's owed to us." He blabbed excitedly as he let his guard down momentarily, but his facial expression changed as soon as the last word left his mouth. At that moment Lewis knew he had said the wrong thing.

"What do you mean?" Rodders wondered if he had latched on to the rouse. Lewis was now thinking quickly as to how to back track on his words. He began to talk about the day's events in a vain attempt to divert the conversation away from its current path.

"It's nothing really, just a buy and sell thing with old banged up cars you know, doing them up and selling them on. Anyway, how are you holding up? It's been a bit mad for the past day or so hasn't it?" The focus was now on Rodders and he knew he couldn't return to his previous line of questioning. The conversation was over and Lewis was aware he had dropped the ball, big time. Now it was his turn again to make it look as though he had missed the comments about money and look disinterested in the whole conversation.

"Ah, nice one, easy money if you do it properly. I'm OK but tired, nothing is really sinking in right now, I can't even remember most of what's gone on today, but I'll be fine. Listen why don't we have a brew and try not to think about your situation, especially out here, it'll drive you mad in the end." Lewis watched as Rodders stood up, trying his best to make it appear he had forgotten Lewis's comments not sixty seconds earlier. He looked around aimlessly and started walking towards his bed. Squires stood in front of him, stopping him in his tracks. He braced himself for aggression but when Squires spoke, he was knocked off-guard momentarily.

"I'm sorry about earlier." He didn't mean it and Rodders knew he didn't. He had overstepped the mark and was pretending to make amends.

"It's fine," said Rodders. "I'm just narky about everything and we're only a month in and I miss home already. I never, EVER thought I would actually miss rain. But hey, you were out of order reading my stuff mate, don't do that again, OK?"

"OK, I was wrong, I admit it...truce?" Squires held out his hand. Rodders looked at it, took it in his and they shook. As he looked Squires in the eyes he thought, *you murdering bastard. I'll get you, you reptile.* The act was still holding up but his nerves were shot to pieces. *How long will it go on for?* He thought. Deano stood and cleared his throat.

"I heard the boss say they were auctioning the Sarges kit this evening," he announced. "Everyone is expected to bid for something with all the cash going to his missus. Should be a decent amount raised if we're not all Scrooges."

Rodders lay down on his bed. He tried to close his eyes and maybe catch some sleep, but the note kept prying its way into his thoughts. Writing about cars? Keeping my feet on the ground. It didn't sound like Dave at all. Maybe that was the whole point, writing something so obviously cryptic that it would spring out instantly. It didn't and he lay for over an hour thinking. It started to hurt his head and he decided to get up, have a brew and get his laptop out and watch an episode of 'Game of Thrones.' He had seen them all before but was a bit of a geek when it came to fantasy shows and there was also the added bonus of ogling some beautiful women on show.

He swallowed the last of his sugary sweet tea and pulled out his laptop from its case. He opened the screen and it sprung into life. As he reached into the bag to get his memory stick, he realised it was missing. He inspected the whole bag back to front but couldn't find the stick. He wasn't worried as such, there wasn't anything personal on it, only TV shows and films but it annoyed him that he had mislaid it.

"Bollocks," he muttered to himself and put on his shoes and headed to the toilet block for a pee. He wondered where he could have put it: in his locker? In his wallet? He dismissed his thought finished his business and went to the basin to wash his hands. He looked like he had aged five years in 36 hours, but he would be ok. He threw some cold water on his face and headed back to his bedspace. He picked up the laptop case and put his hand into the front pocket. The memory stick was there. He had checked thoroughly and found nothing not five minutes ago and now it had miraculously appeared out of thin air. He didn't register anything on his face and acted as though nothing was wrong. They had taken the stick and replaced it when he had left the tent but he knew it wasn't worth anything to them. However, it proved one thing, they were still watching him. They were waiting for him to screw up and if he did then they would make a move and something would go down. He wondered if Lewis had spoken of their conversation and admitted to Squires that he had talked out of turn. He had let his guard down but he wouldn't make the same mistake twice.

He opened the laptop, inserted the pen drive, and started watching his TV show. But it was a cover. It gave him some quiet thinking time to work out what the note meant. About thirty minutes into the show, he had it. He looked up and without knowing it shouted "Holy shit!" at the top of his voice. Having headphones on he hadn't released just how loud he had been and everyone in the tent stopped and looked directly at him.

"Holy shit what?" Deano looked confused.

"It's just a good part in the show." Rodders thought quickly. "You know, the bit with the big dragon thing?" They all nodded in agreement and turned back to their card games and magazines.

Rodders had cracked the code. Not really a code but he was certain he had it. He was looking at the answer right in front of him. Writing about cars. PEN DRIVE. But not this pen drive. This one only had films and rubbish on it. He skimmed through the files but found nothing new and neither would Squires after he had undoubtedly scanned its contents.

Another pen drive. If he broke the first part of the conundrum, he was sure he could break the rest. He wracked his brains but came up blank. He took off the headset and lay down flat. He slipped into a light sleep only to be woken an hour later by Bairdy.

"Rodders?" He whispered. "Are you awake mate?"

"Yes."

"They're auctioning the Sarges gear in half an hour, I just thought you would want to know," he said sheepishly.

"I totally forgot about that Bairdy. Thanks mate."

Bairdy seemed pleased he hadn't been chewed out for waking the Corporal and sat drinking tea until it was time to leave.

"How are you Rodders? OK? I know the Sarge was your mate and all. I liked him as well; he was a good guy."

"He was that Bairdy" Rodders looked into his mug of tea, "he was that. But anyway, it's done now. Makes you think about life though, doesn't it? What's your plans for when we get home? It's a few months away but things like this make you want to get home quicker." Rodders was attempting to make Bairdy comfortable in the hope he too might slip up like Lewis who he thought would not have mentioned his indiscretion to anyone other than Squires, making him look like an idiot to the group.

"You know me Rodders, I don't mind it here. As long as I can get a decent tan and save a few quid for when I get home, I'm happy. As soon as we get leave though that's me away, I'll be in Ibiza partying like there's no tomorrow." Rodders knew Bairdy was a party boy and he was known for his alleged conquests with the opposite sex. He was young and carefree and although he loved the Army it was a source of income to fund his Bacchanalian lifestyle. If he had had any decent qualifications, there was no chance he would be sitting in a tent in Afghanistan.

"You still doing lines?" He enquired.

"Just a bit to be social, you know, nothing heavy or anything like that. A few lines of coke never hurt anyone did it? You're not going to report me are you? Because I'll deny everything and you won't be able to prove a thing." Drugs had been a problem in the armed forces for years and although it was punishable by jail time or court martial, it still ran rife. If the military police charged and acted on every suspected drug taker the personnel count would diminish drastically meaning it was overlooked a lot of the time. Rodders decided to buddy up to Bairdy and use this to his advantage.

"Come on mate, you know me by now, of course I won't. Listen, if I wasn't a Corporal, I would be joining you. I've never tried any kind of drug before but I'll tell you what, if it can help me take away the thoughts of what's happened recently, I'll give anything a go and from what you say it puts you right on your uppers. Who knows, maybe when we get back, I might just let my hair down a bit more, you know? Live life like every day could be your last. Maybe you could line me up with a decent bird and a bit of the old Charlie. What do you say?" Bairdy's eyes lit up. He had never seen Rodders like this before. He was always so professional and, in Bairdy's eyes, uptight. He liked Rodders beforehand, but he liked him even more now.

"Ah, man, that sounds great: let's do it." He replied, laughing.

"But it's expensive though isn't it? How the hell do you afford it? Have you been moonlighting when we're back at base?" Rodders winked at him, deciding to play his ace as soon as he saw a chance.

"Nah mate, I've got some extra cash coming but don't worry, I'll see you alright. It's going to take a while for it to come through but I'll hammer my overdraft until I get it." Rodders didn't need to push any further. He had heard enough and didn't want to go too far in case Bairdy became suspicious. But judging from that answer he was sure he was involved. He let the conversation drop away and suggested they left to attend the auction.

Rodders and Bairdy carried on chatting about nothing important on their way over to the cook house where the auction would be held, the private totally forgetting about his mention of money coming his way and focusing solely on the fact he thought he had found a new friend who he could party and get high with without any kind of reprimand. When they entered the dining hall almost the entire company was there, give or take the odd straggler. Lots of eyes appeared to be watching Rodders as he took a seat at the back of the hall. Maybe they weren't, maybe it was paranoia; everything was starting to get on top of him a bit. He shrugged it off and tried to forget it.

Five minutes later Nolan appeared. Following him were two of the company privates hauling two large cardboard boxes full of Dave's military gear behind them. This was a good opportunity for some of the younger guys who weren't well-equipped. Soldiers who had done a good few years' service tended to invest in some non-issue equipment which helped them in their daily duties such as thermal clothing, torches, knives, and other essential kit. Rodders remembered that Dave had bought a cracking pair of brand-new Danner Gore Tex boots recently. They would hardly be broken in and they cost almost two hundred quid new. That didn't mean someone was going to get a bargain, this was a charity auction after all. Then like a light bulb moment it dawned on him. Keep your feet on the ground. The boots. The pen drive. Had Dave hidden a pen drive in the boots?

"You sneaky bugger," he whispered to himself with a wry smile. *I'll bet that's exactly what he's done*, he thought. Rodders had to buy those boots.

Firstly, came the SAS smock, sixty quid that went for. Jumpers and socks next, twenty quid. Torches, knives, and ammo pouches made a decent amount too and after half an hour Rodders thought the boots would be up soon, but he was wrong. They would be last, the star of the show and there were lots of people interested.

"Well gents," said Nolan. "Look at what we have here. An almost brand-new pair of Danner Boots. Not the cheap rubbish though, noooo, the good ones, top of the range Gore Tex no less. Only three months old so not even due their first service. Who will give me sixty for them? Can I hear sixty?" There was an audible groan from the room mainly from the high percentage of people who thought they could get a quick purchase at fifty pounds, maximum. Sixty pounds was a lot for a pair of boots considering they get issued for free but then again, these were not military issue and anyone who had a pair would agree, they fit like gloves on your feet.

A hand went up. "Sixty pounds," said Nolan. The hand belonged to Squires.

"Seventy." Said Rodders

"Eighty," said Squires. As usual, he was skint but there was no way he was going to let Rodders get the boots. It was a war of attrition.

"I'll go one hundred pounds, Sir!" Shouted Rodders. Squires didn't move. He was thinking about what he would do next. He didn't want to look a fool but he didn't want Rodders getting the better of him.

"One hundred and twenty," proclaimed Squires, puffing out his chest signaling that he was going to be the victor of this duel.

"I'm out," said Rodders calling his bluff. Squires almost went into shock. He felt a lump in his throat and he started to panic. He didn't have the money and he was going to look like a complete fool in front of the whole company. Nolan lifted the hammer, and in what seemed like slow motion to Squires, it came crashing down on the table.

"Sold for one hundred and twenty pounds to Corporal Squires. Right gents as you know, in these situations all accounts and monies owed will be paid to Cpl Harris the company clerk by midday tomorrow. Does everyone understand?"

"Yes Sir." They all exclaimed in one loud voice.

"Then thank you for your time and money and enjoy the rest of your evening." And with that, Nolan strode off stage like a second-rate Bruce Forsyth and everyone stood up and started to exit the dining hall.

Rodders watched Nolan as he left. Jesus, he was good. He had just ordered the murder of one of his own soldiers and he's standing there like nothing is wrong.

In the warm evening air outside, some of the guys had gathered and were having a general chit chat when Squires broke away and steamed towards Rodders.

"Can I have a word?" Squires was direct. Rodders grinned to himself, he knew what he wanted, and he would relish watching him squirm.

"How can I help you?" said Rodders in a very light tone.

"You know how. You had to get one over on me didn't you, you knob? I can't afford the boots but you had to try and make me look a dick."

"Why on earth would I do that Squires?" asked Rodders. "If you didn't have the money, you shouldn't have started a bidding war with me to show off, should you?"

"Because you're an arsehole that's why," he replied

"Careful now Squires or I won't buy them off you. I take it that's why we're having this conversation, because you want to offload the boots? Nobody else can afford them and you need to save face by handing the money in tomorrow. You're calling me arsehole and all the names under the sun, but you still need me to pull you out of the shit... Am I right?"

"You know I do. Do you want them or not?"

"Of course, I do, otherwise I wouldn't have bid on them."

"Right then, that's a ton twenty," Squires seemed deflated.

"But I've only got one hundred. That's why I bailed out Squires. I capped at a ton. You should have thought about that before you jumped in with both feet... with your new boots on." Rodders was now openly laughing at the dejected Squires.

"I'll take it," he said through gritted teeth as he scanned to see if anyone was witnessing this embarrassment.

"Deal." Rodders slapped him on the back and walked away with a smile on his face.

The tent was baking hot on that particular night. There was no respite from the heat. The air conditioning worked but it didn't have the power to have any effect on the atmosphere, so it hummed away pointlessly. There was the usual milling around. The kettle boiled, cards shuffled and Squires, who had already lost the money he won from Lewis, was trying to win more money so he could keep the boots and get one back over Rodders. The attempt was futile and he ended up losing more than he had on the table.

Rodders lay, looking at the ceiling and thinking of when he could get time to inspect the boots and check to see if he was correct about his hunch..

What is on the drive? If there even is a drive, he thought. I've just spent a hundred quid on an assumption there's some evidence that can help me nail the lot of them. He had the feeling something bad was coming. His hunch wasn't wrong.

CHAPTER 4

It was cold outside but not freezing. One of those days where you wear a thick jacket in the morning only to become too hot in the afternoon and end up carrying it wherever you go. Jenny decided to wear a light fleece to work, slipped it on over her NHS uniform, had a last check to make sure the house was secure and headed out of the front door. She gave the handle a good tug just to make sure the latch had engaged and once she was satisfied no burglar could break in, she got into her car and began the thirty-minute drive to the hospital.

She hadn't enjoyed a solid night's sleep for about a month since Dave's company had left for Afghanistan. She hated him going away and although being used to it after years of marriage she still couldn't settle without him in the house. She thought about him for a second whilst at traffic lights and sighed, not necessarily unhappy but just fed up with the lifestyle that came with the army. Both Dave and Jenny desperately wanted kids. They had been trying for a couple of years without success. They had both been checked out and everything was fine. They put it down to the stresses of life, both their hectic jobs and fatigue whenever Dave came home from deployment. She was now having second thoughts. Dave was away for months at a time and she loved her job in the healthcare sector. Was there time for children? She put the thoughts to the back of her mind. She would need to have a serious discussion with her husband when he returned beck to civilization.

The lights turned green but Jenny sat, staring at the road ahead until a sharp toot from the vehicle behind interrupted her thoughts. She snapped back, gave an apologetic wave to the driver, and slowly moved away. As she drove, she listened to her favorite radio station. The familiar oldies mixed with the newest songs was pleasant but whenever the news bulletins came, she feared she would hear of some shooting or roadside explosion in Afghanistan. Today was a good day, for her anyway. There was no mention of action in the middle east but news about the rising cost of living were headlines and she caught something about a storm brewing in the Atlantic which was close to making landfall on the eastern seaboard of the United States. When the Rolling Stones started chirping away in the background, she went back to thinking about Dave.

Twenty-five minutes later she arrived at the hospital. It was a great place to work but an awful thing to look at. Dull grey brickwork and some fancy attempt at modern art stuck to the front made it look like a bad attempt at cubism or surrealism or whatever that famous Spanish guy did. Whoever dreamt up the idea of strapping it to the front of a hospital had poor judgment. It was supposed to cheer the place up. It didn't.

However the hospital looked, Jenny loved her job and she couldn't wait to get inside and start her day. She had always wanted to help people. She wanted to be a doctor when she was a child but was convinced by some of her teachers in high school that she wasn't 'doctor material' and should concentrate her efforts on something else, like shopwork or a 'something in administration.' Neither of those jobs were bad, they just weren't for her. So, when she did leave school, she decided to push her detractors from her mind and aim to become a nurse. Ten years later, here she was, still doing the job she loved and had been doing since the age of twenty-one.

She stepped through the main entrance door and was hit immediately by the hospital smell, feared and hated by many, loved by so few. The antiseptic and disinfectant aroma never leaves a hospital, no matter how many windows or doors are opened. It seems to be ingrained into the very fabric of the brick and paintwork in every ward and theater throughout the country. Jenny loved it. Some people love the smell of cut grass or new shoes but for Jenny it was the smell of the hospital and when she inhaled it, she knew she was where she was meant to be. After the obligatory 'good mornings' to everyone, Jenny took up her workstation, chatted to her colleagues and looked at her roster for the day on the mental health ward. As she thumbed her way through her patients' folders she came across a familiar name. Her shoulders slumped slightly as she recalled their last encounter. This was followed by a slight tinge of sadness, before eventually returning to a smile remembering the bittersweet nature of their meeting. This really was a job where you could feel a whole range of emotions in the space of a minute. Jenny knew that the patient had taken a backwards step in their rehabilitation to be returning to the ward and eagerly set off to hear how she could help.

As Jenny strode purposefully down the corridor she couldn't help feeling slightly impotent in her role. She was good at her job and had considered moving up the chain in the mental health sector but questioned her abilities. Empathy and sympathy weren't enough to move forward but she knew deep down she had so much more to offer. As she entered the patient's room the sympathy she had thought about moments earlier came flooding into her mind.

Raymond was sitting in his chair, knees drawn up to his chest, staring blankly at the ground in front of him. Jenny could see he had been self-harming, the cuts on his forearms shallow but deep enough to draw blood. His toenails were long and yellow, and he appeared slightly scruffy even though his file said he had bathed that very morning.

"Raymond?" Jenny's voice was soft, "Raymond, do you remember me? It's Jenny... Jenny the nurse from the last time you were here." He slowly lifted his gaze upwards and smiled. He closed his eyes for several moments before returning to look back at Jenny.

"Jenny?" He whispered, "I'm so pleased to see you." He began to gently weep.

"Come on now Raymond, why don't you tell me what's bothering you?" Jenny felt a compelling urge to help Raymond, more than any of her other patients. He had been a soldier in a previous time. Smart and highly motivated in his duty he had returned from a tour in Iraq to find his wife had taken their two sons and moved in with a man she had been seeing for almost a year behind his back. He was dishonorably discharged several months later and had since fallen into drink, drugs and homelessness followed by bouts of crippling depression. As a military spouse, Jenny knew that such things happened but she was upset by the lack of support from the Ministry of Defense for its veterans and vowed to herself to help Raymond as best she could. Raymond stretched out his arms and although she knew she shouldn't Jenny walked over to him, bent down on one knee and hugged him tightly.

"It'll be OK." She sighed "let's see how we can get you better." As she sat and listened, Raymond explained how he had turned back to drugs to help him forget everything but inevitably crime went along with that. Before too long he ended up in the police cells and from there he came to the hospital. She felt so helpless. She was a nurse and wasn't in a position to offer advice, that was the job of a doctor or counselor but she was a good listener and for over an hour that's exactly what she did. When Raymond finished, he felt a weight lifted from his shoulders and thanked Jenny for being an ear to talk into. As Jenny was leaving the room, she took one last look over her shoulder. Raymond had pulled his knees up to chest and was staring blankly at the floor again. *And the cycle begins all over again*, she thought, as the door closed silently behind her.

After a long day, Jenny sat in her vehicle for the arduous drive home. She hated the boring commute but what it did offer was time to think; whether that be about Dave, plans for the coming days or focusing on what she really wanted to do with her life. She had ideas and aspirations but as she contemplated her future, she was reminded that, as usual, it would all depend on where Dave was posted and for how long. The upheaval of a posting every three years had, at times, taken its toll on their relationship but they were still as tight as ever. Of course, there had been some blazing arguments but she was still happy with her marriage. Her mind wondered back to the events of the day and in particular her appointment with Raymond. It made her think of how fragile and delicate the human mind and body are. If something so traumatic could happen to a strong, proud soldier then it could happen to literally anyone, herself included. She reminded herself of how lucky she was and how much she loved and longed for Dave to be safe, at home by her side.

She pulled up to her house, walked up the path and put the key in the lock. As she pushed open the door, a chill ran up her spine and Dave's face flashed in her mind. She felt like someone was watching her and she looked around to check before stepping inside and pushing the door shut behind her. She had never done that before and she was perplexed as to why she had done it then. She shrugged it off and made her way to the kitchen, a little shaken. Jenny was not a big drinker; she never had been even though the culture was part of the armed forces. When the men were home there was always a BBQ or event going on and as Dave was a Senior Non-Commissioned Officer there would also be dining in nights in the Sergeants Mess. This usually meant dressing up to the nines in a ballgown or summer dress and partying until the small hours, something she enjoyed but not something she wanted to do every weekend. But this evening, she fancied it.

She walked toward the wine rack and removed a bottle of nice but inexpensive red wine, smiling to herself she looked at the price label: Four pounds and fifty pence. *I'm a cheap date,* she thought. But she knew her tastes and if she liked it, she drank it and if she didn't, she didn't. She didn't know the slightest thing about vintage or BIN numbers. If its red I'll have a go, that was her outlook on the whole thing. She unscrewed the lid and poured herself a medium glass, spilling several drops on the worktop as she up-righted the bottle. She sat down in front of the television and switched to the twenty-four-hour news channel to catch up on what she had missed throughout the day when the front doorbell rang. She wasn't expecting anyone. She rose from her seat and made her way to the door. She peered through the spy hole see who was there, making out two men in uniform and opened the door to see they were from the Kings, although she didn't recognize either of their faces. They must have news about the lads coming home.

"Good evening Mrs. Edwards," said one of the men. "I'm Major Harris and this is Major Smith, may we come in please?"

"Of course," replied Jenny, starting to tense at their impromptu visit..

Both men entered and Jenny ushered them into the lounge. They sat on the sofa but Jenny remained standing, too anxious to sit.

"Mrs. Edwards," Major Smith spoke slowly. "Were here in regard to David." Nobody called him David. Not even his mother.

Jenny suddenly noticed he has crosses on the lapels of his uniform: the station Chaplain. The dread hit her instantly and her eyes welled up. "Dave," she uttered as she put her hands to her mouth, "Is he OK, what's happened? He's OK, isn't he? Tell me he's ok... Christ WHATS HAPPENED?"

Both men looked at her with genuine remorse in their eyes.

"Mrs. Edwards... Jenny," said the Chaplain. "I'm sorry to inform you that David was shot and injured today. He was taken by an evacuation helicopter back to base but later succumbed to his wounds. I'm so terribly sorry, I really am."

Everything went into slow motion. Jenny felt herself falling but could do nothing to prevent it. As she fell, she caught the wine glass which smashed on the floor beside her, a large shard flying free and cutting Jenny on the side of her right ankle. She didn't feel the pain. Harris and Smith lunged forward to catch her but it was too late. By the time they reached her she was sitting amongst the wine and broken glass, blood pouring from her leg.

The men helped her up and got a tea towel to stem the bleeding as Jenny sobbed uncontrollably. They sat her down on the sofa and wrapped up her leg."What happened?" She managed to ask eventually, talking through sharp intakes of breath.

"From what we know," said Harris, "there was a contact, erm... a fire fight and Dave got shot. At this moment that's all that has filtered down but more precise information will be coming in the next few days I'm sure."

Jenny sat and cried for an hour, both men trying their hardest to console her.

"You need to get that looked at," Major Harris pointed at her ankle. "It looks like it will need a stitch or two."

She gazed down at the bandage that had been applied by the Chaplain. It wasn't a very good effort but she was grateful he had been there to help; she was grateful for both of them in fact.

"Is there anyone we can call to come and be with you?" Asked Harris.

Jenny paused. "No.... thank you, I'll be fine."

"Are you sure Jenny?" He continued. "You may be in shock."

That's an understatement, she thought, but she didn't want to be around anyone right now. She stood resolutely and held out her hand to Major Harris.

"Thank you Major," she said. "I appreciate the sentiment and you both taking your time to see me tonight but I think I would like to be alone now if you don't mind."

She showed the men out who gave her one last conciliatory look before they turned and walked away. As Jenny closed the door she slid down onto the cold tiled floor and began to sob. *Dave is gone,* she thought, *and so is my life.* She stayed there until morning.

Jenny awoke on the cold tiled floor, aching both in body and in heart. She looked through to the kitchen and saw the clock on the wall said 6am. She stretched out her legs and stood slowly but as soon as her eyes adjusted to the light she started crying. She felt so lost, so helpless and had no idea what to do next. She climbed the stairs and considered slipping into bed and crying herself back to sleep. But that wouldn't do. Instead, she stepped into the bathroom and turned on the shower. She looked into the mirror. Remnants of yesterday's make-up were streaked down her eyes and cheeks. Her hair was like a bird's nest, and she looked drawn.

She stumbled into the shower half asleep and let out a loud sigh as the hot water stung her skin. She stood for five minutes and did nothing except soak in the warmth from the pulsating water on her head and body. Thoughts of Dave rushed around inside her head. His smile, the looks he gave her when he didn't think she could see him and the laugh he bellowed when he heard a good joke. She remembered their first date, their first kiss and how he looked in his uniform the day they married. They had been together since high school, childhood sweethearts. He was her rock and she was his soulmate. There's was a bond which nothing could break, except a sniper's bullet.

She had never contemplated that this could happen to Dave. He was such a good soldier and his back was covered by the best men he knew; or so she thought. She climbed out of the shower, went to bed and sobbed, eventually falling into a shallow, restless sleep.

The phone rang and she awoke, startled, not knowing the time and feeling uneasy. The ringing stopped and looking at the handset she wondered who it was. She didn't recognize the number. The phone once again came to life, and she gathered herself together before answering it in a low, quiet voice. "Hello?"

"Hello, Mrs. Edwards. Its Major Smith. How are you holding up today?"

"Hello Major," Jenny took another moment to get her bearings, "I'm tired but awake. Everything seems very... fuzzy if you get my drift."

"I do," said Smith. "I know exactly what you mean. I've been in your position, myself, and it's the hardest thing I've ever had to deal with but it's not about me, it's about you and how you're coping. I know it's only been a day, but I must speak with you regarding David and his return the UK. Are you ok to do that now?" He asked.

"Yes, of course," she said letting out a heavy breath that Smith could hear. He decided to comment, "If you're not up for this right now I can call another time?"

"No, please carry on, I'm just a bit stiff and my leg stings a bit from cutting it last night, but I'll be OK, please continue." She swung her legs out of the bed and noticed the bandage on her ankle. As she slowly peeled away the layers of material, she came to the injury itself. The cut was about an inch long and had been sliced clean by the glass. It should have had at least two or three stitches but Jenny couldn't face going to the hospital. It had already started to heal over but would leave an ugly little scar: one more reminder of the worst day of her life.

As Major Smith went into detail regarding Dave's repatriation, she began to tear up but held back her tears. She had to try and switch on to what was being said and she struggled to understand everything that she was being told but eventually pulled herself together to glean the important information she required. Dave would be flown home to the UK on a military flight. His body would be taken to a funeral director of Jenny's choice and then the funeral would take place at a time suitable for her. The government would pay for everything. The armed forces still had one decent benefit left, she thought. She could, if she chose to, have members from the Kings present at the funeral, in full uniform to honor Dave's commitment to the regiment. She decided this was something he would have definitely wanted and in the space of just over an hour everything was arranged. All she had to do now was turn up.

CHAPTER 5

The day following the auction, the tent rose at 06:00 and were on parade at 07:00. Nolan would highlight what the company, and 4 platoon in particular, would be getting up to before going out on patrol again. Vehicles needed to be looked over, washed, and made ready for operations. Weapons had to be drawn, ammunition issued, and routes had to be planned. Rodders headed to the medical center for his 10:00 o'clock appointment with the medical CO.

"Hello again?" He greeted the pretty Lance Corporal from the day before. "I'm here for my appointment with the Head Med. Hopefully I've got the right day this time," he said smiling.

"I'm sorry Corporal Trotter, he left this morning on a course. It was short notice and we didn't have time to tell everyone about their cancellations." She replied.

"When is he due back?" Rodders wanted to know if there was any way he could get to see him before he went back out on patrol.

"Erm...four days, so Friday coming."

"OK, I'll wait until then. Thank you." Rodders flashed a flirtatious smile. He was seriously thinking of telling someone in a higher authority about what he knew. If he told the Head Med, it would go one of two ways. He would either lock him up in a mental hospital and throw away the keys or he would call the Military Police and then who knew what would happen. He didn't know who else was involved, so, after quiet deliberation he decided against telling anyone for now.

The platoon had been given the afternoon off for sports as they would be heading out on patrol the following day. Some decided to play football in the air-conditioned inflatable hangar, some went to pay table tennis in the gym, and some went to sit on their back sides and do nothing. Rodders would head over to the weight training room and do some light lifting until Squires went and got the boots and handed them over in the afternoon.

As he entered the gym, he didn't hear a soul. Mind, it was expected, only 4 platoon had the afternoon off. He was relieved it was empty.

Then he heard muffled voices. He couldn't quite make out who they belonged to but he was definitely not alone. So much for peace and quiet. He crept into the changing room and heard the spray of the shower hitting the floor and two men speaking quietly. He decided to chance it and made his way forward to see who was speaking, obviously using the noise of the shower to hide their conversation. He started to make out words but couldn't string them together. He needed to get closer. This conversation could be important. The stakes were high but he needed to know.

Rodders moved forward by one more row of lockers towards the open showers.

"No cubicles here," the head Physical Training Instructor used to say. "You're not on your Daddy's yacht." That expression always brought a smile to Rodders face and he nearly let slip a snort at the thought of it but held his nerve and reminded himself why he was doing this in the first place.

The steam was intense and Rodders started to feel the heat from the shower now. As he peered through the steam, he could make out Deano, naked in front of another man. He was stroking his head gently and telling him it would all be over soon. Rodders couldn't believe what he was witnessing. Deano with another bloke. There must be some good reason behind it. Maybe he was trying to coerce him into something. He watched as the other man told Deano, "I know it will be over soon, but I want out and I want to be with you."

"We will be together, I promise." And with that Deano kissed the man on the lips. As Deano's head moved to the side Rodders could see it was Billy Stevens. He pulled his head around the corner so as not to be seen by Billy. Rodders took in what he was watching and he realized that's why the two of them are involved. Squires or Nolan must have found out about them and blackmailed them into doing the dirty work for the group. He needed to get out, *now*.

Rodders was stepping back slowly taking care he wasn't seen by Deano and Billy. He reached the door and without taking notice, kicked it with the heel of his shoe. Deano swung around, startled. He saw Rodders and both men's eyes connected. Rodders swung the door open and ran out of the gym and into the direction of the tent. He had no idea what to do now or where to go. If he went to the tent Deano and Billy would show up at some point. Did he go to the guard room and tell the Military Police what he had seen? His thoughts were racing and his head was pounding. He was in so much trouble now. He was either going to take a massive beating or wind up like the Sarge. He decided to head to the tent. The other two would be in no hurry to see him again out of sheer embarrassment. He would get the boots, check to see if his theory was true and work it out from there.

He walked briskly down and saw Squires and Hayes were waiting for him outside. Rodders noticed the boots. As he went to pick them up to inspect them, Squires pulled them out of reach.

"Ah, ah, hold on now there Rodders me boy," he said. "Where's the reddies? You know the score, dosh, then boots." Hayes gave a short, forced laugh at the comment whilst giving Rodders a look of disdain. Rodders threw an angry gaze in return. Hayes was unmoved and stared angrily, chewing on a stick of gum as he smiled.

"I've got it in my foot locker. You know I'm good for it, let's see them first."

"Nope," came the stern reply. Rodders let out a sigh.

"OK, c'mon," he said, entering the tent.

"I'll wait here if you don't mind," said Squires. "It's a nice afternoon and I'm in no hurry. You jog on and I'll stay here."

"Whatever suits you best," replied Rodders. He entered the tent, opened his footlocker and took out some money he had hidden in a pair of socks. He counted it out. One hundred quid. It was all there. At least they hadn't nicked his money when they rifled through his belongings. He could hear, but not make out, the hushed chat between the two men outside. He strained to pick up on their words but their tones were lost over the incessant whirring of the inadequate fan, spinning like a record stuck on the needle. As he stood to walk outside, Davis slowly walked past towards the exit.

"I know what you're looking for corporal," he whispered without stopping. "I can help you but I need away from here for good, it's not safe for me or you right now. Watch your back." Davis left the tent and Rodders followed, returning to where Squires and Hayes were waiting. A look of suspicion came over both men as Davis walked past.

"There you go." Rodders handed over the money. Just as Squires was about to take the cash, Rodders pulled it away at the last minute.

"Ah, ah, hold on there now Squires me boy," he copied what Squires had said earlier. "Where's the boots? You know the score, boots *then* dosh." He was goading him, trying to get a rise and Squires knew it but didn't have the time or the inclination to take him on. He handed the boots to Rodders and the cash changed hands straight after.

"Nice doing business with you, thanks for the boots. I'll give them a trial run now I think."

"Piss off." Squires turned to walk away. Hayes stopped him before he could take another step and gave a nudge and a wink to his friend.

"So Rodders, how are you doing since the Sarge was popped? OK are you?" There was no attempt to hide the sarcastic inflection in his voice. He meant his words to hurt and they did exactly as intended. Rodders stopped still and stared deeply into Hayes' eyes, making him, for the first time, uncomfortable and vulnerable.

"What did you just say? Popped? Don't you mean killed or maybe even murdered?" Both men's attention was sharply heightened by the words and Rodders instantly knew he had let his emotions get the better of him. "If you ever, and I mean EVER speak about Dave like that again I will rip your throat out you arsehole. Have you got that?" Hayes was stunned. Not by Rodders' actions but more by the word 'murder' and he stood defiantly staring back, chewing his gum. He tilted his head to spit on the ground, narrowly missing Rodders boots. He moved closer to within a foot or so and leaned forward, the two men almost touching noses.

"Anytime," he replied, side nodding at Squires to move on and away from the situation. Rodders began to tremble with anger and began to take his first step towards Squires and Hayes but then thought better of it. This could turn out very badly for all three of them. Using sound judgment, he decided to throw in one last remark before standing down.

"I'm watching you both," he snarled. "Piss me off again and it'll be the worst and last decision you ever make." A look of anxiety came over both men. They had never seen Rodders in such a rage before. They knew, on this occasion it was best to retreat with their tails between their legs. Rodders paced for a minute or so until he regained his composure. He let the repulsion sweep over him and out of his system as he watched the two figures disappear into the distance.

Rodders put the boots on, size ten, an exact fit for him. They were comfortable and as he walked around getting the feel of them on his feet, he became sad. The thought of literally walking in a dead man's shoes brought no joy, even when he knew Jenny would benefit from the money he had paid for them. He opened the tent door, threw his old boots down next to his cot and started to walk away, in no real direction, just to give the boots a try and attempt to find somewhere he could have a look to see if Dave had hidden anything in the sole.

Fifteen minutes passed and Rodders found himself close to the armory. He sat down by the pavement on a bench and proceeded to unzip the boots. He felt around the left one but there was nothing he could make out. He ripped out the insole and scraped around to see if there was anything loose on the inside. No joy there. He put the boot back on and started to unzip the right boot. As he removed the boot, Captain Nolan came around the corner of the armory building and headed for Rodders.

"Corporal Trotter," his voice sounded surprised. "What are you up to in this neck of the woods? I thought you would be playing football or whatever it is you gents do with your time."

Rodders looked up with a start. "Good afternoon, Sir," he blurted. "I was going to go for a run but remembered the boots I bought at the auction last night and decided to give them a try out before we go on patrol tomorrow."

"Why aren't they on your feet then?" Nolan sniggered but Rodders didn't smile.

"I've got a stone in them Sir, I was just emptying it out before I carry on with my walk."

"Let's have a look at them then Corporal." He ushered Rodders to hand over the right boot.

He did so and hoped and prayed nothing fell out onto the ground. If it did, he was finished. He held his breath while Nolan inspected the footwear.

"Very nice indeed Corporal. I should have bid on them myself but the thought of wearing someone else's boots quite frankly repulses me." Rodders wanted to punch him square in his smug face but let the thought wash over him, knowing his career would end there and then. Not that he had one for much longer, knowing what he knew.

"Beggars can't be choosers Sir, you know that." He replied, trying to make himself look small to appease his boss.

"Quite." Nolan looked at him with mild disgust and then back to the boots as if they were infested with some disease. "Run along now Corporal, I'm sure you've got lots to do before heading out tomorrow."

"I do Sir, you're right. Have a good evening, I'll see you in the morning." He didn't get up and Rodders could see Nolan was irked by that, but he said and did nothing except give him a snotty look before walking away.

"Prick." Rodders muttered under his breath before turning his attention back to the right boot. He removed the insole as he had done with the other one. Nothing. He ran his hand around the inside. Nothing. He tugged at a loose thread connected to the main leather insole of the boot and it came away from the body where the stitching had been. He pulled it out and there inside the rubber was the pen drive. I little one gigabit USB sitting under a piece of clear sellotape holding it in place. He tore it out, slid the leather sole back and then the softer insole on top of that. Then he tied the boot back on and started walking towards the tent.

One hundred yards or so from the tent came the cry "Rodders". As he turned around to see who was shouting, he saw Deano and Billy coming towards him. He wasn't expecting a confrontation so early after witnessing their act in the shower. He gathered himself, ready to go on the offensive.

"Why the hell were you sneaking around the gym? Why were you spying on us? What's wrong with you man?" Deano was angry.

Rodders couldn't believe what he was hearing. They were making him sound like some kind of voyeur. This really got his hackles up.

"Firstly," bawled Rodders, "who do you think you're talking to? Don't talk to me like that...EVER! I'm a Corporal and you had better start getting a bit of respect in your tone or I'll march the pair of you down to the guardroom, tell them what I've seen and throw you in pokey until they decide what to do with you. Don't EVER talk to me like that again, do you understand?"

His question was met with silence.

"DO YOU FUCKING UNDERSTAND ME BOTH OF YOU?"

"Yes, Corporal," they replied in tandem.

"Secondly," continued Rodders, his tone softening and his voice lowering to just above whisper, "I wasn't watching you. In case you've forgotten it's a *communal* gym for the whole camp to use. It's your fault you were stupid enough to go there for your meet up wasn't it?"

More silence.

"Wasn't it?" He reiterated.

"Yes, Corporal," again in unison.

"Listen, I don't care what you do to be honest. I don't care if you're straight, queer, gay or whatever you want to label yourselves. You can do what you want. I'm not your judge, if that's what you want good luck to you both. You know it's frowned upon so if you're going to carry on you had better find a better way of covering your tracks. I'm not going to say anything to anyone, you have my word... as long as you both don't try to shag me."

They both looked at Rodders and smiled at his joke.

"Thanks." Billy looked relieved. "It's our intention to get out and live an open life outside but there are a few loose ends to tie up before we hand in our notice. It should be about six months after that, and we will be out and free to live how we want."

"Hey," said Rodders, "I hope you get everything you want; I really do. Good luck to you both. My lips are sealed... and so should yours be, gobshite," he pointed towards Billy. They all laughed and headed towards the billet, Rodders still quietly confused as to what had just unfolded. Another thing to think about. He didn't know Billy well. He had only been in the army for a short while and was quiet and unassuming, but now he understood the predicament he and Deano were in, or at least he thought he did.

Once inside the tent and on his bed, Rodders removed the pen drive from his pocket and slipped it into the laptop. He loaded the only file on the drive, it was a video. He had to be ready to click the screen off in case anyone came too close, but he was alert and on his guard. He slipped on his headphones and pressed play on the file.

Dave's face appeared on screen. Rodders felt a lump in his throat as he looked into the eyes of his murdered friend. He had one more look around to make sure no one was watching and carried on with the video.

"Hello Rodders. I'm guessing that if you're watching this something serious has happened to me and you've found this drive in my boot. If this isn't Rodders, and it's one of the others then I hope you all burn, you murdering bastards".

"Anyway mate, if I was met with a grizzly death there's a one hundred percent chance it wasn't an accident. You've probably got a million and one questions you want answering so here goes. Nolan, Squires, Deano, Bairdy, Lewis, Stevens, Davis, and Hayes are into smuggling up to their necks. Nolan runs the show and Squires is his right-hand man. Most of the lads are into it either because they've got money problems or a few of them are being blackmailed. I'll come to that later. This is how it started.

During our second tour, do you remember we spent most of our time in the cities going house to house? Well, the boys were finding some nice stuff you know. Gold and watches, that kind of stuff. I mean quality stuff like Rolex and Cartier. That's how the enemy were spending their ill-gotten gains. We were finding *lots* of expensive watches, thirty in the first month alone. We had the stuff, but we didn't know how to get it back to the UK or what to do with it after that."

Rodders felt his fists clench as he listened to Dave. He was talking like he was involved in this racket but there's a big difference between fencing watches and smuggling opium thought Rodders. He needed to know more and carried on listening.

"We started asking questions about how to get rid of it and then we found out about Nolan. *You're going to love this.* He wasn't drafted in from another company within the Kings. He was in the Blues and Royals beforehand and nearly got kicked out of the Army altogether a few years back for theft. His father is a retired Major General and had his record and conviction expunged by another high up officer and that's why nobody really knows about him. Apparently, he was trying to show off to his officer pals and wanted to impress with a new shiny sports car so they could all go and drink Pims at Henley or whatever they do on their days off. Anyway, he stole a land rover and sold it to a bloke in Hull. However, he forgot that the Army driver training school is in Hull and the vehicle popped up soon after as nicked and the trail led to Nolan. He's nothing more than a common thief and that's how we hooked the greedy bastard."

Rodders couldn't believe what he was hearing. Stolen Land Rovers and sports cars. He had no idea about any of it.

"This is where it gets interesting. The boss has a friend in the city who deals in fine art, paintings and such, and told him he could get rid of the haul for thirty percent. We agree and the boss is in with the rest of us, me included. We were finding hundreds of watches and gold jewelery on our searches. Some were crap but lots were high end brands. In the first four-month tour we made just over £200,000 pounds."

Rodders gulped as he listened. Two hundred thousand pounds? That was life changing money but the worst was to come.

"Anyway, we were making big money until we end up getting the current posting out in the desert and we have to find a new income stream. Do you remember the village we went to where I got bitten by the dog? The real cesspool. Well, we found a community leader who made money growing opium. When we looked at his hut, he had about three kilos hidden under the floor along with an AK 47 and a hand grenade. He wasn't the enemy but he did turn out to be very useful. That's when Hayes was recruited. He came with us and was the one who did all the talking and arranged amounts and times and everything else we couldn't. He gets a big chunk. The same as Nolan to be exact but it couldn't run without him. He's a dickhead but he's vital to the operation.

"We had a new income stream but no way of getting it home and nobody to sell it onwards when it reached the UK. So, we did a bit of digging last time we were at home and came up with a plan and made some new contacts.

"The actual smuggling part is the easiest bit. We get the packages, wrap them in vulcanized rubber tape and cover them with grease. Then they're placed into the tyres of vehicles that are being rotated back to base at home and one of the mechanical workshop guys collects it at the other end. He then moves it to our dealer. And here is where we found our trump card: Mavis Davis.

"Mavis' old man isn't a scrap metal merchant. It's a front. He's a drug dealer and a big time one at that. Mavis has tried to escape it his whole life and even joined up to get away from it but once Squires found out, he passed it along to Nolan and now he's snared up in the whole thing. He is the lynchpin of the whole operation. Without him it collapses overnight. The thing is that the poor lad hates being involved. It's ruining his career and neither his dad nor the boss gives a shit about him. He's the odd one out of the group."

Rodders was stunned. Davis' speech explained a lot now. The quietest one of the whole bunch and probably the whole platoon was so involved in smuggling and distributing opium that he couldn't get out now, even if he wanted to. Rodders slowly looked around the room, trying not to draw attention to himself.

What am I in the middle of here? He thought. It was like something from a Hollywood movie. It reminded him of the film where George Clooney and Mark Wahlberg try to get the gold out of Iraq. But this wasn't a film. He was in the deep end with the sharks, the Sarge was dead and the smell of blood was in the water. These once innocent young lads were making so much money that if they found out about him knowing, it would jeopardise the operation, he would wind up dead in a hole in no time whatsoever. It was sinking in. *I'm in deep, deep shit here,* Rodders told himself.

The Sarge carried on.

"When I went home on leave, I was sitting chatting to Jenny. You know she works in the NHS, right? Anyway, she was telling me about the damage drugs do to kids and adults and even babies in the womb. Did you know that? It can screw a kid up before it's even born. So, I decided to get out. You can probably deduce from what I've told you what happens next. If I was taken out by a sniper, I can almost guarantee it was one of Nolan's men and they will never be caught.

I'm sorry Rodders, I really am. I'm sorry I've landed you in this situation and I'm sorry I've left Jenny without me. She will be in so much pain right now I can't bare thinking about it. Please, help me bring them to justice. PLEASE.

"I'm counting on you buddy. Watch your back. Oh, and by the way, I didn't bring you in on this for one reason and one reason only. You're too good for this. I mean it, you're one of my best mates and I didn't want you involved. I don't give a rat's arse about the others, but you are different Rodders. You are a rare thing these days: a genuinely good man. I'm not blowing smoke up your arse, it's not my style, you know that. But this isn't for you mate. Watch your back."

The video ended and Rodders' respect for Dave had almost vanished. Not only was he involved but he had now involved *him* to the point where his life was seriously in danger. Then he thought of Jenny. She would never be the same again and what for? Because of greed and drugs and the actions of Dave. What a selfish bastard. He was in it up to his chin. He had the knowledge and the pen drive but there was no hard evidence. The drugs in Deano's locker would almost certainly be gone by now. It was a dead guy accusing some others of doing a deed that couldn't be proven. He was up the creek without a paddle and he knew it.

The following day started the same as every other except for the fact the platoon would be going on their patrol and wouldn't be in camp for most of the week.

Rodders opened his eyes and thought about Jenny. He couldn't imagine what she was going through and he thought about what would happen if she ever found out the truth. It would come out at some point. It had to. He couldn't keep the information he had to himself and he contemplated how we could use it to best effect.

He decided he would run the risk of being looked upon as a basket case and broach the subject with the Head Med. It might land on sympathetic ears or it could blow up spectacularly in his face but he needed to take the risk. He needed an ally, or maybe two. He had the perfect people in mind but didn't know how they would react. He was in a corner and couldn't see any other way to bring this out into the open.

Tent by tent the platoon started arriving at the meeting point to march as one group to the armory and draw their weapons and ammunition. Everything else was ready to go. The vehicles were fueled and rations had been issued; all that was needed now was to dot the I's and cross the T's.

Rodders looked across in the distance and saw Nolan walking towards the group with Hays by his side. He had all his gear with him and he knew he was coming along for one reason only. They would be meeting with the Leader at some point, and he was there to interpret what plans they had drawn up to expand on their growing smuggling empire. He knew the others still viewed him with suspicion but to what level he didn't know. Once the kit and orders were issued, Rodders decided to make his move. He sidled over to Deano and Billy who were finishing off packing some ammunition into the pouches, took a deep breath and went for it.

"Deano, Billy can I have a quick word?" he asked quietly. They looked at him knowing that if he wanted to speak to them both together it was likely to have something to do with yesterday's events.

"Yeah, of course." Deano gave Billy a nod to follow Rodders. They only walked ten or so feet away but it was far enough to not be heard by the others.

Right. This is it, thought Rodders. *D-Day. No more messing about, say it, get it over with and see where it goes.*

"About last night." Billy and Deano looked at each other expecting him to say he had changed his mind about the goings on in the gym and was duty bound to report what he had seen. But he didn't. It was worse.

"I know about the blackmail. I know about the opium and I know who's involved. I know you're both good guys and are being pushed into this and I want to help. I've got a plan. The Sarge left me a pen drive with some solid intel and we can use it to put a stop to this."

The two men looked at him with ashen faces. Deano stared at him. His blank expression was not the reaction Rodders was expecting. A look of relief maybe, but not this. Billy had the same look. Eventually the silence was broken when Deano leaned forward and whispered in Rodders' ear.

"Who said we want it to end? What blackmail are you talking about? Everyone in our group knows about Billy and me, you're the only one in the tent that doesn't. This isn't about being coerced into anything. You should have kept your mouth shut." And with that they both turned and made a beeline for Nolan and Squires.

A pit opened in Rodders' stomach. What had he done? He had nowhere to run. He was right in the middle of the viper's nest and no matter how quickly his brain went he couldn't see a way out of his predicament. He started biting his lip as thoughts circulated and plans that were scrambled in his head slowly started coming to together like pieces of a jigsaw.

Rodders slowly walked over to his kit and his weapon. He took out an ammunition magazine from his webbing pouch and slid it quietly into the gun. Hiding his actions by turning his back to the group, he cocked the weapon, pulling the working part slowly to the rear so as not to make any noise. The magazine dispensed a round into the chamber and clicked the safety catch to 'Fire.' He stood up, rifle in one hand pointing toward the ground. He could see Nolan, Squires and Hays listened intently to what Deano and Billy were telling them. Like meerkats they all stood bolt upright and swung their heads around to look at Rodders. Davis stared over to Rodders and attempted to make contact but stopped in his tracks he saw the boss and Squires start making their way in Rodders' direction. Rodders waited nervously to see what they would say. He was pumped up and ready to go now. All he could do was think about how they had murdered Dave and left Jenny to be a grieving widow. The hate started coursing through his veins. They both arrived and looked Rodders up and down.

"Well Corporal Trotter," sneered Nolan. "It turns out you're worthy of a best actor Oscar doesn't it? You were doing so well until you dropped yourself right in the shit. Did you really think those two would turn us over to you? They've got a fortune waiting for them at home. You mean nothing to them you moron."

"Thing is Nolan, they don't do they? They've never seen a penny of your so-called fortune. They've only got your word for it and I'm guessing the word of this little turd here." Rodders cocked his head towards Squires who smiled, knowing he had the upper hand and would relish the opportunity to make Rodders' life a misery. It was payback time.

"It makes no difference Corporal. They're in it for the long run and you, you irritating little shit, are the only thing standing in our way. Not that it matters but how much did Sgt Edwards actually tell you?" He quizzed.

"Enough," said Rodders.

"Ah, still keeping it to yourself, even in the face of certain defeat." Nolan pushed his face right up to Rodders.

Rodders brought his face closer so their noses touched. The anger was palpable, and he started to shake as he tried to control his emotions.

"Defeat? Are you threatening me, Sir?"

"I don't need to threaten you Corporal; I have no intention of harming you. Those gents however are not very happy at the fact you are in a position to relieve them of their very lucrative income stream."

Rodders turned and looked at the group. They were baying for blood and he knew that if he went out on patrol he wouldn't come back. He looked at Squires in disgust and whispered, "I'm having you, Squires. Maybe not today but you're mine you worm." He then turned to Nolan, looked him in the eye and ushered him to look downwards. The muzzle of Rodders' rifle was pointing at his groin. He smiled at the boss.

"You're a murdering bastard. Both of you are and you will pay for this I promise." And with that he took a deliberate step backwards, looked at his feet, calculated where he would suffer the least damage and pulled the trigger.

The crack from the rifle took everyone by surprise, most of all Nolan and Squires.

The bullet went straight through Rodders' boot, through his foot and embedded itself into the dusty ground. He fell over instantly, screaming and writhing in pain. Every person within a two-hundred-meter range turned and looked at what was unfolding where 4 platoon were gathered. The blood started oozing from the hole in the boot and into the dirt. Bits of boot and bone were visible and Rodders knew he had lost at least one toe, maybe even two but one thing was for sure, he wasn't going on patrol with 4 platoon.

PART TWO

The Catalyst

CHAPTER 6

Jenny looked at herself in the full-length mirror that hung in the hallway. Dressed all in black bar a small red Kings Regiment badge on her left lapel, she never thought she would be going through this scenario: laying to rest her husband and becoming a widow at her age. She pulled at her dress to straighten it. Dave did the same thing with his uniform every time he left the house. Jumper straight, beret perched at just the right angle and then one last sweep over his shoulder with his hands to remove any lint. She looked at her own reflection and she could see Dave looking back at her. Her breathing was labored and she felt exhausted but if she could get over this final hurdle she could begin to fully grieve and bring some sort of semblance of normality back to her life. She closed the door behind her and walked towards the funeral cortege. She was guided into the front vehicle where members of Dave's family were already seated. His mother, who Dave doted upon, sat sobbing uncontrollably next to Jenny, offered her hand and as the hearse began to slowly move away, she could feel her grasp become tighter, knowing they were heading to her son's final resting place.

Jenny was numb throughout the funeral service but when the gun salutes sounded, Jenny visibly jumped with each loud crack of the soldiers' rifles. She turned to see if she recognized anyone. A few faces were familiar but she remembered that all of Dave's closest companions were still on deployment in Afghanistan. They would have wanted to be here, she thought to herself. She had received a lovely condolence card from Captain Nolan the day before telling her how sorry the men in the company were and how, for operational reasons they couldn't attend but he promised he would come to see her at some point in the future. Dave would have understood. They were doing their duty.

As the day wore on Jenny felt the strain of the situation bearing down on her and after the wake, she headed back to the house to be on her own. When she opened the door, with the post was lying on the doormat. It was mostly junk mail except one which was addressed to her and emblazoned with the emblem of the Kings Regiment across the front. As she began to read, she realized it was an invitation to use the bereavement counselling service offered to family members by the Ministry of Defense. She quickly glanced over the document and without taking much notice placed it onto the fridge door using a magnet. She felt cold. The house felt cold and empty. She missed Dave terribly already and it had only been two weeks since his death. She thought about a lifetime of grief that would be her future and wondered whether it would be worth being alive. She quickly pushed the thoughts out of her mind. *What's the use in that,* she thought? She went upstairs, took off her clothes and ran a hot bath. She looked at the wound on her ankle. It had scabbed over now and had gone red around the edges. She rubbed it and thought about how to cover it up once it was completely healed. She couldn't wear long socks and stockings her entire life. She briefly thought about it until the bath was full and slipped into the hot, bubbly water. The pressure seemed to dissipate from her body instantly when she was enveloped in the water. Sitting on the corner of the bathtub was a rubber duck painted in camouflage colours. It was Dave's. Everything reminded her of him and although she never wanted to or would forget Dave, she had to think of a way to keep her mind busy so as not to go into a depressive state. She lay back, covered her face with a hot flannel and switched off.

The following day started with the usual thoughts and apprehensiveness to leave her safe, warm bed. After twenty or so minutes she decided to rise and do something proactive with her day. She put on the kettle and thought about eating. She couldn't face it and although she had little to nothing over the last twenty-four hours, she knew she wouldn't be able to stomach anything just yet. A cup of tea would have to do. As she opened the door to get some milk, she noticed the bereavement letter hanging by its corner on the magnet. She gave it a tug, the magnet staying in its original position. She gave a smile as if she had achieved the old magicians' trick of removing the tablecloth and leaving the cutlery in place. She slowly made her way to the couch, meandering through the lounge and settling in front of a coffee table covered in cards of condolence. She unfolded the letter and started reading, more intently this time. The bereavement service was there for as long as she wanted, it stated. She could have one to one or group sessions, whichever suited her needs. She decided it would be a good thing for her to talk to a professional about coping with her grief. When she was on the ward, she had seen some of the counselors and knew that they did a stressful but incredibly rewarding job. *Why not?* she thought. *I've got nothing to lose.* After a quick phone call she had an appointment set up for two days later.

The room was large and empty with thirteen chairs in a wide circle, presumably for twelve attendees and a counselor.

Jenny looked around hesitantly, mainly to see if she recognized anyone in the group. She knew it was a longshot but it was better to be safe than sorry. She nodded to people as eye contact was made but no handshakes or introductions were offered. When the door opened again, a man with a clipboard and a tan briefcase entered the room. He was dressed very informally in jeans and a loose-fitting woolly jumper and appeared to be rushed in his actions even though he was five minutes early for the official start time of the session. Jenny stood silently until she was ushered to take a seat of her own choosing. She was flanked on both sides by men, both of whom appeared to be immaculately dressed for the occasion and she wondered if they had come from work or had made the effort especially. She couldn't help but inspect each member of the group and speculate who everyone was and why they were each present. The counselor stood up and began his introduction.

"Good morning, everyone, my name is Jonathan Connelley and I'll be conduction our sessions. To the ones who already know me, welcome back and to those who don't I'll be looking forward to hearing a bit about yourselves as we go along." He kept the introduction short.

"Andrew," he said as he pointed to one of his previous patients, "would you like to start us off please?" A man in a blue t shirt with a beard gave a hello gesture with his hand and began. He looked tired and weather beaten. Jenny guessed his gaunt features exaggerated his age and she placed him in his mid 40s.

Hi. My name is Andrew and I've been coming here for around two months." He paused and took in a deep breath before informing the group of the demise of his wife to cancer and the road to acceptance and recovery he was still on. The anguish in his voice and his general demeanor was of a man in perpetual turmoil, wishing and hoping inside that he could find solace someday soon. Once he had finished speaking his expression changed and Jenny could see the obvious relief on his face. She concluded the whole experience was helping Andrew and felt glad in the knowledge at least one person was getting the support they needed.

Jenny listened with interest as each person offered the group a snapshot of their everyday life and the problems they faced. She, like some of the group, had suffered a bereavement and was finding it difficult to deal with. Others had come through the other end and now attended to offer some form of guidance and help to the rest. She began to grow nervous when it was the turn of the man on her right to convey his feelings and experiences to the group. It only seemed like a minute or so before the baton was passed to her and as she raised her head, the view of twelve pairs of eyes resting on her made her uncomfortable. She observed all the participants, took in a long deep breath and exhaled, controlled and calm.

"Hello everyone, my name is Jenny. This is my first time here and, well, I'm not too sure where to start." She felt embarrassed making that comment until Andrew spoke up.

"Start from the beginning Jenny, that's the best place." He smiled when he looked at her and after taking a moment to compose herself, she began. "Dave, my husband, was killed recently in Afghanistan." As she spoke her voice became more fluid and the words rolled out of her mouth as though she was offering advice to a friend. She could feel a burden lifting with every sentence she expressed to the group and although she felt trepidation to begin with, it was soon overtaken with an overwhelming sense of release. When she came to the end, she saw the group smiling in appreciation of her honesty and vulnerability. She let out a heavy sigh of relief.

After her first two sessions Jenny had no doubt that she was learning more about coping with and coming to terms with Dave's death. She didn't want to ever forget Dave but she had to learn how to deal with her emotions and she was making great progress with the counselling. She decided that maybe she could help others in the same way. She already had a solid footing in mental health work. She could do the course and become a counselor. She had decided, she would go back to university and study. She would use her grief as a learning tool and help others who had been through the same experience as her. Her mind was made up. She would go home and fill in her application form that very night.

CHAPTER 7

Rodders sat up in his hospital bed, took one look at some brown food on his plate and turned away in disgust. He had been lucky, or so the doctor had told him. He had lost his little toe altogether and part of the adjacent one as well. But other than that, he would make a full recovery and would be up and about in a couple of months. He would, however, walk with a slight limp for the rest of his life. As he lay on his bed wondering about his next move, he noticed a uniformed officer heading towards him. *Here we go*, he thought to himself.

"Corporal Trotter?" The man eyed him with cold suspicion.

"Yes Sir?" replied Rodders.

"I'm Captain Mills from the Royal Military Police. Are you busy?" He asked sarcastically.

"What do you think?" Returned Rodders.

"Cut the attitude son," he snapped back. "You're still in the Army, I'm a Captain and you're not. Understand?"

"Yes Sir," said Rodders backing down. "I'm just a pissed off with this," he nodded towards his foot.

"Looks nasty," said Mills. "Two toes, from what I understand." He said.

"One and a half," said Rodders, trying to get one up on the officer.

Captain Mills was in his forties and obviously someone who had come up through the ranks. He didn't seem like the type to pay lip service, and he didn't: he came straight to the point.

"You're in the shit young man," he said. "You told the doctor this was an accidental discharge and not your fault, correct?"

"Correct." Said Rodders.

"But your Platoon Commander… a Captain… Nolan says differently." He scanned his notebook to clarify names so as not to get anything mixed up.

The bastard thought Rodders. *He couldn't get me in Afghanistan so he will screw me over here instead.*

"He says you were desperate to get home. Says you told him you would do anything to get back to the UK. Next thing… BANG… and you're on a jet back to Blighty. How do you explain that one?"

"He's lying Sir," said Rodders. "He's had it in for me for ages."

"You do realise that makes you sound even more guilty, don't you? I'll give you another go, let's see if you can find a slightly better excuse before I tell you what I think happened."

"It *was* an accident Sir," Rodders tried to sound sincere. "I was packing my stuff and before I knew it, I was on the floor and now I'm here. That's the truth."

"Bollocks!" Mills fired back. "Let me tell you something, OK? I've been in this army for almost twenty-five…no twenty-six years and as you've probably guessed I'm either crap at my job and still a Captain or I'm really good at my job and I'm an ex-ranker Captain. In case you're wondering it's the latter. I've been around the block and I know there are some right dickheads who wear the officer uniform but from what I understand your Platoon Commander is a bit of a golden boy. Not a blemish on his record. To be honest I find that a bit hard to believe because he sounds like a right arrogant prick on the phone but there's the facts. So, I've got good news… good news and bad news. Which one do you want first?"

Rodders had an idea of what was coming.

"Give me the bad news first," he said.

"OK" said Mills, "you're out." He looked at Rodders expecting there to be a look of shock on his face but Rodders didn't flinch.

"And the good news?"

"You will be able to claim a military disability pension when you get evaluated by an independent medical professional." *That's a bonus*, thought Rodders. *But if they're offering me a pension then it can't be a dishonorable discharge.*

"They're not charging you," Mills said. "The government are taking flak from all sides about Afghanistan and if the press catches wind of a soldier being shot, charged, and losing his pension there will be a massive shit storm and it won't look good. So, you're off the hook. Personally, I think you're lying through your teeth but it's not my call, so you walk… or rather limp out of here." He said looking at his foot.

Rodders sighed with relief. At least he would have some kind of income, no matter how small.

"Off the record…" said Mills, "did you do it on purpose?"

"Off the record?" said Rodders, Mills nodded. "It was an accident. I clicked the safety off my rifle when it caught on part of my webbing and it went off when I hit the trigger by accident. But you are right about one thing," he continued. "My Platoon Commander is a dick of the highest order, and I had a feeling he would try to screw me over because he's that kind of person. Maybe you should look into his record a little bit harder Sir. It'll show what kind of person he really is." He had said enough to get Mills attention but not enough for him to sit back down and start asking questions. Mills looked at him slightly inquisitively and nodded.

"Good luck son," he said. "Look after yourself." And with that he turned and walked way leaving Rodders with a sense of satisfaction inside.

Rodders picked up the daily paper and scanned the headlines. The usual political party squabbling was the lead story of the day. Not a mention of the war in Afghanistan on pages two, three or four. He kept thumbing the paper until he came to page nine and the first mention of any military action the UK was involved with. The story made Rodders take a deep breath. The lead line read: "Kings Pay Tribute to Fallen Hero." It was the story regarding Dave's repatriation and subsequent funeral. Rodders had a slow look around the ward to make sure nobody was watching him and when he was satisfied, he wasn't he started to silently weep. He lay on his side, away from the door and reflected on what had happened over the last couple of weeks. Dave's death, the uncovering of the smuggling enterprise and his eventual shooting just to escape the almost certainty of ending up in the same situation as his friend. It became overwhelming and he started to openly sob. It didn't last long. He reached for a tissue, blew his nose and pulled himself together. Jenny needed to know what had happened but he had to get his own life on track before making inroads with her. He was prepared to wait and during that time would plan how to make the others pay.

CHAPTER 8

The letter box slapped against the door with a clang and the envelope dropped to the floor. Jenny was sitting on the second to bottom stair waiting on its arrival and watched it as it fell through and hit the doormat. She went to retrieve it then sat back down again. She had been biting the skin surrounding her nail and inspected the damage she had done before deciding to stop prolonging the inevitable and open the envelope. She took a deep breath and tore open the letter. She quickly perused the contents and smiled broadly then gave out a loud "YES!" and a strong fist pump into the air when she saw her university results. She read out loud, "The Diploma in Grief and Bereavement Counselling with Distinction is conferred upon Jennifer Edwards." Dave would have been so proud to see this day.

It had taken eighteen months of hard work, juggling studying and her job, but she needed something to occupy her time following Dave's death and she had now become a trained counsellor, able to help others in their grief process. She had taken the day off, knowing the letter would arrive: if she passed she could celebrate but if she failed she could be grumpy in her own space. Deep down she knew it would be the former rather than the latter. She had worked hard and today lunch with friends, a takeaway, and a bottle of red would help her celebrate her happy day. She picked up her handbag, keys and coat and left the house to meet with the "Ladies That Lunch" with a spring in her step not seen for many, many months. *Nothing can spoil today*, she thought to herself.

When Jenny arrived at the Outside Inn bar, she realised this was the first real day out she had attended since Dave died. She pushed through the door and could immediately see her two work mates, Olivia and Isla, waiting eagerly for her at the bar. When they spotted her a loud "YAY!' filled the room. All eyes turned their attention to the ladies as they ignored the glares of the other patrons and continued their ebullient greeting.

"This, girls..." exclaimed Olivia, "is going to be one hell of an afternoon...and evening...and maybe nighttime as well!" They all laughed.

"Let's see," replied Jenny, scratching her chin pretending to seriously think about her answer, "so far, it's a yes from me." She was intent on having a good time. She had a milestone to celebrate and if that meant going all out today then so be it.

"So?" Asked Isla, inquisitively, "what's the result?" Jenny opened her bag and slowly removed the letter, then replaced it into her bag again and repeating the process several times like a burlesque dancer doing her final 'reveal.'

"Get on with it woman!" Yelled Isla, eager to share in her friend's news. Jenny removed the letter and opened it with a loud "TA DAAAAAA."

"It's a pass," she announced. "But... ahem... not any ordinary pass... no no no, but a pass with a distinction."

"That's amazing Jenny." Gushed Olivia, "I'm so proud of you. Well done girl."

"Same here Jen." Beamed Isla, "we couldn't be happier for you." The girls huddled together into a group hug and then tried to get the attention of the bar staff to order some well-earned aperitifs.

As the drinks flowed and the chat continued, Jenny began to feel like her old self again. Thoughts of Dave flashed through her mind but only when she had a recollection of a good happening and the afternoon was a happy event and one to be remembered for a long time. As the afternoon wore on into the evening Jenny noticed that Olivia was getting more than her fair share of attention form a tall good-looking man at the bar, accompanied by an equally handsome friend.

"Aye aye," said Jenny, "eyes on you six o'clock." The comment was aimed at Olivia who quickly spun around to see who Jenny was referring to.

"Don't look you fool," she said, laughing. "Now he knows you're onto him."

"I don't care," voiced Olivia, "I saw him ages ago anyway when you two were at the loo. He's a bit of a dish mind and I'll bet his mates got skills as well." Laughter rose from the table as the three friends collapsed onto the table in fits of giggles.

"Get yourselves away the pair of you," pushed Jenny.

"No," sighed Isla, "this is a girl's night out."

"Listen you two," said Jenny, "it's been great, but this is my first night out in a long, long time and I'm ready for my bed." She was being completely honest. It had been a long afternoon and evening and she had drunk her fair share of booze. She genuinely wanted to be wrapped up under her duvet watching TV. She urged them to carry on without her and stood up from the table. She gave a slight wobble and a snigger and began to put on her coat.

"I'll be very disappointed if neither of you pull tonight," she smiled. "Now, go get 'em tigers... tigers?... tigressess?? Oh,

I don't know. Go and get laid the pair of you." Olivia and Isla agreed to follow her wishes and walked her to the door.

"I can't tell you how good this has been," comforted Isla, rubbing Jenny gently on her upper arm. "I've absolutely loved this."

"Me too," said Olivia.

"ME TOO," yelped Jenny as she hugged the friends individually and she left with a broad smile on her face; something that had been missing for far too long.

During her short twenty-minute walk home she decided that her night wasn't quite over and stopped for a bottle of wine from the local corner shop. Exiting, she stood outside in the cool evening and filled her lungs with clean fresh air, slowly exhaling, watching her breath rise and dissipate in front of her. She loved this time of year and after pulling her collar up around her neck to deflect the cold she continued in the direction of home. As she walked, she smirked to herself, remembering funny anecdotes and stories told throughout the afternoon and made her mind up that she must do it more often. She needed to regain a social life at some point and this was the start. She was in a happy mood.

Suddenly and instinctively, she looked over her shoulder thinking she could hear evenly matched footsteps behind her. There was no-one there and she lingered for a few seconds to make sure she wasn't being followed. She continued slowly, ever attentive of her surroundings and then... there it was again, footsteps behind her. Moving away from the dimly lit streetlight she turned sharply to see the outline of a person, dressed in black some fifty meters away on the other side of the street. Swiftly she began to pick up her pace wishing she had worn her flat shoes instead of the heels she had put on this afternoon. As she attempted to walk even faster, she continuously looked behind her to catch a glimpse of the shadowy figure stalking her. She was frightened now and began to look for the keys to her house. As she fumbled in her handbag she began to fluster, resisting the urge to turn and look one more time. The keys were pulled from the bag and in her haste, she dropped them onto the dirty, chewing gum laced pavement. Now she was becoming scared, and an acute feeling of anxiety swept over her. The keys were in her hand and once more she turned to look but there was nobody to be seen. She let out a sigh of relief but as she did the figure stepped out from behind a tree which lined the street. She kicked off her shoes and left them in the gutter at the side of the road, breaking into a sprint. She could see her house in front of her and continued running until she thought her heart would burst from her chest. She swung herself around the gatepost for purchase and arrived at the front door. She jostled with the keys. *So many keys*, she thought, *so many useless keys*. Finally, she found the one she was looking for and she scrambled to get it into the lock. The key slid into the slot cleanly and Jenny began to turn it clockwise. As she did, she spun around one more time to analyze the situation and there, stood motionless, was the person she guessed had been following her. They were dressed in jeans and a dark green waterproof jacket with their head hidden behind a hoodie pulled tightly around the face. She was about to scream when a familiar voice spoke to her.

"Jenny?" Said the man. "It's me, its Rodders." He removed the hoodie and looked at Jenny.

"Rodders," she gasped, "oh my god it *is* you.". Her welcome turned to anger. "What the fuck are you doing following me like that? Are you stalking me? What on earth are you doing here?" Rodders looked at her sheepishly.

"What are you talking about?" He said, stumped by her question.

"You, following me up the road there," she pointed in the direction she had just come from.

"I didn't come from that direction," he stammered, "I came from down there." He pointed down an adjacent street. Jenny began to question herself. Had she really been followed or had her mind, in a semi drunken state been playing tricks on her?

"But if you came from that direction, who has been following me?" Rodders stepped onto the street and looked up and down in both directions.

"There's no one here Jenny," he said. Jenny stared and turned to open the door. She stood in the porch and studied Rodders for a moment.

"Jesus, it's been, what, just over a year and a half since I've seen you. I heard about your accident. Are you OK?"

"I'm fine Jenny," he uttered. "Can we speak inside?"

"Sorry where are my manners, of course, of course come in." She guided him through the door in front of her. Jenny had no reason not to let Rodders into the house. She had known him for years and he was always a great pal of Dave's. She was genuinely pleased to see him after such a long time.

They stepped through the door and pushed him into the lounge as she headed for the kitchen to open her wine.

"Do you want a drink?" came the shout from the back of the house. Rodders was expecting it. There was always a drink offered at the Edwards house. They always made him feel welcome and at ease when at home. In fact, they were known as being the perfect hosts.

"I'll have what you're having," he replied.

"I'm having wine but I've got some beers if you prefer?"

"No wines fine." Rodders made himself comfortable on the couch.

She came through minutes later, drinks in hands and handed Rodders his glass.

"Cheers," she said. The toast was reciprocated and she stared at Rodders.

"Wow," said Jenny. "You look great. How's life been treating you?" She felt a bit silly knowing that he had been shot in the foot but didn't have a clue how to start the conversation or why he was there.

"Well," he replied, "apart from having half of my foot blown away, I would say I'm fine." Rodders' joke put her at ease. They both laughed nervously but at least the ice had been broken. After exchanging pleasantries and having a general catch up, Rodders decided the time for small talk was over.

"Jenny, I came here tonight to have a chat to you about Dave," he said.

"Listen it's OK," she replied, "I know you couldn't make the funeral what with being in hospital and that, but it's alright, I know you would have been there if you could."

"It's not about that Jenny. It's something a bit more complex and I think you need to hear what I have to say. But I want to warn you, it's not easy listening." Jenny's brows furrowed as she leaned in to hear more..

"Jenny, Dave wasn't killed by accident. He was murdered." The words were very precise. Rodders had spoken them a thousand times in his head and looked into the mirror on numerous occasions practicing breaking the news to her. Now he had said it, he instantly regretted it. It was straight and to the point, but Jenny started to get agitated, and he wondered if he should have done it in a gentler way.

"What the hell are you talking about? Seriously Rodders... WHAT THE FUCK!?" She was screaming. "I don't hear from for almost eighteen months, and you rock up out of the blue to *my* house to tell me my dead husband was murdered, instead of being shot by a sniper's bullet. How dare you?"

"Jenny," he said in a low voice staying cool as not to upset her any more. "He told me himself".

She stopped dead and stood up from her seat. "What are you talking about he *told you himself?* How could he do that if he was already dead? You're sick Rodders!" She shouted. "And I want you out of here, right now."

"He left a message on a pen drive a few days before it happened. I have it with me if you would like to see it but you must be prepared for what you will hear. It's not a good story."

She looked at him suspiciously and wondered if this had been some elaborate set up or stunt. *Why would anyone do something like this?* She thought. But she had to see, she had to know. She opened up her laptop and he handed her the pen drive. She inserted it into the USB slot on the side of the computer and it played automatically. When Dave's face came onto the screen she began to cry. She paused it instantly.

"I can't do this," she said through tearful gasps. "Why are you doing this to me, what have I done to you to deserve this?"

"You *need* to see this Jenny," he urged. "This is *important*. I risked my life for what's on this drive. I gave up my career for what you're about to watch. Christ, I blew off my own bloody toes for what's on this drive, at least hear me out. Watch the video and we can talk."

She looked at him. He was laying it all out there and she knew in that moment he was being brutally honest. This wasn't any kind of sick trick of wind up, it was serious. She clicked play and watched as Dave told the story of his death.

The video stopped and Jenny tenderly touched the computer screen. She couldn't believe what she was hearing. If it had come from anyone else, she would have dismissed them as being mentally unstable or a crackpot conspiracy theorist. But it came from the mouth of her own husband. He had foreseen his own death and outed the perpetrators of such a heinous crime. Her sorrow turned to anger then rage. She upturned the small coffee table and grabbed Rodders by the lapels.

"Who is Nolan and who is Squires?" She spat, her eyes full of fire.

"Nolan is the Platoon Commander and Squires is one of his Corporals," he answered. "But it's bigger than that Jenny.

There are another six blokes involved in this. I don't think they are all complicit in Dave's death but they're balls deep in the opium deal."

"Bastards!" She shouted. She let go of his clothing and brushed down his shirt. "The Platoon Commander: is he the head of this whole thing?" She wanted to double check that she was hearing this correctly from Rodders.

"Yes," he replied.

"Do you know the rest of them? Do you know their names?"

"Yes," came the answer. She let out some heavy breaths and started to cool down.

She looked at him and touched his face. "You shot yourself to escape these people?"

He nodded, a slight tear in his eyes.

"You've carried this around with you since it happened trying to avoid them?" He nodded again.

"Oh Rodders," she said softly, "you poor, poor man. Thank you, I mean that from the bottom of my heart, thank you." She stared at the blank computer screen and then to Rodders.

"I've lost my husband and you have lost not only your career but injured yourself. And all because of some greedy, filthy, murdering low life pieces of shit." She seethed. "Now... what are we going to do about it?"

"The police are not an option," he said. "There's no physical evidence, that would have been moved as soon as this thing blew open. Even the Military Police wouldn't investigate as they think I'm a self-harming malingerer. I only escaped a dishonorable discharge because they didn't want to risk media attention."

"What about the drive?" She asked. "Surely that could be used as evidence?"

"Not really," he said. "See, its one man's word against another's. Every single one of the Platoon, whether they're in this or not, would state Dave was killed by a sniper. The video only shows one man blaming others for his death. They would look at this as a possible grudge against the boss. After all, officers are only liked by other officers." Rodders drummed his fingers on the table as he thought. "I think going through traditional channels is a closed shop I'm afraid."

"So where does that leave us then?" She asked.

"I'm not sure but we will have to do a lot of investigating ourselves. I've still got friends in the Kings, and they might be able to help."

"Can you trust them?"

"We've got no other choice."

He got up to stretch his legs and began limping around the living room.

"Does it hurt?" She asked.

"What, this?" He tapped his thigh. "Sometimes it does. Sometimes it gets itchy, and you go to scratch and remember your toes aren't there anymore. It's weird but I'm getting used to it. You've heard the old phantom limb theory?"

"Of course" she said. "Have you forgotten; I am a nurse."

"Ah, of course," Remembrance flooded his face. "I've noticed you keep rubbing your ankle. Have you injured it or something?"

"I cut it on a piece of glass the night I found about Dave being shot." She stared into the distance while she said it. "I had a tattoo done to try to cover the scar." She pulled down her sock to reveal a rather striking, beautifully colored Koi Carp on her ankle. "Dave always said that if we ever moved into a big house in the country he would have a pond filled with Koi Carp. I liked it and thought it would be a nice reminder of him. Do you like it?"

"Actually," he countered, "I don't normally like tattoos but that is very subtle and tasteful. I like it, it suits you."

It was coming up to four in the morning when Jenny left Rodders on the couch and ascended the stairs slowly. It had been a tiring night. She had discovered her husband had been involved in drug smuggling. It made her wonder if she knew him at all. But what did it matter now? It was all in the past. She could get over that. What she couldn't get over was the fact his commanding officer, the person he thought he could trust, was involved in his death. She slid under the sheets and thought about how she could get revenge on the people who had ruined her life. She was never going to let this drop. Not while there was a breath in her body.

CHAPTER 9

The sun broke through the curtains of Jenny's bedroom and she stretched out in the bed before rising, wrapping herself in a cozy dressing gown and heading downstairs to see Rodders. He was still asleep, snoring gently. As she looked at him, she felt a pang of guilt towards her outburst at him. Of course, she never really thought he would do, or say anything to hurt her but it was a knee jerk reaction. She felt embarrassed for shouting at him in the heat of the moment. He had given up so much to get this information to her. She didn't quite know how to repay him, but she would in time.

"Tea or coffee?" She said quietly.

"Tea please," came the muffled grunt of a reply.

She went to the kitchen and switched on the kettle.

Steam rose into the air and as the kettle boiled and Jenny snapped out of a temporary trance. She was thinking about ways to find evidence to give to the police but in reality she wanted those involved to suffer like she had. She despised those responsible for Dave's death and was willing to plunge to their level to exact her own form of justice. The difficult part was it had to have no comeback at all.

She carried the drinks through to find Rodders upright and fully awake. He yawned loudly and acknowledged the hot tea in front of him. He sipped the mug and gave her a thumbs up. He took a bite from a shortbread biscuit she had offered him and sat contented. He hadn't really had much of a life for the last eighteen months so this he basked in the feeling of simple pleasure a good brew and a biscuit gave him.

Jenny eventually broke the silence.

"Rodders," she began, "the people who did this, can we find out where they are now? I mean the juniors and NCOs will still be with the regiment at barracks, but Nolan, he will only do two years posting as an officer, correct?"

"Yeah, that's right," he said. "I have contacts I can use. I know a lovely girl in the medical admin section at HQ I used to see casually. I could ask her. She's trustworthy and she will have access to records and such things so I can find out where everyone is right now."

"What about medical records?" She enquired. "Could you get them?"

"Possibly," he said. "Like you said last night about me not forgetting you were a nurse, don't forget I was a medic." He gave her a quick wink, "do you have an idea?" He asked.

"Not yet," she said. "I'm just thinking about what tools and documents we have at our disposal. We have to consider the things we need to start our campaign and believe me; I'm going to destroy every single one of them."

"There's a job coming up with the local authority for a junior counsellor to serve the members and families of the barracks. I'm thinking about applying. I should have a good chance of getting the job, after all I've got lived experience of grief within the military environment. It'll cover all angles; not just grief but I'm more than qualified for the job. I just qualified yesterday but with my mental health nursing and it being a junior role I'm confident of landing it."

"What about running into some of the 4 platoon guys? That's not something you would want to risk, surely?" He looked at her with concern.

"Actually, none of the juniors really know me, do they? I only ever went to functions at the Sgts Mess, so I've never met any of them. They don't know me and that's only going to be an advantage. Where are you staying? We need to keep in touch and figure out where we go from here," she said.

"I'm at the caravan park down by Henley Wood, you know the one with the big lake about twenty miles from here? It's a cash job and they don't know my real name; I'm obviously trying to keep a low profile so that's the best I could do without deposits and references."

"OK" Jenny pondered. "Have you got a mobile number?" He spoke it out and she put it into her phone under A. Rod. After exchanging hers they agreed to call regularly and meet up once a week to talk about progress in their plans to bring down the gang.

After the tea and a bacon sandwich, Rodders got up to leave. As Jenny escorted him to the door, she kissed him on both cheeks.

"Be careful Rodders, please. And thank you again for coming to me."

"Anytime Jenny," he said. "Take care and be safe." He left and Jenny gently closed the door behind him.

Rodders strode as fast as his limp would let him from Jenny's house and down to the nearest bus stop. He had a car but most of the time he found public transport to be a better way of getting around bringing less attention to himself. He may be living twenty miles away but if he encountered any of 4 platoon, at least he would be surrounded by other people and could shout for help. Three buses later and he arrived at Henley Wood Caravan Park. He entered his thirty by ten-foot static home and threw his keys into a fruit bowl sitting on a cheap plywood sideboard. He went to his fridge and took out a can of super strength lager and opened it with a hiss and a spirt of cream-colored foam splashing onto the work top. He put the can to his lips in a vain attempt to stem the flow of beer but as expected, it still managed to spoil in a puddle onto the lino covered floor. He looked down, ignored the spillage and went into the lounge area where he threw himself onto the fitted couch which was a permanent fixture of the caravan. Picking up the remote control he switched the television to any random channel for background noise and began to chug the booze from the can. Three good gulps and the can was empty. He repeated the process until he emptied the fridge and fell into an alcohol fueled slumber. When he awoke, the TV was still blaring and as he squinted at the clock, he was shocked to see it was only eight o'clock in the evening. The sun was setting, and the sky was a cool orange colour which meant the corner shop was still open and he could go and restock the fridge with more beer.

Trudging back to the caravan, holding a carrier bag laden with cans, he reflected on his past life and wondered what the future had in store for him. Following the 'keys and TV' routine he sat with another can of beer and began the cycle again. It started to feel like Groundhog Day. He removed his shoes and socks and stared down at his mangled foot, toes missing and the stump protruding out from the skin. It looked ugly. Although the doctors had done their best, he felt incomplete and stupid. Suddenly, in a fit of instant rage he threw the can at the television set, smashing the screen propelling hundreds of tiny shards of glass onto the floor around him. He sat forward, put his head into his hands and began to cry.

"What have I become?" He said to himself. "I need help." He placed his shoes back on, got up and walked to the fridge, took out the cans and poured them down the drain.

"This is the beginning of a new life. This is the start of a new me." He said out loud to himself as he watched the amber liquid wash down the plughole. With this he vowed to get his life back on track and he would start by helping Jenny in her journey to bring down the opium gang.

A fortnight passed and Jenny hadn't heard anything back from her application for the counselor's role. She was disappointed. She thought that it was perfect for her and she wondered why she wasn't being given a chance. Maybe it was an experience thing, maybe she had overestimated her own qualifications and background. At least she still had a job at the hospital. They knew about the application for the counsellor's post and had backed Jenny all the way. Her boss had given her blessing for the chance for Jenny to move up in the healthcare chain and welcomed the opportunity. She was perplexed, two weeks was a long time. An email had received upon receipt of her application but nothing since. The phone rang.

"Hello?" Jenny said quietly.

"Hello... hi... am I speaking to..." Jenny could hear papers rustling in the background as the anonymous person franticly searched for a name. "...to Jenny, yes Jenny Edwards?"

"Yes, hello this is Jenny. Who am I speaking to please?"

"Oh sorry, of course, how silly of me. Jenny may name is Joyce Middleton, I work for the NHS trust dealing with the counselor's role for the Kings Regiment. How are you?"

Jenny was startled. "I'm fine," she said, "how are you?"

"To be honest," she said, flustered, "I've had better days. I'll get straight to it as I've got a million other things to get on with. Firstly, I'm sorry you've not heard from us. Our I.T. system went down almost a week ago and it's still not working. Not only that but the printer has gone on the fritz as well, *that's* why you didn't get an email or a letter and you're now getting a phone call. I'm sorry it's at short notice but you're in line for an interview, is there *any* change you could do Friday coming? I know it's a big ask but it's a race to get someone in the post as soon as possible." Jenny couldn't believe what she was hearing, she was so excited but was taking a second or two to compose herself.

"Friday you say? Yes, I can do that, what time suits you best?"

"How about.... ten, is that ok?" Replied Joyce.

"Yes of course," said Jenny with an air of confidence.

"You know where to go?" Asked Joyce.

"I do," she responded, "I know the building well."

"Then we will see you then," and after exchanging pleasantries they both hung up.

Jenny dropped her phone onto the couch and made a fist. "YES!"

When the interview day arrived, the drive to the appointment seemed to go by in an instant. Jenny ran through some questions she expected would be thrown in her direction but other than some very light nerves she felt quite calm. As she entered the office and introduced herself to the receptionist, she could feel herself picking at the skin on the side of her right index finger. This was her nervous 'tell.' When she caught herself doing it, she stopped instantly but a small bead of blood had appeared where the rawness was and she took out a tissue to clean it off. As she wiped the blood away, her mind began to wander with thoughts of Dave and she had to snap herself out of her daydream before she became too engrossed and made herself unhappy. Even though Jenny knew the drill when it came to controlling her grief, there were times when she just couldn't help getting emotional. The receptionist called out Jenny's name and she stood and entered the interviewer's office.

"Hello Jenny, I'm Joyce, it was me you spoke to on the phone," came the welcome. Jenny held out her hand and the two shook.

"Of course, Joyce. It's so nice to meet you." Joyce ushered Jenny to take a seat and the interview began straight away.

"So," said Joyce, "why do you think this role is suited to you?" Jenny had endured interviews before in which she was asked exactly the same questions.

"To be honest," she began, "I've been a mental health nurse for over ten years and I've seen people at their lowest. Unless you're a doctor or..." she gestured, "a counsellor, your ability to influence their treatment pretty much stops there. I want to be a bigger part of the patients' journey to recovery and I think I have the experience to offer that," she answered. Joyce perused the paperwork in front of her.

"I see your husband was a soldier. He was shot and killed in Afghanistan I believe? How did that make you feel?"

Jenny started to feel like *she* was in therapy now.

"I felt like I suspect everyone else does in those circumstances," she carried on. "Sad at first, then angry, then helpless, but I went to counselling and they helped me come to terms with my loss and in doing so, I think I can bring to the role the perspective of a person who has lost someone in the military and that, I believe is my greatest asset. I'll never fully get over my husband's death, I mean who would? But I've learnt to control my grief and I truly believe I've come out of it a better person."

Joyce showed no expression as she spoke. She wrote notes and ticked boxes but gave nothing away. This lady would make a great poker player though Jenny.

After almost an hour in the hot seat, Jenny was starting to tire. She began to take longer with her answers but thought hard and methodically before offering up her views. They're not only interviewing me, she concluded, they're testing my resolve and focus. She could do this; she just needed to concentrate and work hard. Something she was used to.

"Well, Mrs. Edwards," said Joyce, standing up from her seat and extended her hand, "that's it for now. Thank you for coming in today, especially at such short notice." She shook her hand. "The receptionist will see you out and we will be in touch in due course."

Jenny expected more from her but didn't want to ask questions and was about to leave when she stopped and turned around. She looked her straight in the eye and studied her for a second before saying, "Thank you, Goodbye."

As the receptionist spoke to Jenny quietly about getting in touch with her, she felt let down at not getting at least a hint of how she had done in the interview. She left, slightly disappointed in herself.

As the door closed the Joyce looked down the short corridor to the receptionist and smiled, nodded, and gave a quick wink.

Jenny wasn't even home when the call came through. She had got the job. As soon as she accepted the role and hung up, she made a call to the girls, "it's time to celebrate!"

The next morning, Jenny awoke to the shrill ringing of her mobile phone. She fumbled for it in the semi darkness and when she failed to subdue the shriek, she opened her eyes and answered it abruptly.

"Yes...hello?" She snapped.

"Hi Jenny," came the cautious reply, "its Rodders. How are you this morning? You sound a bit..." he thought for a second trying to think of a diplomatic word for what he wanted to say, "worse for wear. Good night was it?" He sniggered.

"Hi Rodders," she rubbed her eyes, "actually I was celebrating my new job. Remember the counselors position we spoke about? Well, I start at the end of my notice period and I was out with the girls having a few drinkies. You know the score. I was going to give you a shout out later today for a catch up. What's the latest with you?"

"Well," he sighed, "I've managed to dig up some information on the group but I don't want to talk about it on the phone. Can I come to you?"

"Of course," she hesitated, "good or bad news?"

"A bit of both actually," he replied. 'Still, I would rather see you to let you know what I'm thinking."

"OK. How about two o'clock at my place? Bring biscuits."

At precisely two o'clock, the doorbell rang and there stood Rodders with a carrier bag filled with a selection of biscuits and sweets.

"Well," he proclaimed, "as you've got the job a celebration is still in order. And from the sounds of it, I didn't think you would be in the mood for alcohol." He was right. Jenny was more tired than hungover but needed to be lucid to hear what he had to say about their ongoing plans.

Once the tea had been served and they had taken seats in the lounge it was time to get down to business.

"Right then," he said sitting side on to look at Jenny. "The good news is that Hays is dead." Jenny looked bewildered but quite nonchalant about what he was going to say next.

"He stood on an IED on patrol." he revealed with a smile. A moment after he said it, he looked rather regretful. Jenny felt the same way. They had known people, friends and colleagues who had befallen the same fate over the years and to show a strange kind of happiness over someone losing their lives in a similar way seemed incredibly immoral.

"That didn't come out the way I thought it would." Rodders continued.

"I know," replied Jenny feeling rather upset with herself for thinking the way she did "but as far as I'm concerned, he was one of the bastards involved in Dave's death and he got what he deserved."

Rodders nodded in agreement.

"Right then," he continued, "Deano Martin and Billy Stevens are both out of the army. They managed to buy themselves out after receiving threats from outside of the platoon over the whole gay thing and they apparently live about twenty miles from the camp. I've been led to understand they both go to counselling for PTSD and depression associated with their experiences. I don't know if that involves guilt owing to the fact, they were involved in a drug smuggling ring and murder but hey, who cares? They don't have the protection of either the army or Nolan anymore."

"And the rest?" Quizzed Jenny.

"The rest are all still in and on camp. A few of them visit the camp counsellor once a week, especially after Dave's death and Hays being killed. I think they were all involved now except one: Davis. I've been speaking to a really good mate of mine who knows my predicament but not the whole story. He's a medic on camp and he's familiar with all the 4 platoon guys. He says Davis just keeps to himself and seems very down. I think the burden of this drug thing is really weighing on him. His father is a right bastard by all accounts and is only using the lad to get a supply of gear into the country." He thought for a minute, looked at Jenny and said, "What kind of father would ever use his child like that?"

"He's a victim," she replied, "maybe just as much as you and I are. He's been stuck without a way out for God knows how long. Can we get him on side?"

"I haven't even thought about it to be honest. Leave it with me and I'll have a think," he said.

"OK" Jenny sighed. "Good work by the way," she smiled as she said the words and Rodders blushed slightly. "But we must remember why we are doing this."

"It's not forgotten," he replied with a nod. They finished their tea and then said their goodbyes. Jenny let him out, secured the doors and went back to the couch. She was happy with the way things were going but needed to formulate the plan in advance and not on the spot as they had been doing so far.

She would have an early night and give it more thought tomorrow. Before any of that though she would have to get through a pile of mail that had been left, unread at the table by the front door. There was a letter with the address handwritten in what appeared to be fountain pen with exquisite handwriting.

She was intrigued. She opened it and put her hand to her mouth in shock. It was from Nolan.

Dear Mrs. Edwards,

I'm sorry it has taken me so long to contact you in regard to David's death. I hope you received the card of condolence sent by myself from the platoon when David was buried. We were, regrettably, on detachment and unable to attend, much to our frustration. After I returned from detachment I was seconded to another unit for a period of time and foolishly, I believed the Company Commander would have contacted you. Please accept my sincere apologies.

David was a valued member of our company and an excellent soldier. The men miss him terribly, not only because of his guidance but also on a personal level. Although still young, he became a father figure to many of the younger soldiers.

Jenny could feel the anger coursing through her veins, and she had to force herself to carry on.

This letter is not an official correspondence from the Army Mrs. Edwards, but more of a plea for help. One of our platoon was seriously injured during our time in Afghanistan and we are deeply worried about him. I'm sure you are well aware being a mental health professional that PTSD and depression are common within the armed forces and we would like to help and be involved in his recuperation if possible. I know he was a very good friend of David and no doubt yourself as well. We think he may have contacted you directly at some point. His name is Andrew Trotter, although you will probably affectionately know him as Rodders as we all did.

Please, if you have seen or heard from Andrew can you contact me on the details given.

Kind regards

Capt. Merlin Nolan.

Jenny was now livid. Her mind was now running overtime with questions. How did they know she was a healthcare professional and why did they think Rodders had made contact? Was it them following her after her night out or was that her own mind playing tricks? Were they watching her now? She peered out of the window to see if she could notice anything strange or out of place on the street.

"Stop it!" She yelled to herself and closed the blinds. This is what they want. It's intimidation. They hadn't been in touch before because they weren't worried about the pen drive or the 'proof' Rodders had. Now, she guessed, they think he would contact her and tell here everything and she might attempt to take it further by any means necessary. She looked at the letter and read it one more time. When she had finished, she rolled her eyes and shook her head.

"Merlin.... says it all really." She spoke aloud before launching her right foot at the small table, smashing it into pieces as it hit the wall.

CHAPTER 10

As Jenny entered her office, she was still thinking about her letter from Nolan when Siona the receptionist gave a sharp knock on her door.

"Jenny?" She began, "your ten o'clock will be five minutes late. She's called to say she's stuck in traffic. Is that OK?"

"Yes of course," she replied. "Just give me a shout when she appears, thanks." And with that the door closed shut.

Jenny sat silently while she contemplated how to move forward with her plan. It governed her thoughts day and night, and she wouldn't find inner peace until she had retribution. She had a few things floating around in her head but nothing solid. Rodders had imparted some ideas he had but they needed a firm direction and a fool proof strategy to make It work. She stared at her diploma on the wall in its new frame and pride bubbled up within her. She had a wry smile on her face when there came a knock on the door.

"Jenny, it's your ten o'clock," informed Siona.

"Thanks, send her in will you please." What Jenny or her patient didn't realise is that the next hour would shape their destinies in a way neither of them would have ever thought.

"Hi, how are you, please come in and take a seat. My name's Jenny and I believe you are –

"Laura," she cut in, "Laura Henderson."

"It's very nice to meet you Laura, please sit down. Would you like a cup of tea or coffee?"

"Go on then," she said, "tea white, no sugar. Thanks."

As Jenny made the tea, she watched Laura closely. She was nervous. She wasn't shaking but she was agitated, like she didn't want to be there, or wanted to be there but didn't know what to say or expect. Jenny needed to put her at ease and quickly.

"I understand the drive in was a bit of a challenge today. Terrible traffic. It's a real pain this time of the morning. It's the flexi-timers you see. They think they're avoiding the traffic by coming in later and then they create their own traffic but an hour later than normal. It's a Catch-22 isn't it?" Laura seemed to react to a bit of idle chatter and as she was telling Jenny about the drive in, she appeared to relax slightly.

So, thought Jenny, the ice has been broken and now it's time to see how I can help this girl.

"Right then," Jenny started, "Again, I'm Jenny. A little bit about myself. I was a mental health nurse and about eighteen months ago I decided to become a councilor. My husband was in the Kings Regiment, and I decided to try and help people in, or connected to the military and see if we could work together to come to terms with some problems as a start and carry-on forwards from there."

Laura looked at her and listened carefully for the minute or so Jenny spoke. When she discovered her husband was in the Kings, she seemed happier as if she was going to chat to a friend who was in the same situation or understood the military lifestyle the same way as she did.

"OK," she commenced, "I'm Laura. I'm thirty-one, I've got no kids..." She suddenly stopped. She took a deep breath as if she was trying to suppress an outburst of tears. She regained her composure.

"Ahem..." she cleared her throat and looked directly at Jenny. "We wanted kids but Tony erm... you know he couldn't hold on you know." She raised her head a bit and continued clear as day. "He hung himself." Laura let out a long sigh. She had said what she needed to in those short few sentences. "He hung himself... hanged himself, I'm not too sure which it is but he did and anyway, that pretty much put a stop to us having kids, and a life and growing old and.... Shit." She stopped. Jenny could feel the pain she was suffering inside and had a feeling that this may have been the first time she had let out her feelings to anyone other than family or close friends.

"What happened?" probed Jenny, offering her a tissue from a box on the table.

"He was bullied from the first day he arrived at his new company in the Kings. She gazed at the floor as she spoke. "He had been hit and beaten on numerous occasions. He had been ostracized and pushed out since he joined. He had possessions taken from him and over a period of about a year he was treated like a dog by two members of his unit. They made his life hell and the army did absolutely nothing to help him. He tried to hide it from me but I knew what was going on. They found out I used to be in the army as well and he got even more hassle after they told him like most army girls, he had married a second-class skank. Those bastards killed my husband and I never got the chance to see them suffer. The army did nothing, NOTHING even though I had complained. They didn't care about me. I was just some army wife. They claim to be an organisation who cares about the welfare of their soldiers and their families but in reality, they couldn't give a shit." Laura's anger was palpable now. Jenny could feel the hatred towards the army and the two individuals responsible for her husband's death. She would delve a little but deeper but not too much on their first meeting.

"What happened to the two men who instigated the bullying, Laura?" She queried.

"One got killed in Afghan. He stood on an IED when out on patrol and the other crashed his car. Apparently, he was three times over the drink drive limit. Its sounds terrible but I'm glad they're dead. Those bastards ruined our lives." Jenny latched onto the last statement. *I wonder,* she thought, *killed by an IED.*

"Do you know their names?" It had nothing to do with her treatment method, but Jenny needed to know.

"The drunk driving guy was called O'Neill and the bloke who stood on the mine was called Hays. Why do you ask?"

"Oh, I'll come to that part a little later Laura, it's all part of the process and how we can move on in life. You will see soon enough." Jenny was elated inside. Not just for herself but for Laura as well. This lady had a big grudge against the army for her husband's treatment and every fiber of her body showed it. The contempt was almost contagious. So, Hays was a nasty piece of work in more ways than one. Not anymore, she thought.

The hour wore on and Laura opened up to Jenny more and more once she realized they shared a common background. Then the question came from Laura that Jenny wasn't quite prepared for.

"So, you said your husband was in the Kings. What does he do now that he's out?" she asked.

Jenny spoke softly. "He's not out as such. He got killed in Afghanistan almost two years ago... shot by an enemy sniper."

"I'm sorry... I shouldn't have..." but before she could finish Jenny interjected.

"No not at all. Listen, if I can come to terms with it then so can you, OK?" She wasn't *really* upset. It was part of her life now. She could openly talk about Dave without tearing up. It was something she had learned to control and it was now something she was trying to impart onto others who wanted her help. It showed Laura that there was more than common ground between the two of them.

"I'll tell you more when we next meet but for now I think we should leave it there." Laura agreed and they made an appointment for next time. Out of interest, Jenny asked, "What did you do in the army yourself Laura?"

"Oh, I was in the Royal Signals. I was at the Joint Service Signals Unit in Cyprus. I loved it there. Its where I met Tony actually." She smiled as a memory came to mind and then broke off.

"Wow," said Jenny. "I know that unit, all a bit hush hush isn't it?" She tapped the side of her nose.

"Yeah, but isn't everything in the army? It got me a cracking job when I got out though. I'm now a Field Operations Supervisor for BT. Good job, good pension so I landed on my feet career wise. Anyway, I'll see you next week yeah?"

After Laura left, Jenny felt a bit better herself but she wondered if she had maybe gotten too close by sharing information regarding Dave dying. It wasn't, after all, about her. She convinced herself she had done nothing unprofessional and decided to head for lunch before seeing her next patient.

The drive home for Jenny seemed quicker than usual. Before she knew it, she arrived but wasn't sure how. She had been thinking so hard during the journey that she had almost gone into remote control without a thought of anyone else other than the road directly in front of her. She opened the door, kicked off her shoes and gave Rodders a call.

"Hey, you," he exclaimed on answering the phone. "How's things? I was going to call you later; you must have read my mind. Great minds think alike and all that rubbish."

"Rodders," she was direct and to the point, "Davis. You think he's unwillingly involved in this whole scenario?"

"I do." came the similarly direct answer.

"Can you get to him, I mean, do you think you can get him to me? I think we can use him if we can get him onside. I think I have an idea and Davis could be pivotal to the success of that scheme. It's been bubbling around in my head all afternoon. I met a girl today who could also help us, I'll have to work on it but..."

"Whoa.... hold on a minute Jenny. The more people who know about *anything* could be detrimental to the whole thing. This started off with you and me, why would we bring in others to help us?"

"Because," she said matter of factly, "we all share a common enemy. The others have all suffered at the hands of the army. They've also been failed at the time when they needed them more than anything and they were offered nothing. No support, no justice, nothing. In fact, I'm guessing Davis is still living in fear of his father and Nolan. Once Dave was out of the way did you honestly think they would stop? He was gone. The only weak link to the whole opium gig was out of the picture. It should be plain sailing for them to start up; that's if they haven't already. It might blow up in our faces but if we can get them onside, we actually have a chance at getting our own back on that bunch of bastards."

"Where does the girl come into this?" He questioned.

"She has skills," she hinted. "Do you have a bit of time to talk, and I'll run something past you?"

"Sure," he said, "what have you got?"

Jenny spoke for over an hour and explained how they could use Laura and Davis. Not only for their own ends but for their own benefit as well. Some of the plan could have come out of a James Bond novel and the whole thing was very audacious but, it could work. It would have to be done very quickly; the timeframe would be crucial but if it came off the whole elaborate plot would be very hard to prove. Rodders was impressed.

"Jesus," he gushed, "who am I talking to and what have you done with Jenny? I don't know how long this has been stewing inside your brain but, you know what, I think if everything aligns properly, we could pull this off."

She smiled. It was high praise from an ex-military man, even if he was used to saving lives instead of ruining them.

"Before you go there's something I need to talk about. I didn't tell you last time we spoke as I was still figuring things out in my head, but I received a letter the other day about Dave and a strong mention of you as well."

"Really? Who from?" Jenny paused.

"Nolan," she replied. There was silence at the other end and after what seemed like an age Rodders spoke, his voice breaking slightly.

"Nolan? Captain Nolan? Our Captain Nolan?"

"Yes, that Captain Nolan."

"They're looking for me, aren't they?" Said Rodders, matter of factly. "They're asking you if you've seen me, I'll bet?"

"That's pretty much it in a nutshell," replied Jenny. Rodders didn't seem surprised when Jenny read the contents of the letter.

"I had a feeling this would happen to be honest," he began, "but I didn't think it would be so soon. I mean, I know it's been eighteen months or so but if they're asking if you've seen me, it's because they're thinking about starting up again and they're worried in case I've opened my mouth to anyone, and when I say anyone, I mean you."

"I told you I was sure someone was following me on the night you first came to the house, remember? Why didn't they approach you then?" Asked Jenny.

"I know exactly why," he revealed, "it's because they didn't see me limping like a man with three toes, that's why." I've been trying to train myself to walk straight, without a limp for almost a year. If Nolan's lot are keeping an eye out for anyone, it's a bloke with a heavy limp, so, I trained my body to walk straight without a sign of my injury. It's not perfect but you would really need to look or know I definitely had a wound to notice it. That's why I wasn't approached by your mysterious person. They're expecting me to be using a stick or crutches."

"What's the plan for moving forward?" Queried Jenny.

"Carry on as normal but stay sharp. If you think you see someone shady try to remember their faces. They won't do anything to you. Killing someone in the theatre of war offers lots of scenarios to make it look like an accident. Murdering a civilian is a completely different ball game. Anyway, it's me they want." Rodders was only being ninety percent honest but he didn't want to put undue stress on Jenny. If they found out about their meetings, then they would come for her. For now though, she was safe.

"Let's just be very careful and watch our backs, OK?"

"Right then," she stated with the clarity of a battlefield commander. "Can you do your bit with Davis and I'll speak to the girl?"

"I'll get on it and call you when I have something." They hung up, both knowing what they had to do.

A gentle tap on the door indicated it was time for Jenny to have her second appointment with Laura. Her head slowly appeared as Jenny ushered her in.

"Hello again," she greeted her with a friendly smile and an offer of a handshake.

"Hi," Laura shyly replied, taking the hand which Jenny also used to shepherd her to a comfortable seat to begin their session. Jenny had thought about the appointment all week. How could she broach the subject without breaking any professional standards? And then she checked herself. The whole thing would be breaking professional standards. Christ, the whole thing would be tantamount to a lengthy prison sentence if the plan was discovered. She would have to be careful and cleverly introduce trigger words into the conversation until something clicked with Laura and a sign was given to elaborate on what she meant.

"How was your week Laura?" She began.

"To be honest... not too good." Jenny paused and then questioned, "would you like to tell me about it?"

"Well," she began, "after I saw you it brought a lot of things to the forefront. I mean, it's always there bubbling beneath the surface, it never goes away. But this time, after chatting to you I started to really feel it, you know?"

"Feel what?" Asked Jenny, "what was bubbling under the surface?"

"Hate." Laura's face was dark. "Hate, anger, resentment, rage, call it what you will but I can't help it, Jenny. I despise the people who did this but underneath it all I hate the whole system that did nothing at all to help me deal with Tony's death. Especially their ineptitude in instigating any kind of investigation. I can't help thinking about it. I have dreams about how I would tear down the whole thing. I have terrible thoughts about it, Jenny, I really do. But you and I both know there's nothing I can do. The people who were personally involved in Tony's death are now dead themselves which I think makes it worse because I have nobody to take my anger out on and trying to take the MOD to court, well, that's never going to happen. So, here I am, in limbo, constantly thinking about something I have no control over. I don't suppose you know how that feels though do you?" Jenny did not respond directly to the rhetorical question.

"Tell me Laura, what would you do if you knew someone who was going through a similar situation? Would you help them? Would you go out of your way to make sure that person got justice, or at least some kind of victory over the ones who committed the act?"

Without hesitation Laura swiftly replied, "yes, without a doubt. One hundred percent because I wouldn't want someone else to go through the pain and anguish I've been through. I would bring those people to justice any way I could."

Jenny didn't flinch. She sat, looking at Laura and thought, *I'll never get another opportunity like this.* She inhaled deeply and began.

"Actually Laura, I do know what you're going through. I literally know *exactly* what you're going through." Laura eyed her with suspicion.

"How's that then? Your husband was shot in Afghan wasn't he, how's that the same?" She spoke with bitterness in her voice.

"Because Laura," Jenny hesitated slightly, thought for a moment, and decided it was time to say what she had wanted to the first time she heard Laura's story, "Dave, my husband, wasn't *just* shot. He was murdered by two people in his platoon." The admission was met with silence as Laura looked up to see Jenny welling up.

"What?" Laura was shocked to hear the words coming out of Jenny's mouth. "What do you mean he was murdered?"

Jenny took out a handkerchief and dabbed her eyelids to prevent the mascara streaking down her face. She pulled herself together and proceeded to tell Laura of her ordeal. How Dave had left the message for Rodders who had mutilated himself to escape certain death and how, after all the time that had passed, she had a plan to make sure they didn't harm anyone again.

"The people who did this to my husband are still out there Laura. They're still doing their jobs and getting on with their lives like nothing happened while I am, as you said yourself, in limbo. The only difference is I could walk into one of my husband's killers in the street at any time. The Military Police cannot help me. The civilian police can't help me, and the army cannot help me so, what do I do? What do *we* do, people like you and I are cast aside and forgotten with all our rage and anguish, to do what exactly? Try to start new life like nothing has happened." Jenny was out of her chair and pacing around the office now like a caged animal, walking from wall to wall of the office while Laura sat and watched her.

"I'll help you get them," came the soft voice. "I'll help you get the people who did this to you. I can help. Let me help you, Jenny. I know how you feel, Christ I've been telling you since I met you." Jenny looked at Laura knowing she meant every word. She did have a role for her which wouldn't implicate her in any wrongdoing should they be found out.

"There's another thing you should know, Laura." Jenny looked her straight in the eyes. "One of the guys who bullied Tony was also involved in Dave's death: Hays."

Laura's eyed widened, "what.... How?" She questioned.

Jenny went on to explain how he was the go between for Nolan and the gang with the local tribal leader due to his intelligence background and language skills. Laura stood, went over to Jenny, and held her by the shoulders. "One down, several to go" she said with a solemn look.

On completion of their appointment, Laura walked to the nearest coffee shop to let what she had just experienced sink in. As she sat and stared at the bubbles swirling around her large cardboard cup, she realised she had agreed to be complicit in the downfall of a group of people she had never met or heard of. As she sipped her piping hot drink, a wave of contentment swept over her. *A good cup of coffee can cure all ills,* she thought. She liked what she had heard from Jenny and had no reason to disbelieve her. They both wanted the same thing, all Laura had to do was decide just how far down the rabbit hole she wanted to go.

Arriving home, the house felt icy. Laura never liked it too hot, she always kept it cool whereas Tony would turn the thermostat up to its highest. She smiled at the thought of him sitting in the lounge, watching television in shorts and t-shirt while she sweltered, fanning herself next to him. The lounge itself was adorned with photos of the two of them together on holidays, friends' barbecues and at family get togethers. She picked up a picture of them together, lifted it to her mouth and kissed the image of Tony. The house was immaculately clean. Like Tony, she didn't want clutter, to her it implied laziness if a woman couldn't keep up the appearance of a nice home. She sniggered knowing it was actually Tony who did most of the housework. The house seemed empty and without Tony, it was. Thoughts turned to selling the property and moving on, but where to? She didn't know and although they had a happy and loving life, the house echoed sad memories without him around. She slumped onto the couch, stared mournfully at each and every photo on the walls and placed carefully on the furniture and let out a loud sigh.

"To hell with it." She said out loud and stood up to go to the kitchen. She opened the fridge door to be met with the depressing sight of only enough food for a single person. She ignored last night's leftovers and removed a cold bottle of Chardonnay, popped the cork, and filled a glass to the brim, laughing to herself as she did so. As she walked back to the lounge, she eyed the thermostat on the wall. She turned the dial to maximum, switched on the TV and took her place back on the couch.

CHAPTER 11

The meeting, it was decided, would be held away from town. Somewhere quiet and out of the way so as not to draw any kind of attention to themselves. There was a large open park area about thirty minutes away from Jenny's place where the gathering would take place. After that they would have to be careful where and when they got together but that was a bridge to be crossed when they came to it.

Jenny arrived first. She sat for about five minutes and drank a takeaway Starbucks coffee from a large cardboard cup with a plastic lid, trying not to scald the roof of her mouth. In the distance she could see Rodders walking calmly to the picnic table she had commandeered for their liaison. She noticed that he did appear to limp, but ever so slightly and only because she knew of his injury. She mentally applauded him for the work he had put into it. He greeted her with a nod and sat down at the table.

"How are you doing?" He asked.

"I'm actually quite well as it happens. And you?"

"I'm hobbling along, you know.... or not," He laughed and Jenny smiled to see it; at least he could laugh at his situation now.

"So, have you got anything to go on concerning Davis?" She led.

"Actually, I have," he replied. "I know the poor lad is seeing the doctor for depression. He's been taken off certain duties which means he can't get his weapon issued to him and if you're an infantry soldier that's not the best thing really. My contact in the Medical Centre also claims he's attempted suicide once but stopped and called an ambulance when he couldn't go through with it. He was taken to the General Hospital and needed to have his stomach pumped. I don't know what he took or how he got hold of it, but he was on suicide watch for a couple of weeks afterwards. He's not been the same since apparently. They can't kick him out for the same reasons they couldn't charge me. He now has a history and dumping him would look callous in the eyes of the press. So, he's in no man's land until they can find a way to offload him and make him someone else's problem. I feel sorry for him. Even if he gets out where would he go? His Dad is a bastard and the army don't give a damn, at least while he's in he has a roof over his head."

"Yes," replied Jenny, "but at what cost? Nolan and Squires will still be bleeding the poor kid dry to get his dad to courier more gear for them. He's like a drugs mule but without actually carrying any drugs. It's information and contacts he's hauling around with him twenty-four hours a day. He knows the inside story better than anyone else involved because he's dealing with both sides of the same coin. Christ, I hate to think about the amount of stress and pressure he's under. It must be unbearable, no wonder he tried to top himself." She paused for a moment and took another sip of coffee.

"He needs our help. He can help us greatly but we need to get him away from the situation he's in." She thought for a minute.

"Can we somehow get him referred to me instead of the counselor he's been with over the last few months? He must be with someone on camp. Let's see if we can persuade them to try him with a new counselor. Can you do anything to pull some strings?"

"I'll try," said Rodders. "Of course, I've got no leverage whatsoever in this whole thing. All I can do is ask my contact to slip in a note into his records and pretend she knows nothing about it. It could work, we've got nothing to lose."

After ten or so minutes, Laura appeared and made her way to the table. She had intentionally been asked to come slightly later, offering Jenny and Rodders time to catch up. As she approached, Rodders stood first to greet her.

"Laura," said Jenny, "this is Rodders, Rodders Laura." The two shook hands and they all sat down.

"So Rodders," Laura asked, "is it actually Rodney or are you going to keep me guessing?"

"It's Andy actually," he stated, "Trotter."

She rolled her eyes and laughed, "of course. I should have picked up on that straight away. Mind with some army nicknames it could have literally been the most tenuous connection couldn't it?"

"You're right," he replied, "I've known some guys with the weirdest nick names that have absolutely no connection to their real names. However, mine is boring old Rodders Trotter." Laura inspected his face as he spoke. He had gentle features, was attractive in a sort of 'normal' way and spoke gently in a relaxed manner. She knew he had a slight limp, and she knew the reason why but would wait until he told her about it rather than appear being rude and asking him outright. She concluded that she liked him. She liked Jenny as well and deep down she hoped they liked her. She wanted so much to help and be accepted into a group who shared a common purpose, a common goal. A group who shared a common enemy.

"So," Jenny kicked things off, "we all know why we are here."

"Yes," said Laura enthusiastically, "what do we have so far?"

Jenny nodded to Rodders to begin and share what he had with Laura.

"OK, so here we go," he explained "I'll take it as read that Jenny has informed you of all the major players in this whole situation so far." Jenny confirmed with a nod.

He continued, "Nolan is on a course at the Defense College. That is due to end shortly when he will be returning to his unit. Squires is still with 4 platoon as is Phil Lewis and Bairdy. Hays met with an untimely and erm... 'unfortunate' death." They all smiled at his sarcastic delivery.

"Davis is on light duties and is undergoing treatment for depression. It could be PTSD but I'm not sure how they're classing it right now. He is our way in. He, if we can get him onside, could be the skeleton key to opening so many doors and to giving us information that we would never be able to get by ourselves. I believe there is only one way we can get him onside and that is to guarantee him it will be his way out of the whole sordid affair. If he feels we can genuinely help him, I think he will go for it."

Jenny and Laura looked at each other approvingly.

"What do you need from me?" Asked Laura.

"Firstly," started Jenny, "if we can get surveillance equipment, could you install it so we could record and watch a chosen location live and remotely?"

"That's easy," replied Laura.

"OK," said Jenny, "this next one might sound a bit strange. Is there such a thing as a device that can change my voice, so it appears to be someone else on the end of the phone? I've seen kids' toys that do it to make you sound like a robot and I've seen them in films but do the real ones actually exist?"

Laura's face lit up. Now they were talking her language.

"They do exist. I mean, it's not going to change your voice from your own to Morgan Freeman's, but they can change the tone and make your original voice disguised to the point that if you heard them both together you would never know they were in fact the same person. It's not difficult technology to get hold of but, and here's the but: a good quality version can cost around two thousand pounds."

"That's fine," said Jenny, "money can be found for everything we need." She wrote the numbers down in a small notebook.

"Here's another one for you, is there such a thing as a machine that can switch from one number to another number without the person making the call knowing?" Laura looked at her intrigued, not really understanding what she meant.

"Can you elaborate on that one? Say exactly what you want slowly, and I'll get my head around it."

"Right. Let's say I call a helpline with a number I've been given, say The Samaritans but when that number is called certain numbers are screened and put through to another number like McDonalds. Call Samaritans, get switched to McDonalds, do you know what I mean?" Laura still looked puzzled.

"What I don't want is fifty people getting the number to our hotline thinking its genuine. I need to screen the numbers of our targets and only let those through and the rest will get an engaged tone. Now do you know what I mean?"

"I do know what you mean. Again, yes, they do exist but if you want that second number to be untraceable, you're talking about military grade communications interception equipment. You can get stuff like that through certain dark web sellers but it's *very* costly."

"How costly?" Jenny's eyes narrowed.

"Top of my head.... six to ten grand depending on how we get it and who we get it from..

Rodders whistled.

"That's a lot of dough but if it's needed then it's needed. Im glad I'm not forking out for this lot."

'What about encrypted phones like the ones...." Jenny paused, "like the ones drug dealers use, the ones that cannot be unlocked or traced? Can you get them?"

Laura was taking a mental note of the equipment and thinking about a contact or a supplier she could get hold of.

"Yes, I can get almost anything you need," she replied. "What you want is the ability to intercept calls and route them to an encrypted phone, which I'm guessing will be the one you will have control of and be able to talk on the phone with a disguised voice and for it to be untraceable. Correct?"

"Yup," was the short answer Jenny offered up.

"That's all-doable Jenny. There will of course be hardware involved and if anything happens it will have to be disposed of. I can make your calls and everything you need encrypted but if the authorities get hold of the devices and link it to us there could be repercussions and a lot of explaining to do."

"The surveillance equipment we mentioned. It's got to be top quality and crystal-clear picture and recording. Can we fit hidden cameras into my office and my home? It needs to be so discreet that only if you really looked hard you could find it. Could you do that?"

"Bread and butter stuff that Jenny. A good system with hidden devices could come in at around four to five thousand pounds. I could fit the devices into lamps, wall sockets, clocks: you name it, I can do it."

Jenny added up the figures. "So, best case scenario we're looking at around twelve maybe fifteen thousand to cover all costs for surveillance stuff, yes?"

"About that," relayed Laura. Jenny pulled out a velvet bag from her handbag, looked around to make sure no one was looking in their direction and emptied the contents of the bag on the table. Out spilled six Rolex watches of varying styles. "Will those cover it?"

The eyes of the two others widened.

"Jesus Chris Jenny!" Gasped Rodders, "where in the hell did you get that lot? Actually," he said, "don't tell me, I know already."

"I don't," piped in Laura.

Jenny looked at her directly.

"I found it hidden in the loft in an old kit bag of Dave's," she began. "He obviously creamed them off the top when the platoon boys started their little enterprise before opium and trafficking became the next big thing." She looked embarrassed when she said it. As far as she was concerned it was stolen goods and blood money but for their plan to work, they needed funds and she just didn't have twenty thousand pounds sitting around, not until she discovered Dave's 'rainy day' stash.

"I haven't even started looking through stuff he's got in storage yet. God knows what else he's got hidden away. There might be more, or this might be the lot, I just don't know but if these will cover our expenses for now then this is what we will use. Now do either of you know anyone who could shift this lot?"

"I know one of the pawnbrokers in town is a bit shady," said Laura. "I've known some of the army wives pawn stuff when they've gotten into debt and need a quick way out. I'm sure he will take them but we won't get half of what they're worth."

Rodders picked up a watch. He was by no means an expert but like a lot of blokes he liked his watches and knew a little bit about them.

"This is a Submariner," he revealed. "A new one will sell for around twelve thousand pounds. This one without any box or papers and no provenance will go for around... four grand I reckon. If it's genuine of course but the pawnbroker will know that."

Jenny looked at him as if he was an expert on the antiques roadshow.

"Get you," she beamed. He took the compliment and polished his fingernails on his jumper jokingly.

"Ah, but there's a problem," observed Laura. "One of us can't just walk in and dump six high end watches on the counter.

That's going to look pretty suspicious isn't it?" She had a point. "I've got a better idea. Why don't we take a couple each and try going to different towns and pawning them? I reckon Jenny and I will have a bit of an advantaged being women especially if we put on the old 'husband pissed off and left me and the kids' look about us. The only thing we need to do is a little bit of homework about the watch movements and talk a bit of shite and that might deter them from taking advantage of the fact we're women trying to punt on men's watches. What do you reckon?"

"It's a great idea," chimed Rodders. Jenny was equally impressed.

"Well," said Jenny, "that sounds like a definitive plan. Here Rodders you take these two, Laura you take those, and I'll take these." She divvied out the watches. "Let's see what we can get for them and either talk next week or as soon as we get the cash and we can start ordering equipment, OK Laura?"

"I'm all up for that," she said but then followed on, "don't forget though, I have an appointment with you at your office. We can use the time to pick locations for the surveillance microphones and cameras if you want?"

"Let's do that." Jenny smiled. They said their goodbyes and each headed off in their own direction. Jenny wandered to her car, in no hurry or rush to get anywhere. As she walked, she thought about how productive the day had been. She needed Rodders contact to get young Davis assigned to her for counselling but in the meantime she thought, the plan was coming to fruition.

Laura had been assigned to look into a problem at a junction box located at a small exchange in the center of town. She finished her task, changed her jacket into something smarter than her uniform, locked the building and her van and chained the door to the compound and made the five-minute walk to the high street. She made her way onto Evans Street, a well-known area for jewelery shops and pawnbrokers. She had a particular dealer in mind and could see the traditional three golden balls hanging outside, a sign signifying the trade. She was confident, but she needed to have a bit of cockiness ready to fend off the pawnbrokers attempts to lower the asking price for her items. She entered the premises and unlike many mainstream commercial lenders who have equipment showrooms this was a safe, secure shop with protective glass on three sides and a man sitting on a stool behind a sliding hatch.

"Good afternoon madam, how can I help you?" He asked. Laura gulped slightly and began her spiel.

"I need to sell some of my husband's watches. You do buy watches, don't you?" She enquired, sheepishly. The broker's face did not change. He sat with a blank expression saying nothing, egging her on to expand on her request.

"Anyway," she continued, slightly flustered at his lack of response, "I need to sell two watches." She moved toward the hatch and the heavy glass slid aside as the man spoke.

"Let's see 'em," he bawled. Laura removed the watches from her bag and handed them over. The broker gave them a quick look and offered his opinion.

"They're fake love," he concluded, pushing the watches back through the hatch. "They're good fakes mind so I'll give you a hundred quid for the pair." Laura was hoping this would happen and smiled to herself before beginning her monologue.

"Do you know anything about watches?" She demanded. He glared through the hatch.

"Of course, I do." He snapped, angry at his competency being questioned.

"So, you're telling me that if you opened the back of the black Submariner Date 16610 you won't find the classic caliber 3235 movement? Or are you going to tell me that the ceramic Cerachrom bezel is also fake? Would you like me to give you a bit of information on the 40mm case and bracelet or do you know about that already?"

The broker's expression changed into one of awe then embarrassment. He had been rumbled.

"Let's take a quick look at 'em again," his tone now more subtle. He removed the backs and inspected the watches with military precision. Once he was satisfied with their authenticity, he offered Laura a price. His first offer made Laura remove the watches from the counter, place them in her bag and turn to walk out of the shop.

"Five grand the pair," he growled.

"Six and a half, no less and no questions," she replied. The broker huffed out loud and began counting out the cash slowly and methodically in front of Laura. She took the envelope, stuffed it into her bag and turned to leave.

"Have a nice day," she said as a parting gesture, waving behind her as she left the shop.

The following day, Jenny's phone beeped to notify her of an incoming text message. She glanced at the screen:

'CALL ME WHEN YOU GET 5. L X'

Jenny couldn't answer straight away because she was in the middle of an appointment but as soon as she finished, she picked up her phone and called her.

"Hiya," Laura's voice was excited. "You're not going to believe this. I've flogged the watches already! To the small pawn shop on Evans Street in town. You know the one next door to the pizza shop?"

"Yeah, I know the one. Holy cow, that was quick. How much did you get? Please tell me it's good news."

"Six and a half grand... cash, right there and then. He tried it on of course telling me they were fake and all that garbage but I called his bluff, came out with some drivel I read on the internet about serial numbers and movements and ceramic bezels, and he thought I knew my stuff and caved. He tried for five, I told him to ram it and went to walk and he asked what I was after, I thought about seven but we agreed on six and a half. What do you think? Did I do OK?"

"OK? OK? It's absolutely brilliant Laura. WOW! That's more than I thought we would get for them. Will it be enough to get the surveillance equipment we need for the office or the house?"

"It's a start, we should be able to buy the cameras and some other bits and bobs with this." Laura was pleased that she had done well on her first task.

"What's the timeframe from ordering to receiving the goods, roughly of course?"

"I reckon a week, maybe less. I know a company in London who are very discreet where I could get the stuff quickly and slightly cheaper as were paying in cash."

Jenny was also feeling excited but never took her mind of the long game and why they were doing it. She calmed her voice down to a more serious tone.

"Would you mind doing that? If we can get the stuff this week, we could start installing the equipment on Friday. I can make your appointment an hour and a half instead to give us a bit more time?"

"Leave it with me. I'll get it sorted for you. OK, chat soon. Bye for now." The phone went silent as Laura rang off. Jenny was astounded by the speed and productivity Laura had achieved. She was turning out to be a great asset to the team.

CHAPTER 12

"Christ! Rodders, I knew you were up to something. I should have known," yelled Debbie, Rodders' ex. "Ah, c'mon now Debbie, you know it's not like that. I just need a favour on top of the other dozen you've done already," he gave her an impish grin. He liked Debbie, he always had and when they used to see each other, before his accident, they had enjoyed good times together. She knew it was never serious, she wanted a little bit more but never pushed, he thought it was unfair to ask someone to sit around at home whilst the boyfriend or husbands went to the desert for four months at a time. She could probably handle it, but he couldn't get over the fact he wouldn't be giving her a full meaningful relationship, so he cooled it down much to her disappointment. Now, after almost two years he walked back into her life, out of the army and expected to start where they left off. Debbie thought the world of Rodders but didn't want to get burnt so was getting more cautious now he was asking her to do favours for him which included going through the medical center records for details about patients. It was wrong and she knew it, but he had a boyish charm about him and sometimes she just couldn't resist.

"If I get found out, do you know what they will do to me?" She exclaimed.

"I do, but I really need this Debbie," he said, being honest with her. "I can't tell you everything just now, but I put my hand on my heart when I say this, I'm doing it for the lad's good. I'm trying to help him get the right help and I know a woman who can assist him better than the lot at the Medical Centre."

Debbie scrutinized his face and caved. "Last time" she announced, "I'll do one more favour and that's it. Do you understand me Rodders?"

"Yes, I understand," he replied. "Listen, I appreciate everything you've done so far. I know I've asked a lot from you, getting information, and trying to help me and everything else but I promise it's all for a good cause and I'll explain it more in time but not just yet, is that OK?"

She put her hands on his cheeks and gazed into his eyes. She really did like him and had always thought they had great chemistry but was wary of what he was doing and why.

"OK," she said gently to his face, "but, remember, you owe me big time. Now, what do you want this note to say?"

Rodders grinned and kissed her on the lips.

"Have you got a pen?" He asked, and she began to write down exactly what he told her.

"Corporal Jones." Came the bark from up the long corridor to the reception desk in the medical center.

"Yes Sir?" Debbie replied to the doctor, an army Major who had been dealing with Davis's case.

"Can you pop into my office for a moment please?" He asked. Debbie quickly got out of her seat and walked calmly to the Major's open office door.

"Yes, Sir?" She announced, "you wanted to see me?"

"Yes corporal. Why are Private Davis's records on my desk? He's not due to come in until a week tomorrow."

"I don't know Sir, maybe he's been referred elsewhere? It's the first I've known about it." She sounded convincing as he opened the notes and scanned the appointments section. Then he came upon a typed note saying Davis had indeed been referred to a new therapist who was attached to the Kings, a Mrs. Edwards.

"Alright," he said, "cancel his next appointment and show in my two thirty will you please?" The Major didn't even give it a second thought. He saw so many men and women coming through the surgery with mental health issues that he, or the rest of his staff could hardly keep up. Davis was one less case and one less burden on his already overworked and over stressed shoulders. Debbie exited the Major's office, went back to her seat and proceeded to call Davis and inform him of his new appointment.

"Jenny, Mrs. Henderson is here for her appointment," said Siona.

"Of course," she replied, "send her in please. There was a tap on the door and in walked Laura.

"Ah, hello again Laura, so nice to see you," began Jenny, offering her a sneaky wink as she entered the office, "please, come in and take a seat."

"Thank you very much," Laura grinned. Once the door was closed and they were both happy they couldn't be heard they greeted each other warmly with a quick hug.

"Great job with the watches by the way!" Jenny gushed, "that was a result. Have you ordered what we need?"

"Ordered it, I've already got most of it. I took the train into London to see the guy I told you about and he had pretty much all the surveillance equipment we need in stock. I still need to find the voice modulator but I've found a supplier on the dark web who can sort that and the splitter and phones I'm still working on. I'll need more cash from you or Rodders to get those items."

"Good news on that front," said Jenny. "I managed to get rid of my watches to a pawn broker in Salisbury. I didn't get as much as you, five thousand two hundred quid but it's better than nothing, eh?"

"Better than nothing? It's great Jenny, well done. It all goes into the coffers, now we just need Rodders to come up trumps and we're in business." Laura spoke with great certainty when it came to their plan. She knew it was going to work. They were planning it with literal military precision and she wanted to punish not just the army but the scum who had hurt Jenny and Rodders. Indirectly, it was her fight as much as theirs and she had the bit between her teeth and nothing or nobody was going to take it away from her now. Jenny got the impression that even if she and Rodders got cold feet Laura would still carry on alone. She admired her tenacity and strength.

"Right then, I've got some goodies with me. This is what a couple of thousand pounds gets you." Laura delved into her oversized handbag and pulled out a box containing several small disk-shaped objects.

"Are they the bugs?"

"Yup," said Laura, "cool aren't they?" Each one was no bigger than a one pence piece and each either had a magnetic or sticky backed cover.

"These link directly to the wi-fi and this small recording device will pick up everything crystal clear. I'll put one under the desk and one underneath the base station for the telephone." Laura was getting quite excited about the new tech she was showing Jenny.

"Now, here's a little beauty Jenny," she said excitedly. "Look at this magnet. It's a simple thing that you would put on your whiteboard to hold up a chart or map or anything really.... Except it's not. Look closely." Jenny leaned forward to inspect the small gadget. In the center it had a tiny little hole.

"What's the hole for?" She asked.

Laura paused.

"It's a wide-angle camera. Top of the range but that's not all, watch this." She opened an app on her phone and gave it to Jenny as she took the camera and waved it around the room. The picture came up on the phone in superb definition.

"Whoa!" She cried out trying not to get too over excited, "that is absolutely brilliant. Does it record as well?"

Laura turned to her and in true sixteen-year-old schoolgirl style, she replied, "er...yeah." Once the fascination with the new gadgetry was over, Laura got to work setting the equipment up and tested its suitability. It was perfect for what they needed and it wouldn't be long before it was put to its intended use.

The three met again a week after their first encounter in the same place as before. Rodders kicked off the meeting and shared his progress with Laura and Jenny.

"I've sold my watches... take a guess... go on take a guess," he teased.

"Four grand," said Laura

"I'll go five, three," chimes Jenny

"Both wrong," he proudly puffed out his chest and said, "five, seven. Not bad, eh?"

"Not bad at all," said Jenny, "not bad at all." She was very happy with the effort he had put in, not just with the watches but everything in-between. He was in deep and even though he had made enemies and was still in danger he never lost his optimism throughout the whole ordeal. Jenny could see why Dave had liked him so much.

"What do we need to do with the rest of the equipment Jenny?" Asked Rodders.

"I think we need to get a clear day in my diary first. I'll give Siona the day off and that's when we will bring in Davis. He won't be any the wiser, he will just think it's a standard appointment. Laura, you will be my 'receptionist' for the afternoon and Rodders you hang about out of sight until he's in, then we can ask a few questions and find out where we stand with young Davis. Does that sound like a plan?"

They all looked at each other nodding in agreement. Jenny was a little nervous just talking about it and Laura sensed her trepidation.

"Don't worry about it, Jenny," she reassured her. "I'm feeling a bit on edge as well and I'm sure you are too Rodders, yeah?" He nodded. "It's expected. None of us are bad people, we're normal people who have had bad things done to us. Life changing things by horrible, evil individuals who didn't care or have the slightest thoughts about us when they shot your husband, bullied mine into suicide and threatened you to the point where you felt the only way out was to shoot yourself. We are the victims. We are the people who have suffered injustice and you know what, I'm glad we're doing what we're doing. Each one of those scumbags deserves everything they get. If the authorities won't or can't help us, then we will bloody well help ourselves!. Her impassioned speech was felt by all of them. She took a sharp intake of breath while she composed herself. "I've had enough of crying myself to sleep, not just because I miss Tony but because since he died, I've felt so helpless, useless, without the power to control what's happened or the ability to get those responsible to pay for their actions. This will give me peace of mind. This will bring me the justice I want... in fact not the justice I want, the justice I bloody well deserve." Jenny leaned over and hugged her.

"You're right, you are one hundred percent right. We *were* victims... but we're not going to be victims anymore."

CHAPTER 13

"Siona, can you please clear my diary for the fifth please? Something personal has come up and I need to cancel all of my appointments. If you call the people due in the morning, I'll call the people with afternoon appointments and let them know. Is that OK?"

"Of course, Jenny," replied Siona. "What about me, will you need me on that day?" She asked.

"No, I won't. Take it off. I'll say you looked a bit pale when you came in and I sent you away, then it won't be classed as a sick day but keep it to yourself until someone asks... *if* someone asks, OK?"

Siona gave her an understanding nod of the head, pleased at this development.

Jenny had managed to intercept the referral letter before Siona had time to open the post. Now that a date was set, the rest would fall into place.

The day came around quickly. Everything was ready. Laura took up her place at the reception desk. Rodders was down the road in his car waiting for a call to come to the office. All they needed now was the man of the moment to appear. At two thirty exactly there came a knock on her door.

"Jenny, your appointment is here," said Laura in her best telephone voice.

"Thank you, Laura, show him in would you please?" Came the reply.

A short, skinny almost gaunt looking young man entered the room. He was wearing beige chinos trying to look smart for his civilian appointment. His clothes hung off him. Jenny could see he had obviously lost weight judging by his attire and wondered if it was the stress of his situation which had caused it.

"Good afternoon," she greeted him with a reply.

"Good afternoon, Ma'am." Davis replied.

"No, no John. No Ma'am here. My name is Jenny, I'm a civilian and you don't need to address me like an army nurse or doctor. Jenny is fine."

"Erm.... hello then, Jenny," he said nervously.

"That's better. Sit yourself down John. Take a comfy seat. Would you like a cup of tea or coffee?"

"No thank you."

"Are you sure? I'm having one. Just as easy to make two as it is to make one." She urged.

"OK," he replied, "tea white with two sugars please."

"Ah," she smiled, "N.A.T.O standard. Yes?"

He smiled back at her. It was the most commonly drunk brew in the armed forces and had affectionately been known as NATO standard for decades. He smiled, impressed by her knowledge. She went through the door.

"Laura, can we have two teas please? My usual and a white with two sugars as well." While she spoke her order to Laura, she also gave the signal of the phone to give Rodders the call to come to the office. "Thank you." She closed the door once again.

"Now John, why don't you tell me a little about yourself?"

He looked up at her and she saw his eyelids were red. It could be from sleep deprivation, stress, drugs, or several different causes. Now she was a bit closer to him she could more clearly see his cheekbones through his skin. This wasn't right. *He's either on drugs or he's scared of something, or someone.* As he began to tell her some basic information about himself, she decided to interject.

"John, are you feeling alright? You look rather pale and, I'll be honest you look a bit thin to me. Are you eating OK?"

"Yes, I'm fine," he replied looking at the floor. She briefly studied his body language for a 'tell' but he gave nothing away.

"I know you attempted suicide recently. Can you tell me a bit about that?"

He was reluctant to speak at first but she could tell he wanted to. He wanted to release himself from the burden of everything he knew and everything he had experienced from both his father and Nolan. He spoke very carefully so as to not give anything away but Jenny needed to gain his trust, and quickly before he discovered what was going on and the whole plan collapsed around them.

"My Dad," he was visibly shaking as he spoke, "he abuses me and my Mum. He always has. He threatens me unless I do things for him."

"Sexually?" Jenny was gentle.

"No, nothing like that, ever, but other things. I don't want to talk about it." He shifted uncomfortably in his chair.

"What about the army?" Asked Jenny, "how do they treat you? Do you like it? You've been in a few years now, tell me how that's been."

He started to well up as he looked at the floor. Jenny felt sorry for the way Davis had been treated and she would let him know soon enough but she couldn't at the moment. She had to judge her timing perfectly.

"I wish I had never joined. I hate it. I can't handle it anymore but they won't let me leave. I'm stuck here and I've got nowhere else to go. I don't want to go home and I don't want to be here." He looked at her. "Where else is there?"

"Why do you hate the army, John? Do you get bullied at all? Is there a particular group who make life difficult?" Jenny hoped the right trigger words would hit home and he would open up to her.

He rose from his chair and began to pace around the room running his fingers through his shortly cropped hair.

"I can't get out. I'm trapped here in this dump. I just want away from the whole thing." His breathing became shallow and he started to cry. Jenny knew she had to calm him down somehow.

"John... John, come on sit down." She urged him. "Come on sit down, it's OK, you're safe here. Nobody can bully you or get to you while you're here with us." He stopped and looked around.

"Who is *us?*"

"I mean me John, the practice, you know me and the other therapists. Listen, don't worry about that now, what would you need to be out of the situation you're in?" Davis was looking around the room with squinting eyes, starting to get suspicious.

"Look John let's start again. I'm only trying to figure out what is best for you. I've only just met you, and do you want to know something? I'm nervous too. I'm new to this. I've only been a counselor for a short time. I used to be a nurse but wanted to help the military guys a bit more so ended up doing this. I'm trying to be as good as I can but I'll make mistakes as well so you must bear with me. Can you do that John, please?" She needed him to open up and there wasn't a lot of time. Once he was out of her office, she might never see him again and then they would be back to square one. He sat down and sipped his tea and wiped his eyes on a tissue. He exhaled a deep breath as if to calm himself and start again.

"Is everything we say in here private Jenny?" He asked.

"Of course, it is John. I can't talk about your situation to anyone, that includes your boss or anyone else, I can only recommend treatment to the Senior Medical Officer on camp, nothing else."

"So, if I tell you things, they have to stay secret, confidential like?"

"Yes," answered Jenny, "totally."

"I joined the army to get away from my dad. He's old school, you know, a scrap merchant, manual labour bloke. Big hands and a bad temper and I despise him for the way he has treated me and my Mum. It was either leave or I would have killed him, I hate him that much. He's into all kinds of shady stuff that I can't talk about but he's a nasty bastard. He always has been and he always will be." The venom spat off his tongue as he spoke.

"When I joined up, I loved it at first. I had a great bunch of mates and life was great. I had a girlfriend but that went downhill like everything else when I joined 4 platoon." *We are getting somewhere now*, thought Jenny, as Davis started to open up slowly.

"There were some great guys in the group but somehow trouble found me and now I'm stuck in the middle and I can't get out. Some of the lads are real nasty pieces of work. Two of them, Hays, and Bairdy along with another bloke from a different unit were bullying some poor fella called... What's his name now...?" He thought for a few seconds. "Henderson, that's right Henderson. He ended up hanging himself, can you believe that? He killed himself over those three bastards. Loads of people knew they had given him a hard time and nobody did a thing to help him. Hays and Bairdy are in my platoon. Well Hays was, he stood on a mine a while back and died in Afghan. I suppose he got what he deserved in the end but it shows you the kind of people I'm talking about and once they had me, I couldn't walk away." Jenny's facial expression didn't change when mention of Bairdy came up.

"Why not?" Asked Jenny, "why didn't you go to your Sergeant? What was he like?"

"He was a great bloke the Sarge." There was a fondness in his tone but also a tinge of sorrow as he spoke of Dave.

"He got shot almost two years ago in Afghan. A sniper took him out." He stared blanky at the office wall for about ten seconds until the gaze was broken.

"Why couldn't he help you, John? Was he getting hassled from people above him?"

"I don't know anything about that. All I know is he was shot and that was it, he was gone. There's been so much shit going down since then I don't know who to trust anymore."

This was it. Just as she had done previously with Laura, she decided the time had come to stop beating around the bush and let him know who she was and why he was here.

"John?" He looked up at her, "were Nolan and Squires involved in the Sarge's death?" His head shot up and stared at her trying to figure why she had said that. He started frantically, scanning the room. He didn't know what for, maybe for another exit but it was an instinctive thing to do.

"What?" He yelled, "what are you talking....? What....? Who are you? Why are you asking me that?" Jenny got out of her seat as Davis rose.

"John?" Her voice was very slow, very calm, and very precise, "do you know if Nolan and Squires were involved in Dave's death?"

"Dave...the Sarge, do you know him, who are you?"? He was seriously agitated now.

"I know everything John. Nolan, Squires, Hays, and the rest of your little gang. I know about the drugs. I know about the smuggling and I know about Dave being killed by your gang. That's right, isn't it John? You all knew about the Sarge being shot on purpose, didn't you?" She was coming across very direct but not laying off until he broke. "Did you know about the Sarge John?" She wasn't backing down. "What do you know John? What about Rodders John? What happened to him?" He looked at her confused.

"Rodders? What about him? He shot himself to get out of the army. What's he got to do with it?" He started to rub his head as if the information he was taking in was overloading his head.

"TELL ME ABOUT THE SARGE JOHN!" She shouted at him.

He sat down again and held his head in his hands and started weeping uncontrollably.

"I only found out what had happened, or rather how it happened about two months after he was killed. I was threatened by Captain Nolan and told that if I didn't keep my end of the deal, I would be next. I'm reminded every day of what happened to the Sarge. It's constantly in my head that Nolan and the rest will come for me. You see..."

"I know your dad is a drug dealer John and not a scrap metal merchant," Jenny confessed.

"How? Who are you? Are you the police? Am I going to jail? Anything is better than living like this."

"I'm the Sarge's wife John," her voice now back to the low quiet tones she had shown earlier. He studied her face for a few seconds and he knew she was being honest with him.

He fell on his knees in front of her.

"I didn't know. I didn't know, really, I'm so sorry, I didn't know. If I did, I would tell you just to get it off my chest but I didn't, please believe me." She did believe him. She felt guilty for pushing him to this but needed to know the truth about Davis and what he knew about Dave's death. She helped him to his feet and wrapped her arms around him. He put his head on her shoulder and wept like a child.

"I do believe you John and I'm going to help you get out of the situation you're in, OK?" He nodded.

"Do you trust me, John?" He thought about the question momentarily.

"Yes," he stuttered.

She put her hands on his shoulders and looked him in the eyes.

"I have a solution to your problems, and it means you will walk away from the whole thing unscathed, but you have to be completely honest with me and I'll be honest with you, OK?"

"OK," came the reply.

"I don't work alone John. I have two friends who have also had dealings with the group. I need you to work with us and tell us what you know. Going forward you must be able to hold your nerve but if we get through this, you will be away from all your troubles, and you can start fresh wherever you please. That's my promise and that's what I'm offering. Are you in? A simple yes or no right now." He didn't hesitate for one second. "If I can walk away from all of this then I'm in."

"Good," said Jenny. "You had better meet my friends then. She walked to the door and ushered Laura in.

"John, this is Laura. She is the wife of Tony Henderson." John's eyes widened but he gathered his manners together and held out his hand. Laura took it and gave it a firm shake.

"Good to have you onboard John," she said.

"Thanks," he replied.

"Now John, you may be surprised when you meet our next colleague." Jenny went to the door, opened it and Rodders entered.

"Jesus! Rodders!" Gasped Davis, "what happened to you? The last time I saw you, you had shot yourself to get out of the army and rumor was that you ended up on the streets somewhere."

"Hello Davis," Rodders winced at the story. "It wasn't like that mate. Like you, I discovered what happened to the Sarge.

He told me on the chopper back to camp the day he was shot. I knew too much and I was told that my time was up. The only way out…" He made a pistol with his fingers and aimed at his foot, "boom."

"Holy shit!" Davis's fear lifted now he knew there were others who not only knew but were trying to bring down the gang, "I don't know what to say."

"Don't say anything. Listen to what we have to tell you. Rodders, can you bring him up to speed? Me and Laura will make the teas and coffees." Rodders nodded and started telling Davis all about the plan and how he fitted into the grand scheme of things. As Laura and Jenny began to make the drinks, Jenny went to say something but Laura interrupted.

"I know about Bairdy. I was watching it on the camera app on my phone," said Laura.

"How are you? How do you feel knowing that one of the group involved in Tony's death is still out there?"

"Focused," she replied, "very focused."

PART THREE

The Reckoning

CHAPTER 14

Davis knew as soon as they were discharged that Deano and Billy had rented a place away from town. As requested by Jenny, he started to do a bit of homework on their movements. He knew Billy was employed at a local petrol station and when he worked out his shift patterns saw that Deano often walked him to work before sliding into the off license on the way home to pick up his daily supply of booze and cigarettes. The time to step up to the plate came just after Deano had left the shop carrying a plastic bad laden with alcohol. He positioned himself on the opposite side of the street in readiness for the chance meeting he had planned.

"Deano? DEANO!?" shouted Davis, hastily crossing the street. Deano looked up from his phone to see Davis walking briskly towards him.

"Mavis Davis! Hey man, how are you doing? It's good to see you," he replied, genuinely happy to see his old platoon comrade. "What are you doing in this neck of the woods?" Davis had his excuses for being in the vicinity all planned out in his head ready to answer and questions with confidence. He laughed at the question.

"Ah man, it's a long story but I'll give you the short version. I'm actually here seeing a girl I met on Tinder. She's a nice girl, not long-term material but I've only gone and hooked up with another one and they only live two streets away from each other," he sniggered. "I'm seeing the other one later in the week, so I had better be discreet, you know? Hell hath no fury like a woman scorned and all that jazz." Deano laughed and thought for a moment.

"I wouldn't know," he hesitated, "not my thing really." Davis let the penny drop for a second or two before they both cackled out loud.

"I've been meaning to catch up with you at some point but, I'm not sure if you've heard, I'm under the shrink so a lot of my time gets taken up with all that stuff." Davis said and Deano nodded.

"It's good to see you're getting some kind of support; they threw Billy and me to the wolves and chucked us out without so much as a penny to our names." He looked sad when he spoke and Davis understood a lot of what he was going through. Then without warning his mood changed to one of anger and resent.

"It's dickheads like you who get all of the help when people like me and Billy are treated like crap," he snarled, spit flying from his mouth as he spoke. Davis stood shocked at the sudden change. It was as though a switch had been flipped and some kind of Mr. Hyde character had been released from Deano's body. Davis took a step back waiting for another assault, but it never came. Deano's demeanor reverted back to the way he was when they had met just moment ago. Davis wondered if he was high on something.

"I'm sorry buddy," Deano mumbled, "I don't know what came over me there." He took a deep breath and looked around, embarrassed but as if he didn't know how to break away from the situation.

"Listen, why don't I pop around and see you and Billy when I come back to see this other girl? I'll sit and have a chat before the date, how does that sound?" For a moment Davis thought Deano was going to decline the offer but after a moment's thought he abruptly appeared to rejoin the conversation as though for the last ten seconds he had been in a completely different place and time.

"Erm... OK. I'll see you later," he replied and without another word turned on his heels and walked back in the direction he came from. Davis let out an audible sigh as though he had escaped an encounter with a football hooligan from the opposing team. He knew there was a deep-rooted psychological problem with Deano that you didn't need to be a doctor to see. He walked to the bus stop, glad to be leaving.

In the waiting room, Davis sat quietly, patiently waiting for Jenny to ask him to come into her office. Siona looked at him and smiled. *Poor lad,* she thought. He looked downbeat and defeated, like not only his problems but those of the world hung over him, waiting to drop on his head like the Sword of Damocles. He was a new patient to Jenny, but his record showed he had been under one of the counselors at the barracks. *Hopefully Jenny could do more for him* she wondered. The office door opened, and Jenny poked her head through into the waiting room.

"John," she cheerfully called, "would you like to come in now?" He stood, stooping as he walked slowly into the room. As the door closed behind him, he instantly straightened and stood upright without the slightest sign of a slouch. He gave Jenny a smile and she reciprocated with a short, stifled laugh.

"Nice acting there, John, you should be on the stage," she teased.

"I thought so," he replied "but in all honesty I do feel a lot better since I spoke to you and the others, Jenny. I was bottling everything up and I just couldn't cope. Now, at least I can see a light at the end of the tunnel and it's not a train heading towards me."

"What have you got?" Queried Jenny.

"Well," he began, "I 'accidently on purpose' ran into Deano in town the other day and told him I would be passing his place this week as I was going on a date with some bird I met…. sorry, young lady, I met on Tinder. Told him I would swing in past for a brew before going to meet her. He seemed up for it, so I said I'll come past about six tomorrow. He looked like death warmed up and I doubt he'd seen a shower in about a month. He was in a right state. He had a bag full of cans as well, so I'm guessing he's pissed for most of the day. I could have told him to run off a cliff for a bottle of vodka and he would have done it." He didn't show any emotion as he spoke about Deano. He had been instrumental in the Sarge's death and the breaking down of any kind of normal life *he* could have had. As far as Davis was concerned, he was fair game and he was getting his comeuppance.

"Perfect," came the thrilled reply. "You've done very well so far John," she went on "but the biggest hurdle for you is yet to come." David was excited but cautious as to what was coming next.

"This is what I need you to do." He listened intently now.

"I need Deano and Billy's mobile phone numbers. Do you have them handy?" He fumbled in his pocket for his phone and brought the screen to life with a swipe.

"I would password that phone before you leave the office John," she advised. "You never know when or where your phone might be scrutinized by one of the gang. You know the type of people we are dealing with here. Don't let our plan be compromised because of something as simple as an unlocked phone." He nodded in agreement and did it straight away. He then flicked through his contacts before he went to send the numbers via text.

"Stop." Jenny scolded. "Think about the digital trail John. I might be your counselor with a legitimate reason for my number being in your phone, but everything has a footprint so whenever you can, write something down on paper. Do so from now on, alright?" *She's getting good at this,* thought Davis.

"I need you to memorise this number and give it to Deano. You need to sell this to him, John or none of us get anything from this, do you understand?" He nodded.

"Right," she continued, "I need you to tell him you have been speaking to a specialist who gives therapy to military guys over the phone free of charge. Tell him I'm from a military background so know what the guys are going through but most importantly I want you to tell him I left the forces over bullying because I was a lesbian. You must stress the fact that I was gay John, or he won't latch on to what you're telling him. He has to really believe that there's someone out there who understands him and Billy's situation, has been through the same thing and can help him with his depression. Tell him you only know my first name. Tell him I'm called Maggie but you don't know my surname as we like to keep a level of anonymity to our callers. Have you got that?"

"Yes, I understand completely,", he nodded.

"One more thing," she continued, "you must tell him that as this is a privately funded operation manned by volunteers, he can only call on Mondays, Wednesdays, and Thursday between six and ten in the evening. Try to get him to call while you're with him. This whole thing hinges on how successful you are tomorrow. You want out of the predicament you're in, this is how we get out. All of us."

"You can count on me Jenny. I won't let you down." She believed him. He needed a way out of the life his father and Nolan had created for him and he understood the importance of his role in the scheme. All he had to do was play the part and hold his nerve.

"Oh," as he turned to leave he remembered something. "The whole company has a week off prior to mobilizing on a big exercise on Salisbury next month so we have from Friday to do what we need to do." *That could work out in their favour,* Jenny thought. They could carry out parts of the plan and nobody would be any the wiser until people started failing to report for duty the following week. *Things are getting better already,* Jenny concluded.

The rain lashed against the windows of Jenny's house. It was getting dark earlier now and the weather had taken a turn for the worst. It hadn't let up and that meant people had closed their curtains and the streets were almost empty. Laura knocked on the door followed by Rodders ten minutes later.

"Christ it's throwing it down out there!" He said as he took off his jacket in the foyer. As he went into the lounge, Laura was sitting on the floor with a bag in front of her filled with what looked like electronic equipment. Rodders presumed it was for the incoming calls to the number that Davis would provide Deano that very evening. It didn't look complicated at all. The voice frequency modulator was about the size of a cigarette packet and the encryption device not much bigger. She took the equipment out of the bag and three encrypted phones.

"Why so many phones?" Probed Rodders. "This is like the electronic version of a Tupperware party," he joked.

"Well," began Laura, laughing and rolling her eyes at him, "we will need two at a later date and one now to hook everything up to. If we hook up the encryption box to the phone line, then to the modulator it will link up to the phone via Bluetooth so anyone calling in thinks it's a landline number, but it goes through to a mobile phone. It won't show up on any bills, it will only come up as a withheld number; although the mobile will show us its whoever we give the number to. It's very simple but very sneaky and effective. It's also very expensive. The two boxes I managed to get for six grand, but the phones are fifteen hundred each and everything we see has to be disposed of when we finish. There can be no trail of crumbs to the four of us.

That is where you come in and your contact at the medical center, but I'll tell you about that when we've finished using it." Rodders looked slightly confused at the but Laura seemed to know what she was doing.

"Once this is set up," Laura continued, "all we need to do is wait. Only one person has the number, so we know who is on the other end when it rings." Jenny stood up in front of them.

"You both know why we are here." They all nodded to one another.

"When the phone rings I need you to leave the room and let me speak to him alone. I need to do this on my own," she stressed. "I need to go to a place I've not been to before and I can't do that with you guys here with me. I need to see a bigger picture and to be honest, I don't think either of you would want to hear it anyway."

"Agreed," said Rodders. Laura gave a compliant look and they sat in silence for a minute or so to take in what was about to happen... if Davis had done his part.

As Davis headed towards Deano and Billy's flat, he tried to shield himself from the oncoming rain. His jeans were wet and he attempted to keep his head dry by pulling up the hoodie he had on underneath his waterproof jacket. He was in a rough part of the town known for drug deals and third-rate prostitutes although there wouldn't be much business going on in tonight's rainstorm. He arrived at the small block of flats. It was six stories high but luckily Deano's residence was on the second floor so there weren't many stairs to climb. He rang the doorbell without any response. He knocked hard on the wooden, glassless door and waited. After a minute, he heard a shuffling of feet from behind and a chain being removed from its lock and the door swung inwards to reveal Deano, stood in a dressing gown looking as though he had been drinking since early afternoon. He greeted Davis with a look of bewilderment. He waited a moment before shaking his head and recognising that it was one of his old platoon in the doorway in front of him.

"Mavis?" He spoke "how are you doing mate?" His face went serious as he put his head out of the door and looked left and right before pulling it back into the passageway of the flat.

"Why are you here?"

"What do you meant why am I here, you doughnut?" Davis was thinking quickly before Deano could close the door on him.

"I saw you in town just the other day, don't you remember? I'm going on a date tonight with a girl I met on Tinder... I said I would pop by... you told me you would look forward to it... no? Nothing there mate?" Deano searched hard for the memory but couldn't find it.

"Ah well, you're here now so you might as well come in bud," he murmured. Davis entered the flat. The drawn curtains didn't look as though they had been opened for a while and there were cans and bottles strew around the living room. It smelt of stale body odor, cigarettes, and marijuana.

"Christ buddy is it the maid's day off?" joked Davis, trying to lighten the already dour mood.

"Yeah, mate she only comes in on Mondays to give it the once over you know," he replied. "You want a drink? I've got a few beers in the fridge."

Yeah, but what else is living in the fridge with them? Thought Davis.

"Er, yeah, go on then," he begrudgingly said.

As Deano left the room, Davis scanned around to see if he could find anything that could help Jenny and the others. There were letters from debt collection companies and bills from the electricity and gas providers. Davis took care not touch anything in case he left any DNA evidence behind if it all went a bit pear shaped.

"How's things?" He shouted through to Deano as he carried on perusing the room.

"I'm OK, you know. Not too bad. Had better times like but hey, everyone falls hard on their arses at some point, don't they?"

"Yeah, mate I know what you mean." Deano came back into the room, handed Davis an opened beer and clinked his half pint glass of neat vodka against his bottle.

"Jesus mate, how long have you been drinking that stuff for? I always thought you were a beer man?" Davis asked.

"Ah you know mate, its cheap and gets you legless, best way to be don't you think?" He was laughing. Davis gave a slight laugh back and began his well-rehearsed monologue.

"How's Billy doing mate? OK is he?" It was a loaded question.

"Yeah," slurred Deano. "He's working in some shitty petrol station until ten o'clock tonight then he'll be back."

"Cool mate, I'll have to catch up with him sometime."

"Aren't you hanging around Mave?" Asked Deano.

"No mate, I've got a date, remember?"

"But you're soaked through bud, you're not going to meet this bird like that are you?"

"I don't intend to have my trousers on that long mate, know what I mean?" He quipped as they both laughed at the thought.

"Give us a look then," asked Deano, "what's she like?"

"Nah mate, I don't want to jinx it you know," replied Davis.

"Go on show me," he pushed.

"Nah mate, it's private you know," he pretended to be chivalrous. Deano's mood turned in an instant.

"Fucking show me now you little dick." He snarled, "or you won't see her at all." Davis was scared now. Davis had witnessed Deano's instant change in personality the last time they had met. He was taken aback then but he was even more shocked now. Luckily, he had set up a quick date for that evening in case the very situation cropped up.

"OK, OK calm down, you miserable sod," he said, trying to diffuse the situation. Once the phone was out and the Tinder profile shown, Deano started to mellow.

"Looks like a little slag," he mocked "I don't think a little wanker like you will have much trouble getting into that later."

Davis was trying to think fast on his feet in an attempt to bring the situation back on script.

"Yeah," he said nervously, "that's the plan eh?" Deano took no notice and slumped beside Davis on the couch.

"Tell me how you've been Mave," he said, "what's been going on with you?" It was clear Deano hadn't remembered any of their last encounter at all. Davis repeated the story he had told him previously.

"You won't believe this, but I've been referred to a shrink because the army think I'm mental," he started. "They won't let me have a gun so I can't go on detachment anymore and they've got me doing shit jobs until they can dump me mate. I'm pissed off but what can I do? It's over for me mate." Crocodile tears appeared on cue.

"I never knew it was that bad Mave," he said, genuinely concerned. "It's crap, isn't it? Me and Billy have been hounded for ages and nobody has lifted a finger to help us, the bastards." Davis gritted his teeth but kept his temper. *You were one of the people who did this to me,* he thought. He calmed himself and reminded himself why he was there in the first place.

"This shrink I'm seeing, you know? She ex-Navy. She got bullied and then attempted suicide and eventually thrown out under a section eight, but she reckons it was because she was gay." He waited for a response, but none came.

"She was given so much shit but managed to overcome it. She says she's fighting for gay rights and helps out anyone who wants it but she covers everything really. In all honesty mate she has been brilliant for me. I can get out of bed in the morning now without wanting to throw myself under a passing tank," he giggled childishly.

"Yeah mate, the way they treated us for being gay was shocking," snapped Deano. He was on the hook.

"She is fighting tooth and nail for some bloke from the Kings at the minute but obviously she didn't give names or anything.

She is very good to talk to." He waited. "You should give her a go mate but her group only work on a Monday Wednesday and today so if you want her number, I'll write it down for you." He scribbled the number down trying to disguise his handwriting but make it still legible enough that Deano could read it while drunk. He finished his bottle and looked at the clock. It was almost seven, but he still wasn't sure he had done his task well enough to persuade Deano to make the call.

"Tell you what," Davis said "let's have one more drink and shoot the shit for a while. This bird can wait an extra half hour, eh?" Deano gave a smile. "I'll get them."

He went into the small, dimly lit kitchen. There were plates stacked in dirty, greasy water and pot noodle tubs everywhere. There wasn't a clean surface in the place and he could see drug paraphernalia on the windowsill. Nothing bad, just a bit of dope but neither Deano or Billy had even bothered to try and hide it. Davis looked in the fridge. As soon as he opened the door, the smell of rotting food hit him. The milk in the bottle had soured and there was an unidentifiable bit of food, half eaten on a plate, covered in mold. He didn't gag, he had seen worse things in his young life than decaying food and mold but thoughts of how these two ex-soldiers could turn out so filthy was something Davis couldn't comprehend. At the end of the day, he didn't care one bit about either of them. They were scum that had made his life hell and they were going to pay for it. He took the vodka from the fridge and almost filled the half pint glass, carefully cleaning that and the bottle with a handkerchief to dispose of any prints. He then removed a bottle from the shelf, popped the lid with a bottle opener on his keys and went through to the lounge.

"There you go bud," he handed the drink to Deano.

"Cheers," Deano replied and gulped a huge mouthful of the cheap, harsh spirit, shaking his head as it went down. Davis took a small sip of the beer.

"Here's that number mate," he urged Deano to take a look.

"Yeah, I'll get round to it, stick it on the table," he answered. If it went on the table, it would never get looked at, thought Davis. He pushed his luck and decided to face Deano head on. It was a gamble that could go either way but the plan wasn't going as well as he thought, and he had to come through for the others.

"Deano!" He yelled. Deano snapped his head up. "I'm doing this for you for fuck's sake mate," he stressed. "I've got a date tonight, but from what you told me the other day about having a hard time and all that I took time out to come and see you. At least acknowledge the fact that I'm here trying to help you." Davis was taking a gamble alright. Deano looked shocked and for a moment Davis thought he was going to punch him, but then his face softened.

"Shit mate, I'm sorry, you're right. Let's have a squint at the number," replied Deano.

"Tell you what mate, if you call her now, I'll wait outside and cancel this date with Tinder bird and when you're finished I'll pop to the shops and get a massive carry out for you, me and Billy and we can get shit faced for old times' sake. How does that sound?" Deano's face lit up. He was half drunk but managed a smile and a thumbs up. As he reached for his phone, Davis went around and cleaned everything he had touched in the kitchen and all of the door handles without getting noticed. He took his empty bottle and the full one, gave Deano an 'I'm outside' head gesture and left the flat. He looked to see if anyone was watching. The street below was empty as the rain and wind battered down on the town. He pulled the door shut gently until he heard the click, wiped the handle, and slid into the dark night unnoticed.

CHAPTER 15

Back at Jenny's house, the trio sat in the living room in silence with the TV on but muted. Jenny was fiddling with a Bluetooth headset while Laura and Rodders played a game on Jenny's iPad as if they were simply enjoying a fun night in. They didn't know if Davis had succeeded in his task, the phone might not even ring, but they had to be ready just in case it did. And it did. The mood in the room changed instantly. The ringtone was soft and melodic and once it started to chime, the three all looked at each other in a state of shock. Rodders and Laura stood, gave Jenny a consolatory look and exited the lounge. She took in a deep breath and exhaled in a calm, cool manner. She inserted the Bluetooth earpiece, checked the encryption equipment was on and clicked the answer button.

"Action for Veterans, Maggie speaking," she said in a controlled, soft voice. It was silent for a moment or two then a voice came down the line.

"Hi...hello." Deano's voice was wobbly at the end of the line.

"Hello, who am I speaking to?" She answered, clear and composed.

"I'm a friend of Mavis.... Davis, sorry, John Davis."

"Ah yes, John, of course. He did mention he had a friend who could use some help. What's your name again?" She asked.

"It's Deano," he was slurring.

"Yes Deano, I had to ask just to be sure I was talking to the right person. How are you tonight, Deano? Are you feeling OK? I'm guessing you need to chat with someone, hence the call?" The question seemed obvious but she needed to know Deano wasn't just going to rant on then slam the phone down. She wanted confirmation he was going to be receptive to what she was going to tell him.

"I always need someone to talk to," he mumbled.

"Then Deano," continued Jenny, "I will try my best to help you. You may not always like what I say but I speak from experience. I've been in your situation, so I think I know how you are feeling."

"What experience is that then? What's Davis been telling you?" He snarled. Jenny picked up on her mistake straight away and she scolded herself for being so nonchalant in her approach to the conversation. She needed this chat to start on her terms and keep it that way.

"All he said was that you had left the army. You and your partner had set up home together after being on the end of some grief from the soldiers in the company and you could do with a bit of help getting over some problems you were having. He didn't go any further than that. Am I correct in thinking you've been harassed because of your sexuality Deano?"

"Yes," came the single word answer.

"Would you like to tell me about that?"

"The guys in 4 platoon, that's the one me and Billy and Davis were in, they were OK, but the rest of the company were bastards. They treated us like shit all the time," he sniffled.

"Why did the boys in 4 platoon treat you well but everyone else didn't? Why was the relationship different with those guys?" Quizzed Jenny.

"We had a thing going on you know. A little sideline where we all made a few quid. Where money is involved it makes people treat others in a different way, I reckon," he said.

Jenny was straining not to lash out and let him know that she knew exactly what had gone down in 4 platoon but that wouldn't help her cause. She could blow the whole thing to pieces too soon if she couldn't control her emotions. She lingered on her next question.

"So, is Billy your boyfriend Deano? Let's call him your partner, you do live together after all."

"Yes, he is. He's the reason I left the army. He couldn't handle the bullying. I would have stayed in but I gave it up for him. Now we're living in some dump without a pot to piss in and it's all his fault," he wailed. "I've given up so much for him and he doesn't even see what sacrifices I've had to put up with. I love him but hate him at the same time. I don't know what to do.". The cracks were starting to show and he had only been speaking for five minutes or so.

"What time does Billy get in from work Deano?" She asked. "I take it he's at work right now?"

"Yeah," he replied, "he works in a petrol station in town. He doesn't finish until ten, but it'll be about ten thirty by the time he gets home."

"Right," said Jenny sternly. "What are you drinking?"

"What do you mean? Why do you want to know what I'm drinking?"

"Because," she said, "we're going to sort this out like military people do. We will have a few drinks, put the world to rights and say it how it is. How does that sound?" It sounded good to Deano. He reached for the half-drunk bottle beside him on the couch. Thoughts of Davis were long gone, replaced by thoughts of a piss up over the phone with someone he had never met before in his life. It was better than nothing considering he only went out of the flat when he required more booze.

He poured himself another half of vodka and settled in for a session.

"So," began Jenny, "tell me why you hate Billy now?"

"He's just completely oblivious to the fact we're living like a couple of tramps when we could have still been in the army and each of us at least have a wage. Now we live in the worst part of town and we're skint all the time. I can't get a job, so I rely on him. So even though I love him I can't get away from him, even if I wanted to." Jenny could hear him crying now. His resentment of Billy was the weakness she had to play on.

"You know what happened to me Deano?" she fumed. "The same thing. Exactly the same thing mate. I left the Navy and set up with my girlfriend. It all went a bit sour after I had given up everything for her and she left me right in the shit. She did what she did to get back at me and there's not a day goes by when I don't think about what she did to me. I'm so angry all the time. It sorted out her problem but in doing so she got her revenge on me for ruining her life as she saw it."

"What did she do?" Jenny paused.

"She committed suicide Deano. She killed herself to prove a point to me and boy did she do that alright. She wanted revenge on me, and she got it. She left a note which blamed me but really, she wanted to get back at the navy for the way they treated us. No matter how hard we tried we couldn't sort ourselves out. We loved each other but we started to resent each other. We couldn't separate, we had been through so much and the only way out for her was to hang herself. She got what she wanted in the end. I've never told anyone that before," lied Jenny. "I'm going to have another drink, give me a minute or two," she said.

She put the headset on mute and got up to walk around the room. She knew what she was doing was wrong in every sense of the word but as she spoke all she could think of was Dave lying on a gurney dying in Afghanistan and Deano was one of the ones to blame for that. She returned to the call.

"Are you still there Deano?" She asked.

"Yeah, I'm here. Just been to get another drink." He was slurring quite a bit now.

"You like a drink don't you Deano?"

"Yeah, I love a good piss up, I always have. It's one of the things I miss about the army," he lamented. "I used to have some good friends but when me and Billy got out, they didn't come to see us after that. Davis came round today but that's the first time I've seen anyone in weeks. Shit, I think he's still outside. Hang on a minute." She could hear the door opening and closing soon afterwards and the voice returned to the end of the phone.

"He must have buggered off. He did say he had a date with some girl, or did he cancel it? Not too sure, anyways he's gone." Jenny looked at the clock, it was almost eight thirty, she needed to make headway, or the plan would fail. She started to act half-drunk as they continued their chat.

"Listen mate," she slurred, "you know what? I tried committing suicide once. That's the reason they gave for throwing me out of the navy. Section eight, but I didn't really try to kill myself, it was all staged so me and my girl could get out quicker. She had already put her leaving paperwork in, but I needed to go around it slightly differently, see?"

"How did you do it?" Deano asked.

"Pills," said Jenny ,"but I didn't take a lot. It was a fake attempt after all; I knew exactly what I was doing. However, I've been told the best way and quickest is to hang yourself. No pain at all and if you want to make a statement that's how to do it." She felt a lump in her throat as she spoke the words but she kept pushing. "It's the way I would do it now. Get pissed, write a note and boom: it's over. But your legacy lives on and so does the message you wanted to send."

"I wish I had the balls to do it Maggie, I really do. It's the only way anyone would ever listen to me, and it would show

Billy wouldn't it?" He gulped at the vodka. "How would you do something like that?" He asked.

"Well," revealed Jenny, "I would get a long belt, make a loop and with the end tie it in a knot. Slide it over a door so the knot is on the other side, close the door, slip in on my neck and let my feet go. Simple". She was close to getting what she wanted. He only needed a little more persuading and she was certain he would do it. She needed to keep pushing.

"Listen Deano, you don't need to go the whole way. The method I've told you means you can recover if you bottle it at the last-minute." She knew differently. She had read that the technique she had told him meant the buckle dug into your spine at the base of the skull and basically affected you instantly. She pushed further.

"Billy has made your life hell. He's working. He's got money but you have given up *everything* for him and he doesn't even appreciate it. He's a right shit to you. The only way you can get him back is to do it Deano. You can and you will because you need to let everyone know what's been going on. This will get them talking mate. This will prove your point and Billy will go down in flames as well. It's the only way." Her voice was quiet now.

"I'm behind you all the way. I'll even tell you what to write in your note. Have you got a pen?"

"Yeah," said Deano, "hang on a second." "Right, I'm back, I've got some paper as well," he began to scribble what Jenny told him.

"It's simple, this is what to write: THIS IS ALL YOUR FAULT. PROVE ME WRONG. Have you got that Deano?"

"What does it mean?" He asked.

"That's the beauty of it, nobody will ever know. It will have people thinking about it for years. Billy will go crazy trying to work it out and that's how you get him back for what he's done to you. Go and have a trial run. Set everything up and see how you feel." She didn't feel comfortable with what she was doing but she was certain he was getting everything he deserved and she found strength in that.

Deano went to the closet and took out a belt. It wasn't very long but it was good enough for his purpose. He would have to stand on something to make it work but that wasn't a problem. He tied the belt as Jenny had instructed and closed the knot over the door in the spare room. He recovered a small wooden box from beneath the bed, which he kept some of his old army uniform and pictures in. It stood no more than a foot high but it was enough to help him reach the height he required. The drink was overtaking him now and he started to stumble into furniture in the bedroom. He took a long swig of vodka before picking up the phone.

"I can't believe I'm doing this," he bawled. "I'll have a feel and see what it feels like," he continued. He stood on the box and, hands shaking, slipped the looped belt over his neck. The buckle slid down the leather and rested at the base of his neck. He leaned over slightly to feel the loop tighten around his throat. He started to choke and moved his body back upright to relieve the pressure on his neck.

"It feels weird, sort of strange. I can't do it, I love Billy, he doesn't deserve this." He was weeping more now and Jenny could hear him glugging at the vodka.

"You need to do this Dean,o otherwise no one will ever take you seriously. You will just be some loser gay bloke who got shitcanned from the army and who'll never amount to anything." She had to give him both barrels now. The softly softly approach had only gotten her so far, now she needed to finish it.

"Billy fucking hates you anyway, so do your mates so why not just do it and be out of everyone's lives, you leech?" Deano's eyes widened at the insults. Adrenaline shot through him as he became more lucid. He tried to find the words to throw a tirade of abuse down the phone but as he did his footing gave way and the box tumbled over. The belt quickly slid down his neck and the brass buckle dug hard into the top of his spine. There was a loud crack and Deano's body went limp. The choking continued for over a minute as Jenny listened intently on the phone, he had dropped onto the bedroom floor. When the choking subsided Jenny rang off and placed the phone on the coffee table. She sat in silence and felt numb. What she was doing was ugly, there was no doubt about it, but she felt that it was what was right. She sat alone for ten or so minutes before rising and going into the kitchen. Laura and Rodders looked up at her waiting for her to talk. She breathed out heavily.

"It's done." She said.

They sat but didn't speak for at least twenty or so minutes. Jenny went over the scenario in her head but she felt devoid of all feeling towards her actions. She wasn't going to let what she had done overtake her emotions, she had made that clear to herself from the start. She knew the reasons why they were carrying out their plan, they all did, and they had spoken in depth regarding the outcome. He was involved in taking away something from her she dearly wanted to keep. He had paid the ultimate price for his part in the death of Dave and the destruction of Rodders' and Davis's lives. She put it to the back of her mind. Jenny lifted her head to look at Laura.

"You're on next," she uttered stoically.

"It's all planned the way we spoke about it the other night. Rodders, are you totally clear about what you have to do?"

"Yes," he replied. "I'm all set. I've got the stuff in the boot and I've checked a route for you to take with initial minimal exposure to CCTV. All we have to do now is get Davis to do his thing again and we'll be ready."

"OK then," Laura continued. "I need to go to London again to get a few things to help me, but I'll ask John to try to set it up for Saturday night. That bastard won't know what hit him."

CHAPTER 16

Laura was not a great fan of the city, or of any city for that matter. She had grown up on greenbelt land and didn't have the time or patience for traffic, noise, and air pollution. By no means was she an eco-warrior but she understood the effects traffic and carbon dioxide were having on the environment, and she didn't like it. The quicker she could be in and out the better. She had come to visit the West End for some props for her meeting with Bairdy. If she was to be successful, like Jenny, she had be able to overcome and adapt and transform into something and someone she wasn't. The plan for the evening had been divulged to the others who had input into how it could work better or be more covert and eventually the final preparations had been made and greenlit by Jenny. She was, as the others saw it, the leader of their group and had the final word over what happened and when. She was a great organiser and Laura thought she would have made a truly inspiring military leader.

As she navigated the city, Laura dug her hands deeper into her pockets and pulled the collar of her jacked as tight around her as she could. The wind swirled around her neck as she passed by alleyways and shopfronts, the bright neon lights hanging high above the streets in stark contrast to the dark dinginess of the pavements below. She could make out the shapes of the hapless individuals who littered the doorways, like human detritus, forgotten and neglected by society. One man, sitting on cardboard grasping a can of lager, put out his hand in the hope of some loose change. His hands were filthy and blistered, his face weather beaten, covered in a grey matted beard. She felt guilt run through her and at the same time the urge to get away as fast as possible. The thought of helping and being scared of those same people confused her. She put her thoughts to the back of her mind and remembered why she had come here in the first place.

She knew that even with Tony dying and all the problems and stresses that came with it, she was infinitely better off than the majority of people she walked past on the streets of London.

As she entered the shop she was overwhelmed by the sheer amount of props and make up that were for sale. Everything from fake blood to full size costume armor. There was no doubt that she would be able to find exactly what she required, and within a matter of minutes she had what she came for and was out and back onto the litter strewn streets. She had one more stop to make before the journey home.

Davis picked up the phone and proceeded to find Bairdy's number. Once it had been located, he contemplated what he would say and pressed the call button. After three rings the call was answered.

"Mavis?" Bairdy asked in a silly comedy voice. "Bairdy." Replied Davis, in a similarly silly tone. "What's happening dude?"

"Usual crap, you know how it is but I'm buzzing now we've got a week off before we go on exercise at the end of the month. I'm going to get so wasted man, I can't wait. How's life in shit platoon? I'm guessing you're absolutely loving pushing your broom around, eh? You are a malingering sickie." Davis hated being called names due to his depression and being told he would probably never fire a weapon again made him feel useless in the army. It was embarrassing and degrading being on Holding Platoon, but life was life and he had to get used to it. He had never been keen on Bairdy. He had always viewed him as a Jack the Lad, the type who would shag your girlfriend behind you back and blame her if he got caught. He would throw you under a bus to get out of trouble and to Davis, he was a repulsive untrustworthy man. He would take great pleasure in setting him up.

"What have you got planned for today?" Enquired Davis.

"Actually, at this minute in time my usually busy diary is completely empty for the whole of today my old son. Why? What are you thinking?"

"Well," began Davis, "I'm thinking all day session, followed by clubbing, followed by some action with the ladies. What do you reckon? Start off about six o'clock?"

"Where do you want to begin our journey, buddy?" Bairdy sounded enthusiastic.

"Golden Lion... then wherever the evening takes us after that."

"I'm in." Said Bairdy and with that the phone went dead as they both rang off simultaneously.

As soon as the phone call ended, Davis searched for Jenny's number. He rang and she answered quickly. The conversation was short.

"Golden Lion at six," he stated.

"Understood." Came the short reply, and the discussion was abruptly ended. The trap was set and Laura, with the help of Jenny and Rodders, would bring the ruse to fruition. But first, Laura needed to undergo a transformation.

Bairdy had arrived at the bar half an hour early on the off chance he could pick up some drunken girl and cancel on

Davis. He sat at a table on his own. The bar was around half full and it was obvious there had been a football game on that afternoon. The fans of the local team, all dressed in the home strips were drowning out the jukebox by singing loud anthems. After twenty minutes or so the group left for their next haunt and the bar became quieter, at least Bairdy could hear the music now. As he perused the room, he spotted a woman leaning against a table in the center of the room. She had long black hair, arm tattoos and heavy, smoky eye make-up. She was thin, but not skinny, and quite pretty thought Bairdy. She had a tight black top on which showed off her ample breasts and a short black leather mini skirt. Knee high leather boots rounded off the look. Bairdy looked around and once he had ascertained she was alone he decided to make his move.

"Hey there, I'm sorry but do I know you?" He asked, knowing they had never met but deciding to go straight in for the ice breaker instead of wasting his time messing around. Laura shot a look back to him and studied his face.

"I'm not sure, do you?" She replied, smiling but giving him a look up and down as if *she* was the one looking to find a one-night stand. Bairdy studied the body language and instantly decided she was worth pursuing. She gave him a naive come on and she knew from the offset he was on the hook. *This couldn't be any easier,* thought Laura.

"So," began Bairdy, "what's your name?"

"Laura," she answered, "and you?"

"I'm Bairdy," he retorted. "Sounds a bit corny like, but do you come here often? I've not seen you around and I drink here quite a lot."

"Not really," she began "I live on the outskirts of town but don't really get out much. I'm studying to be a child psychologist so that takes up a lot of my time so I really only get to let my hair down once a month. Mind when I do I like to party. I'm sick of being in the house with my nose in the books. Hopefully

I'll only have one more term left and that's me finished. What do you do?" She asked.

"I work on the oil rigs," lied Bairdy. He knew that the military boys weren't always welcome in town either to the women who saw them as mainly shaggers who didn't really want relationships, and to the local men who saw them as out of towners trying to take away their women. An age-old scenario that is encountered in every town where there is a military presence from Lands' End to John O' Groats.

"What's the craic then?" Continued Bairdy. "Are you waiting on your mates coming or have you been stood up by your boyfriend?" He asked, not being very discreet about his line of questioning.

"I was supposed to meet one of my girlfriends here," said Laura, feigning disappointment, "but I got a text saying she's had to cancel so it looks like I'm off home early to watch Saturday evening TV. Deep joy."

"You don't have to go home. My friend has done exactly the same to me. He sent me a text not ten minutes ago saying something had come up so I'm on my own tonight as well. Why don't we have a few drinks and see where it goes, eh? It would be a shame to get all dolled up and not make the most of it. Come on, nothing to lose. Don't worry either, I'm not a nutter or escaped rapist," he said, trying his best to reassure her to stay out, get drunk and hopefully end up in his bed.

"Ok then, why not?" She replied, "and no! I don't have a boyfriend I'm supposed to meet either." She winked at him and Bairdy knew the game was on. He responded in the only way he knew how.

"Right, I'll get the drinks in. What would you like? It's happy hour so I'm going to have a triple vodka and coke."

"Ooh," said Laura pretending to think hard about her choice, "I'll have the same, ta". As Bairdy got up to go to the bar, Laura sent a text to Jenny and Rodders.

IT'S ON.

When he returned from the bar, he announced his intention to go to the toilet and walked off in the direction of the gents. Laura, knowing exactly what would happen, took out a flask from inside her bag and emptied her drink into it, filling her glass again with neat cola from a small bottle she also had. When Bairdy returned she was almost halfway down her drink and singing to the tunes blaring from the bar's sound system. He smirked to himself. He knew he was onto a sure thing. After Laura had bought the second round of triple vodkas, she took her drink to the lavatory with her making the excuse of never knowing when a stranger might try to spike her glass. Bairdy thought nothing of it and while she was away texted Davis to let him know his night would turn out OK after all.

Laura, after throwing her drink down the sink and replacing it with coke returned to the table and the pair continued to drink. She would swap to bottles of beer which she knew she could easily handle while he continued to plough himself with glasses of cheap, triple measure vodka.

"How far away do you live?" She asked.

"About a fifteen-minute walk from here," he slurred. "Just at the end of the high street, you know the old council flats? I rent one of them." The army didn't mind single soldiers living off base as long as they were deemed sensible and could be back on camp within half an hour of receiving a call from their Platoon Commander. Bairdy was one of the lucky few thought to be trustworthy enough to have a life outside of the wire by his O.C, Captain Nolan.

"Do you fancy heading off now? It's just I can't be home too late and I don't want to fall asleep at yours."

"Yeah, of course," he said, grinning. He went to get up and stumbled into the table opposite. The occupants berated him for his drunkenness but he shrugged it off and walked out of the bar, unphased. Laura, attempting to avoid any commotion, was already at the door, trying to be as discreet as possible.

"I'm getting a taxi," she ordered, "my feet are killing me."

"Whatever," came the reply as he quickly tried to gain his composure. He was, after all onto a winner and he needed to be on his game. The thought of scoring some cocaine entered his head but, not knowing his new conquest, decided against calling his dealer. *Maybe next time,* he thought. The taxi was at the curbside within a minute of them leaving the bar. It pulled up ten minutes later to the back of four non-descript flats in a quiet but downtrodden road in a half decent part of town. *A private squaddie can easily afford one of these,* thought Laura as she double checked her escape route which she had done several times over the past couple of days. Bairdy paid for their ride and they both exited the vehicle. Once he had managed to find his key and open the door, he perked up at the thought of getting some action from his newly found friend.

Laura cautiously entered the flat and began taking in as much of her surroundings without showing her nervousness. The door was locked behind her and the key left in the latch, a good sign that she could easily exit from the front if need be. The living room door swung open to reveal a neat and tidy room which Bairdy had obviously rented fully furnished. The furniture was cheap but hard wearing, the kind that adorned many a student rental in any university city. She wasn't surprised. The army very rarely turned out young men who didn't take pride in their appearance or their lodgings. It was drilled into them from day one of basic training. Very few disregarded the skills they had picked up as trainees, unless addiction slid into their lives like in the case of Deano and Billy.

Before Laura had a chance to ask Bairdy if she could freshen up, he was pulling her towards him and squeezing her buttocks through the tight leather mini skirt. As he began to kiss her neck, she felt physically sick. She managed to crane her neck to one side but if she was to keep up the charade and finish what she had started she would have to reciprocate his advances. He started fumbling at the hem of the dress in a crude attempt to pull it up over her hips. She gave off a fake sigh to make him think she was actually enjoying his rough handling of her and he began to slide his hands between her stockinged legs. As she tried to pull away, he grabbed her roughly and pushed her back against the wall. Laura counteracted his movement and as she did, she felt a slap across her face. She had not bargained for Bairdy being a violent man and it had never been mentioned by Davis, but it now seemed that this was more dangerous than she first bargained for. As she began to flail, she swiped at him and caught his chin with a feeble right hook. Although this didn't hurt him, Bairdy responded with a punch to her gut and a slap to the back of her head. She knew she had to think of something to get control and quick.

"How did you know I like it rough?" She spluttered. Bairdy was surprised. It was the last thing he had expected to hear. His face contorted and as he lifted his hand to swipe at her again, she turned to face him full on with a face of defiance and the expectation of being hurt. He stopped short of contacting her body and gazed at her to try to deduce if she was serious or not.

"Do you like a little bit of a livener now and again?" She asked. His mood changed instantly.

"What kind of livener are you talking about?" He replied with a hint of excitement.

"Just a little bit of Charlie," exclaimed Laura, "nothing serious, just a quick toot," she said as she touched the side of her nose with her right index finger.

"Have you got a hit?" He asked.

"I'll tell you what, why don't you cut this into a couple of lines and I'll clean up a bit before we get down to some really rough stuff, OK?" Bairdy could hardly contain himself. As he turned to make sure the front door was locked, Laura removed a small glass bottle from her bag, wiped it clean with a wet wipe and placed it on the coffee table. As Bairdy came back he saw it and as she headed off towards the bathroom, he picked up the container and began to distribute its contents into two evenly spaced lines. He waited impatiently for her to return.

As Laura closed the bathroom door a feeling of dread entered her entire body. Her brain raced with ways to defend herself if the situation took an uglier turn than it already had. As she walked back to the living room through the kitchen, she noticed a granite mortar and pestle on the worktop. She grabbed the pestle in her hand and placed it into her bag. She then stood motionless for a moment, turned back, and went back to the bathroom. As she flushed the toilet, she took a small amount of talcum powder and rubbed it below her nose and faking a drunken stupor, went back into the lounge. He was waiting for her, hovering over the table like a child waiting to open a Christmas present.

"You first," he said expectantly. She pointed to her nose.

"Sorry babes, I couldn't wait so had a snifter in the toilet. I hope you don't mind?". She expected him to be angry but he acted in the opposite way. He appeared happy that this tattooed tart he had picked up with every expectation of shagging senselessly all night was the kind of woman he always wanted. *She doesn't mind a slap*, he thought. *She loves a drink, and she takes the lead when it comes to recreational drugs. What was there not to like?*

"No worries to me," he hollered as he took out a five pond note from his wallet and proceeded to roll it up with great anticipation.

"It's strong stuff that by the way, so watch what you're doing now," warned Laura.

"It's not my first rodeo love," he dismissed her, "I'm not new to this, I'll be fine." With that he bent over the table and took a long snort of one of the lines in front of him. The whole thing disappeared almost instantly and as he straightened up Laura encouraged him to take the other one as well. He happily did so with staggering arrogance and confidence. He felt the effects straight away. The rush was overwhelming and as he sat down in a chair, the buzz was like nothing he had encountered before. He felt like he was paralyzed and as he tried to understand what was going on around him, Laura did what she had been briefed to do by Jenny. She began tracing her steps from the furthest point, going back over. She went to the toilet and sprayed alcohol gel onto everything she had come into contact with and worked her way through the kitchen, remembering to replace the missing pestle and back into the lounge. She got onto her knees in front of Bairdy and looked at him. He gazed at her, bewildered as to what he had taken and why she had done this to him.

"Firstly," she began "I'm Tony Henderson's wife. Remember him?" His eyes widened. "Yeeesss, *that* Tony Henderson, the one you and two of your mates bullied to death. The one who took his own life because you and the other little cowardly shits dragged him down to his lowest point and then made him the target of your insults and ridicule: that Tony Henderson." She began to feel the hatred spilling over and she almost hit him as hard as she could, stopping short to remember the evidence she could leave behind if she did so.

"Secondly, it takes around one to two *milligrams* of Fentanyl to kill a man. You have just snorted half a gram. This is what people like you deserve. You disgust me you piece of shit. I hope you rot in hell and your family with you." She watched as his eyes rolled into the back of his head and his body began to convulse erratically. Foam started to erupt from his mouth and all the while Laura watched without the slightest bit of remorse. Now she knew how Jenny felt. As the poison took hold and his body shut down, Laura rose to her feet and finished cleaning any trace of her visit. Once she was satisfied with her efforts, she called Rodders.

"I'm ready." She and Rodders had timed everything perfectly. Two minutes after the call they were meeting each other in the dark lane by the back of the flats. She got into his car and, as they began to drive, she removed her black wig, peeled of her fake tattoo sleeve, and started to undress in the back seat of the car. She had replaced the dark, almost goth like clothing with bright colours and a short-sleeved top. Rodders eventually broke the silence.

"Are you OK, how did it go?"

Laura looked at him through the rear-view mirror.

"Like clockwork," she stated and turned to look out of the back window as an indication that she didn't want to speak any more. Rodders took the hint and they carried on silently. As covertly as he picked her up, he dropped her off near to the center of town. She gave him a nod and walked directly to an area where she knew the streets were heavily covered with CCTV cameras. She proceeded to go in and out of several bars before hailing a taxi and heading home.

When her front door closed behind her she went directly to the full-length bedroom mirror to inspect any injuries to her body following the attack by Bairdy. Luckily there were no marks to her face but there were a couple of small bruises on her torso, ones that could be hidden by clothes and easily explained if she needed to. She stared at herself and broke into an uncontrollable cry. She had been lucky and she knew it. He could have easily overpowered her at any time and done anything he wanted and she would have been helpless to defend herself from his advances. The bruises she inspected could have been broken bones and cuts had she not used her cunning when she needed it most. She looked at her reflection and galvanized her emotions. At least she had avenged Tony. She was torn between guilt and happiness, and it was a sensation she knew she had to master before she could move on with her life. She knew she was not alone in this conundrum. Rodders and Jenny had their lives ruined and as she stared at herself in the mirror, bruises, and all, reflecting back at her she felt a state of ease, safe in the knowledge she had friends who would help her get through the next few weeks, months, or years if need be.

CHAPTER 17

Deano had died on the Friday yet there had been no mention of it either on camp or in the local news. Why hadn't Billy raised the alarm or called the emergency services? Bairdy, owing to the fact he lived out alone, might not be discovered until he failed to show up at work in a week's time so there was no need to worry on that count. These were the thoughts of Davis as he sat patiently waiting to see Jenny in the plush offices she used for her clients. He was ushered into the main office by Siona. As he closed the door, Jenny made a point of welcoming him with a handshake so the administration staff could see her. Once she was satisfied that all of the pleasantries were over, she sat down, ready to chat about the progress so far.

"How are you doing today, John?" She asked.

"I'm fine but I've got a couple of things running through my mind, like why Deano hasn't been found or Billy hasn't been mentioned on camp. I was just thinking about Bairdy as well."

"Listen," she said in a soothing voice, "you have been doing your role superbly. Let me worry about the rest. Everything will be just fine, trust me." And in that moment, he realized, he did trust her, probably more than anyone else he knew.

"Let's talk about Lewis," she continued. "Tell me a bit about him."

"Lewis is..." he thought for a moment, "OK but a bit hyper. He's got a kid to some girl he met and his girlfriend miscarried their baby after he told her. The stress of the whole thing wore her down and, in the end, she left him high and dry and not a minute too soon if you ask me. He can be alright but he was constantly asking where his money was and when we would get cut in. He started to become a bit of a liability to the boss and I reckon he would have been cut out or met with an accident if he hadn't calmed down and accepted the whole thing was bigger than him and his problems." He looked at Jenny feeling embarrassed after mentioning him becoming another casualty of the whole wretched thing, just like the Sarge had. She knew what he was thinking and gave him a smile and a nod to show it was OK. He went on.

"He knew the ins and outs of what went on with everything, except where the initial money went. Nobody knew what happened to it. My Dad never mentioned anything to me. I'm his son and he still treated me like a drugs mule, just like the rest of his minions so I've got no idea where the cash has gone. That's the one thing that keeps Lewis in the game. He still thinks Nolan and Squires will give him his cut when the whole operation starts up again, and it will, there's no doubt about that."

"How was he with you?" She probed.

"He was fine but he was one of the few who knew my dad was involved and looked down on me because he knew more about the whole thing than I did. He rubbed my nose in it more times than I can count. He thought I was a joke to be honest. A worker bee who would never be anything more. I think my dad actually liked him more than me." He stared out of the window as he spoke the words. Disillusioned with army life *and* home life, Davis was stuck between a rock and a hard place. Every time he spoke to Jenny, he felt invigorated with passion to make the group pay for what they had done to him.

"I'll tell you this," he leaned forward in his chair, "I know he sees the shrink... sorry, counselor on camp. The whole baby thing and debts and everything else he has hidden in his head has taken its toll. If anyone goes against the grain with Nolan and what's been going on, it'll be him." Jenny weighed up the options.

"You want to be in on this one?" She asked.

"I would have been disappointed if you hadn't asked," replied Davis. The plan was easier than the others. Rodders needed to be in town with the car and Jenny would be on the phone. Human greed and the weather would provide final elements.

Lewis sat on his bunk in the barrack block biting his nails to the quick. He had turned from a confident young man with decent career prospects into a nervous wreck, a shadow of his former self. He had been one of the few trusted to live off base but because he owed so much money in back payments for child support and other various misadventures, he simply couldn't afford to have a life outside of the wire. He also knew that his promotion prospects were in the hands of Nolan and, if he wanted to stay in the military, he had to bend to his will and do what was expected of him once the smuggling racket started operating again. He, like Davis was trapped. The only difference was Lewis was a greedy individual who was only out for himself. He was impatient for the smuggling operation to start up again. Even though Nolan and Squires had reassured him the money from their previous dealings was safe, it was implied that it should stay kept away safe until the logistics of setting up again had been completed. He began to doubt there was any money and thought about confronting Nolan, or at least Squires, but wondered what the cost would be.

It was Sunday and Davis knew that Lewis, given half a chance, would catch up for a couple of drinks in the Golden Lion. He made the call and went through the almost identical scenario he had with Bairdy.

"Lewis, its Mavis, how's it going?"

"Mavis!" Came the cheerful reply as though his was the first voice he had heard in months, "how are you doing? What you after bud?"

"I'm in town doing a bit of shopping for crap, you know the score. I was walking past the Golden Lion and wondered if you fancied a couple of beers?"

"Hmmm.... I'm a bit skint," replied Lewis, waiting for Davis to make the offer of paying for his drinks in return for a bit of company.

"Don't worry about that mate," said Davis, "you can get them next time. How about one thirty?"

"Sweet!" Lewis was beaming, "I'll see you then."

"Cheers mate." The toast had come from Lewis in return for his first pint being bought by Davis. Secretly he hoped Davis had more money on him; the thought of languishing in the barrack block wasn't a pleasant one and Lewis needed a bit of a blowout. Fingers crossed, Davis was flush.

"Cheers." Came the reply. "Don't worry about money today fella, I had a win on the horses yesterday, two hundred quid."

"Two hundred notes, that's a great result," cheered Lewis although whilst he was saying the words, he was secretly trying to figure out a way of relieving the money from Davis's wallet.

"How did you get into town?" Davis asked.

"I've got the car; I'll leave it here and get a bus back in to pick it up tomorrow. Rain was forecast and I couldn't be bothered waiting for a bus, it'll be OK round the corner, wont it?"

"Yeah, it'll be fine in town, plenty of police. And anyway, it's a piece of crap so I can't see anyone wanting to nick it, can you?" They laughed at the prosect of some thief stealing a car worth about five hundred pounds and getting caught. The chat flowed as did the beer and after four pints the chat turned to Nolan and the thought of the operation restarting again.

"Nolan is back from his course soon. I know we will be going on detachment to Afghanistan again later in the year, after the big exercise. From what I'm hearing from Squires, the boss is definitely looking to begin exporting again during that time. Hasn't your dad mentioned anything to you?"

Davis gave a look of ignorance.

"Why would he tell me?" He snapped. "He knows I'm useless now that I can't even carry a weapon. There's zero chance I'll go to Afghan with you lot. My counsellor has me down as having PTSD; at least you're not in that bracket. All your problems are money orientated as far as your guy's concerned. You can still go while I'm sat here waiting to be thrown out altogether." Lewis had forgotten about Davis and his circumstances. *What use is he now,* he thought? His Father never gave a shit about him and he was never really in the clique with the boss and Squires. What role was there for him to offer the future success of the operation? Davis had said too much in regard to his uselessness. He had to convince Lewis he still had a place in the group.

"I know my dad hasn't really been there for me or even given me the time of day in the past, but I think he may be coming around to the idea that I can be some sort of middleman once I'm discharged from the army," he lied. Lewis thought for a moment and realised that this could be exactly what Davis needed to prove his worth.

"That sounds like a great idea, I reckon you could make that work for you mate." He had persuaded himself that what Davis was telling him would be the best thing for the whole of the gang, a middleman from a military background they could work with. Someone who understood the chain of command and the problems they would encounter regarding logistics. A man who could paper over the cracks and offer support and grant time when things didn't quite go to plan. He was sure Davis was the person to fulfil that role.

"Brilliant!" he cheered, "I reckon that's a great move. I'll tell you what, when everyone else was calling you all the names under the sun, I knew you would come good." Davis let the words slide off him.

"Let's celebrate," said Davis through gritted teeth. He went into his wallet and purposefully opened it enough to show Lewis it was almost empty.

"I thought you were loaded?" Lewis said with a hint of sadness thinking his drinking session would be cut short.

"Don't worry mate, I'll be taking a trip to the cashpoint later. I'm not finished just yet." The guarantee of more free booze lifted Lewis's spirits almost instantly. As he was at the bar ordering drinks, Davis texted Rodders to tell him to be ready in about one to one and a half hours. He needed to have a few more beers first, just to be sure.

The drinks flowed and conversation turned to the Sarge's death and how Lewis had been told about the plan the day before it had been put in motion. The Sarges death hadn't weighed heavily on Lewis, once he realised there was another share to be divvied up equally amongst the other members of the group.

"I reckon we could be millionaires you know," said Lewis. "If Nolan and your dad can get the supply chain running smoothly, I think we could make a fortune out of this. We could be a major player in the drug trade." Davis looked at Lewis and at one point couldn't hide his smile as he spoke of millions of pounds and smuggling. He was nothing more than a petty thief, a puppet for the people further up the chain, thinking he, himself was a major cog in the drug smuggling machine they had both been part of. Little did he know that tonight would be his last.

"Did you ever find out what became of the money or gear from the first haul mate?" Asked Davis.

"Jesus, mate, I must have asked Squires a hundred times about that. All he ever says is it's safe and we had to speculate to accumulate. I'm not too sure what we needed to speculate or invest in. I mean I know our man who receives the stuff in the vehicles back home needs to be paid but where is the rest of it? I'm going to confront Squires and the boss when he gets back. I mean what's he going to do, kill me as well? That's going to look a bit suspicious isn't it? So I reckon I've got them both over a barrel in that respect. I've got a good mind to ask for a raise in my cut." Davis smiled to himself.

"Mate, if I give you the cash can you get the beers in? I'll go to the cash point and get some more dough."

"Of course, mate, same again?" Davis nodded and left the bar in the direction of the nearest bank. He scrolled through his numbers on his phone until he reached Rodders. He pressed the dial button and waited for a pickup. It rang twice. "Are you close by?" Asked Davis.

"I'm just around the corner about two hundred meters up from Lewis's car. When he gets in, I'll see him and head off up the road. I'll call you in exactly thirty minutes, OK?"

"No worries, I'll be waiting." The call ended and Davis returned to the bar. As he entered, he saw Lewis chatting to a local girl and knew he had to get him away from her and quickly. If he thought he was in with a chance of walking off with her his afternoon of drinking and the subsequent plan would end very quickly. They made eye contact as he entered and as he walked towards the bar, Lewis met him halfway.

"Listen mate, it's been a hoot to catch up but I'm on a promise with this cheeky little minx here. What's the chances of you lending me a few quid and helping me get a bit of action tonight?"

"Shit mate, I'm sorry but I can't," he replied thinking fast on his feet. "The bookies haven't paid the money into my account yet. I've just been to have a look and it's showing that it's pending. But I can go back in an hour or so to double check?" Lewis looked angry but mellowed at the potential of the evening not being a complete write off.

"OK," he said "I'll put her off for a while and tell her I have to chat to you about something and I'll come back to her. She seems keen so I'm sure she'll wait. She would be a fool not to, if you know what I mean," he winked like some kind of Jack the Lad, convinced he had some magnetic pull over women. He wandered over to the bar to explain his situation to the girl. She smiled and nodded in obvious agreement as he ordered two pints and a couple of vodkas for good measure and made his way back to the table he and Davis had frequented for the best part of the afternoon.

"She's cool with that arrangement bud, cheers again," he said as he raised his glass one more time. Davis was hiding his anxiety well. The thought of the whole plan being derailed over a date with a local girl had almost made him sick. He had managed to get back on track but he felt his blood pressure in both temples as his head started ringing due to the stress. Lewis downed his vodka and was halfway down his pint when Davis's phone rang.

"I've got to take this mate, it's my dad calling," he lifted his phone to his ear as he walked towards the exit. Lewis looked on as the conversation appeared to heat up and Davis paced back and forward in front of the window. He walked out of sight and as he did so, Lewis decided to make another visit to the girl at the bar to fill the time. He looked at his watch and realised Davis wasn't in front of the bar anymore. *He must have gone to the cashpoint,* he thought. As Lewis was just about to take the last gulp of lager, his phone rang with a rendition of 'Whole Lot of Love' by Led Zeppelin. He thought it made him look cool although in reality, half of the younger drinkers had no idea what they were hearing. He perused the screen to see it was a withheld number calling.

"Have you withheld your number mate? Don't tell me the money hasn't gone into the account yet, I've got this girl gagging for me buddy," The phone went silent for a moment or two until the worried voice of Davis spoke up.

"This is my other phone. This one is encrypted in case I need to get information from my dad to Nolan, but I haven't got time to explain it now. That was my dad on the phone just now. The Military Police have had a tip off that someone has been running gear from the barrack block. Our gear." Lewis shuddered momentarily.

"But there's nothing there, it's all kept away by Squires. Nobody knows where it is though, do they? That's why I've been moaning for months on end. There's nothing there for them to find."

"That's not exactly true," continued Davis. "Apparently there's about two kilos of gear stashed under a floorboard in your room, mate. I didn't know about it but dad says it's been there for months, Squires put it there thinking it would be safe, he obviously didn't want it outside the wire thinking nobody would find it on camp. Fuck me bud if it's found they will jail you and throw away the key. You had better get back as quickly as possible and get it moved." Lewis felt instantly sick. How could he get back to camp? He couldn't get a taxi; it would only take him as far as the camp gate and he would have a fifteen-minute run to get to his barrack block after dropping off. He would have to drive and take a chance on not being pulled over by the police.

"Where are you now?" Asked Lewis.

"I'm getting away from you mate," Davis replied, "I'm having nothing to do with this, you're on your own this time, sorry but that's the way it is mate." The phone rang off and Lewis stood, alone in the drizzle wondering what to do. He suddenly realised he was wasting time and began running the two hundred meters to his vehicle.

The ten-year-old Golf GTi was falling to pieces. The tyres were on their last shred of decent rubber and the brakes were shoddy. The car had only just scraped through its last MOT, but its engine was sound, and it could still move quickly when Lewis needed it to. It took a couple of turns to ignite the engine and when it eventually started, Lewis gave out a sigh of relief. He revved the motor two or three times to get the fuel running smoothly and slipped the shaking car into gear. The fan belt screeched as it pulled out from the parking space just as light rain began to spatter the dirt-covered windscreen. There was just enough washer fluid to give the screen a good wash but the rain would have to take over cleaning duties for the remainder of the journey.

Rodders had been sitting further up the road in a space ready for Lewis to get into his vehicle. Once he was happy that Lewis was committed to making the journey, he pulled out slowly and once clear of any residential properties, accelerated quickly to build a decent lead on the battered old Volkswagen.

Once the trip had begun Lewis, now shaking uncontrollably due to stress, alcohol and sheer fear began fumbling with his phone in an attempt to call Squires. The signal was bad at the best of times, but it progressively got worse as the weather did. *Maybe a text will get through,* he wondered. The wipers begrudgingly moved back and forth slowly, the rubber blades spreading more dirt than they cleaned off and for the first time he was praying for heavier rain to help him see through the misty glass. All the while he was constantly shifting his gaze from the road to the phone, still trying to contact Nolan in an effort to find out why he had ordered the gear to be hidden in his room. He wanted to find out if someone could get to it before the Military Police did. His fingers started to press the wrong numbers as the shaking began to increase. His heart was racing like he was running on patrol in the Afghan desert rather than driving his car back to barracks on a Sunday evening. The light was fading as the car reached speeds of over sixty miles per hour along the water covered tarmac surface, Lewis constantly making corrections in his course due to his texting at the wheel.

Ahead by almost two miles, Rodders had pulled over at the side of the road and quickly exited his vehicle. In his hand he held a five-litre jerry can of diesel. He ran into the road, just at the beginning of a sharp bend and poured the liquid onto the road surface. Satisfied he had covered the area he intended to, he raced back to the car, drove ahead fifty or so meters and spun around in the opposite direction to where he had come. He took out a small pair of binoculars and waited patiently until he saw Lewis's VW speed down towards his location. He began to drive towards him, and once in the intended position, quickly lit up the road with his headlights on full beam and a loud prolonged push on the horn.

Lewis's head snapped up from his phone at the noise and the glare of the opposing headlights, temporarily blinding him in the process. Instead of braking, he instinctively grabbed the steering wheel tighter and spun it to avoid the oncoming car which by now was twenty meters past him. The tyres spun on the diesel and the car started to move sideways along the surface. Everything happened in slow motion to Lewis. He knew he was spinning but had no idea of direction or speed and his attempt to straighten up the automobile was futile. The tyres suddenly contacted the verge at the side of the road and the vehicle lifted skywards. Lewis elevated from his seat and hit the roof, the seatbelt disconnecting from the broken latch he had meant to fix months previously. The driver's side door caved in and glass from every window and screen showered the inside of the cockpit. The car began to barrel roll over and over like tumbleweed, and as it did, Lewis's unconscious body hung halfway out of the window, his feet caught in the steering wheel. Over and over the car rolled coming to an abrupt halt, upturned on the driver's side on top of the lifeless torso of the soldier. He had died almost instantly. His body smashed and ripped and blood was gushing from massive open wounds which oozed across both lanes of the quiet road. Rodders made a call to the emergency services to inform them of an accident and waited until he could see blue lights appear ahead of him. With that he moved slowly away and drove back into town to call Jenny and offer an update of the situation.

CHAPTER 18

Jenny religiously sat and watched the early morning local news before departing for work. This day was different. The headline of a horror crash and the death of a serving soldier, his life cut short through drink driving and texting at the wheel held more of a fascination that usual. The plan had worked to perfection. No mention of foul play and no harm caused to anyone else with the fuel spill. Jenny breathed a deep sigh. She saw this as simple retribution, an eye for an eye in the words of the bible. She was happy with the way the plan was unfolding. She knew Rodders and the others would need to sit down and come up with a way of luring Nolan, Squires, and Davis's father into their clutches but how exactly to proceed was proving difficult. Nolan, being an officer, could distance himself from the whole thing if he wanted to. There was, after all, no evidence they knew of that could implicate him in any wrongdoing. Yes, it might hurt his reputation and if he wanted to stay in the military, it would undoubtedly follow him around, but it could easily be explained as a vicious rumor created by some ex-squaddie with an axe to grind against his Platoon Commander. Squires was different. He was an NCO and would have to do a lot more explaining if there were the slightest inclination that he was involved in any illegal activity. In military circles, shit rolls down hill and rank has its privileges. Those are two things that would never change. Billy however was proving to be the thorn in their side. He was the loose end. There had been no sightings of him at the petrol station where he worked and nothing had been heard of Deano yet. Jenny began to wonder if Billy had just upped and left without noticing Deano in the spare room, hanging from the door. This would have to be brought up at the next group meeting. Things would have to move fast if they wanted their plan to succeed in the allotted time frame while the platoon were on recess.

Jenny arrived home and kicked off her shoes and rubbed her feet before entering the kitchen and pulling a bottle of white wine from the fridge. Just as she was about to pour a glass, her mobile phone rang.

"Hi Laura, how-" "Have you seen the news?" She interrupted.

"No, what's happening?" Jenny heard the panic in her voice.

"Switch it on now," urged Laura, "channel three, local news." Jenny hunted for the remote control and switched on the TV. The local reporter was standing in front of the flats Deano and Billy lived in. She was instantly glued to the screen. The reporter was just coming to the end of her account of developments at a block of flats in the town.

"The bodies of the two men have been identified as Peter Martin, twenty-seven originally from Corby and William Stevens aged just twenty from Harrogate. Both men had served in the Kings Regiment until recently and were posted to the local barracks. It appears this was a double suicide and according to Police, no foul play is suspected in the deaths. This is the third member of the regiment to die in the short space of two days following the death of Lance Corporal Philip Lewis yesterday in a horrific car accident just four miles from this location. A senior member of the regiment is yet to comment. Back to you in the studio Jane". Little did the public know that the number would increase by the tune of one once Bairdy's corpse was discovered.

Jenny couldn't believe it. So, Billy *had* found Deano and either overcome with grief or guilt had committed suicide in a similar fashion. Jenny called Laura back.

"I think we need to get together and talk about our options moving forward. This is a result for all of us and although it's another one down we need to regroup and find a way forward."

"I agree," replied Laura. "I'll contact the others. Should we say six tomorrow at your place?"

"Yes, that's fine, see you then." Jenny was pleased that Billy had taken his own life. Although they had all been involved in the deaths of Deano, Billy, Lewis and Bairdy there had been no actual physical contact, and she could live with it. But this was just the warm-up; the hardest part was yet to come.

Rodders leaned over and switched off the television. The group were gathered in Jenny's kitchen, huddled around the table eating take away pizza like they were planning a holiday instead of the demise and downfall of three people. Davis had been instrumental in the plan and had played an excellent part so far. However, he would now get his chance at bringing his father down. But to what extent would be up to him.

"To be honest," he began "I can't see any other way out for my mum. I don't give a shit about him and I can come and go as I please, but she is married to him and is stuck. She hasn't got the courage or the will power to move on. She has no money of her own and she knows too much of what goes on. If she left him, she would be dead within a week." There was genuine sadness as he spoke of the situation his mother was in, but also more than a hint of anger. Davis wasn't a stupid man, he was simply used and taken advantage of by people around him. The armed forces were not a democracy, and he could have easily found himself set up and thrown into a military prison at the order of his Platoon Commander, Nolan. All it would take would be an accusation, some planted evidence and another member of staff such as Squires to corroborate the story. It would have been easy to send him down for six to twelve months. He had to tread lightly. And it wasn't just danger from Nolan; his father pulled his strings just as much, using his mother as leverage. As long as he worked on the inside of the smuggling operation there was an opportunity to make money and to Davis Senior, that was his ultimate goal, at the behest of his wife and child.

"I want him gone," seethed Davis. "Out of my Mums life and out of mine forever. I've got no feelings towards the man. As far as I'm concerned, he's a nobody to me, never has been, never will be." This was what the others wanted to hear. The others dying had been personal, but the death of a family member was different, whether you loved them or despised them. Although Davis had a role to play, ultimately, he would have to be disconnected from the final act; the less he knew, the less he could speak about if placed under pressure.

"How do we go about this?" Asked Rodders. "I mean with the others we played on their weaknesses. With this lot we must find a way to turn them on each other. What common denominator do they share?" They all sat and looked at one another.

"GREED," they all said in unison.

"They will stop at nothing to get money and they will go through anyone who stands in their way," said Laura. "How do we make that work for us?"

"I know," said Davis. "The money from the first tour: it exists. I know my Dad got rid of somewhere in the region of fifteen to twenty kilos of pure uncut opium. Once that's been cut with all kinds of rubbish or sent out to be refined into something else, you could be looking at almost three million pounds, maybe more. He wouldn't double cross Nolan, that would be biting the hand that feeds him, so he would try to keep that relationship alive as long as possible. The money will be at one of my Dad's safe houses or on the property at home. The scrap yard covers about one hundred acres, he could hide it in a multitude of places. If I can find out where it is, then we can build a plan around that." They all looked at Davis incredulously. He had come up with the makings of something they could build a solid foundation on without breaking a sweat. Rodders gave him a sly nod of appreciation and he felt good he had contributed something significant to the plan.

As Davis exited the taxi at his parents' house, he could feel the anxiety growing in his stomach before he had even shut the door. There was always a sense of unease when he visited.

His mother was a downtrodden woman who, at the age of forty, looked well beyond her years. She had married Davis senior at a young age knowing he had a previous conviction and subsequent criminal record for violence under his belt but she had been drawn in by his boyish charm. As an impressionable young woman it had seemed exciting and dangerous to her at the time. Little did she know that after only a few short months after marrying the abuse would begin. It started with verbal taunts and jibes about her looks in front of his friends, many of whom would visit the house at the ungodliest of hours, usually carrying some kind of package under their arms. This is when she would be summoned from her bed to make food for his cronies and whilst they drank, her husband would belittle her as she toiled at the oven well into the small hours. Only once they had eaten and drank themselves into a stupor could she eventually climb the stairs. More often than not she would be greeted with the half-naked figure of her husband, strewn across the sheets, his breath stinking of stale cigarettes and alcohol.

When John was born after two years of marriage she genuinely believed things would change, and for a short while they did. Senior doted on the young boy but after a while he lost interest and reverted back to type with the drinking and nefarious criminal activities. After being caught with a small amount of cocaine, a short prison sentence was imposed and during this time, she had planned to leave him and return to her parents with the intention of leaving the area and starting over in a new town. However, he found out about the plan and even from behind bars managed to use his influence. There were threats of violence towards her and the baby and she was forced to stay and live the life of a drug dealer's wife. Of course, there were times when the police would appear and she would be asked a multitude of questions about the business, but she never gave him up to the authorities. There would always be the underlying fear that he could get to her and John whenever he wanted, wherever she was, so for both of their sakes she carried on as normal, suffering verbal and physical abuse whenever he deemed she had stepped out of line. One day she hoped an opportunity would arise for her to leave it all behind, little did she know, that day would come sooner than she expected.

Davis strode down the path to the immaculately laid out house his father had built ten years previously. Senior had money and, as long as he could justify to the authorities where it came from, he wanted everyone to know how successful he was. He built the stunning family home as a monument to his business acumen, previously legitimately dealing in scrap but now, known to the select few as drug dealing. Proud of the property he had built he separated the scrap yard an eight-foot-high hedgerow and as you entered the area no signs of any industrial equipment could be seen, keeping the family home in a clean, well maintained area. Following a downturn several years previous, the price of scrap metal had hit an all-time low so senior had decided to go all in and only use the scrap yard as a front for the drug smuggling and dealing and that was what it was still being used for to the present day. Davis shuddered at the thought of the whole thing. He hated his father and wanted nothing to do with his enterprise but had inadvertently been drawn in by Nolan and Squires. They had discovered his family background through a newspaper article about notorious northern crime families three years ago. He had been coerced into contacting his father and making the arrangements. A meeting between the two men had been deemed too dangerous, so they relied on messages being conveyed. . After the success of the first shipment from Afghanistan, Davis Senior had given the green light to making the relationship official. They had an unexpected hiatus after the Sarge's death but now the plan was to restart the importation of the merchandise and begin distribution as soon as possible. All that John, Jenny and the others had to do was convince them that it was their idea.

Davis rang the doorbell hoping that it was his mother who answered. It was.

"Oh, my goodness John!" She yelled in joy, "why didn't you tell me you were coming? I would have prepared dinner for us all."

He wrapped his gangly arms around his mother and gave her a warm, loving hug. He missed her so much when he was away and tried to talk to her as often as possible if he was on deployment, but things had cooled off since the involvement with the smuggling ring. Any call he made to the house would inevitably be commandeered by his father, demanding updates as to where, when and what was happening with the shipments; anything other than asking about the well-being of his only child.

"I wanted to surprise you Mum," he replied truthfully. He loved seeing the look of astonishment on her face when he appeared without warning at the door to the family home.

She beckoned him in. Once inside, shoes were off and slippers were the dress code of the day. She welcomed him into the kitchen and once the kettle had boiled and the tea had been made, he began to tell her about how he was doing. He avoided discussing his mental health issues, Davis didn't want to worry her. The mood was happy and the chat was uplifting but all that came to an end when Davis Senior came storming through the back door shouting and cursing.

"I thought that pitiful figure I saw coming up the driveway was you," he chided. "What brings you here, need a cuddle from Mammy?" Davis stared at him with contempt.

"Well, it's better than having to look at you," he replied much to the chagrin of his father.

"Listen you..." Davis Senior pointed at his son who turned his head away to dismiss the advance.

"STOP already will you Arthur? He's only just walked through the door and you're on at him straight away. Give the lad a chance to have a cup of tea before having to listen to your insults."

Davis Senior gave his wife a stern look for scolding him and walked over to her. Pushing her against the wall he kept his flat palm pressed heavily on her chest. Pointing a finger at her with his other hand he yelled, "I won't tell you again woman, get some respect in your tone when you speak to me." She could smell the alcohol on his breath and turned her head away in repulsion. He removed his hand from her and began to raise it as if to slap her across the face when Davis shouted at him.

"Don't do it!" Davis senior turned around and saw his son holding a large, serrated kitchen knife in his hand with a look of loathing in his eyes. "I'm warning you, don't do it or it will be the last thing you ever do." Davis Senior could see his son shaking. He felt sure he was bluffing but he didn't want to risk it and stood back from his wife. For once he actually had a hint of respect for his son, it took balls to threaten someone with a knife. Davis looked at his mother who shook her head as if to warn off any more engagement with his father. He placed the knife on the table and proceeded upstairs to unpack his bag. He could hear his father raising his voice to his mother in the lounge below and felt sorry for the fact that he couldn't do more to protect her. He put on his earphones and turned the volume to maximum to drown out the yells.

Davis lay on his bed and waited until he could hear his parents' bedroom door close, knowing his father would be sitting in the armchair watching television whilst his mother went to bed. He went downstairs slowly and opened the lounge door to be met with a look of disapproval from his father as he sipped away at a malt whisky and glared at the TV screen.

"I've got a message for you from Nolan," said Davis. His father's eyes lit up.

"And?" He barked, "what's the message?"

"He says he will be in touch soon. He thinks they should be ready to go back to normal in about a week or so. If you can be ready you're to let me know and I'll pass it along," said Davis.

"When am I going to get to meet this bloke?" Said senior angrily.

"Well, that's the other part of the message. He wants to meet, in person and will contact you soon about how and where. But that's all I've got to tell you." Senior studied Davis's face for a second and showed no sign of emotion towards him at all.

"OK," he replied, "don't let the door smack you in the arse on the way out." He laughed which signified the end of the only conversation Davis had had with his father in almost a year. At one time he would have felt disappointed, rejected even, but now the level of emotion was equal to that of his father. He didn't care one bit about him or his views, he only cared about his mother and how he could remove her from such a toxic environment.

The following morning Davis awoke to birds singing in the trees outside of his bedroom window. It made a change from the blare of helicopters taking off and landing or shooting from the rifle ranges. He lay in bed for a while, dreading having to get out of bed and go into the kitchen for breakfast which his mother prepared every day for his father. He knew he would be up. He could drink a bottle of whiskey and still get up early and do a day's work. It was in the man's nature. He was a lot of things but lazy was not one of them. Davis quickly showered and dressed and lumbered down the stairs and into the kitchen. His mum was at the stove while Davis Senior sat and sipped scorching hot tea from an oversized mug.

"Morning Mum," he said, making a point of ignoring his father.

"Good morning Sweetheart," she replied merrily. He knew it was an act and although there were no physical marks on her he knew his father would have verbally abused her until she was allowed to go to bed and escape his bullying onslaught. He sat at the table, opposite his dad who looked up, shook his head, and continued to fill his face with a bacon sandwich.

"Where are those bloody eggs, Rose?" He yelled.

"What's wrong with you?" Seethed Davis. "Why can't you speak to anyone in a civil tongue, you heathen?" Davis Senior was about to start on one of his rants when mother raised her voice.

"Stop it, the pair of you, just stop it! If you can't speak to your own boy with a bit of civility, then don't speak to him at all." Davis Senior stood up and for a moment Rose and Davis thought he was going to start getting violent.

"Throw the eggs away. You're a terrible cook anyway and always have been. As for you..." he looked at Davis, "tell your man to get his act together and quickly. Understand?" He threw down his napkin and kicked his chair under the table. Then he stormed out of the kitchen slamming the door behind him and knocking off chinaware from the Welsh dresser. Davis's mother carried on cooking the eggs and didn't turn around.

"Mum," said Davis in a soft tone, "come and sit down and have a cup of tea. Leave the cooking for now." As she turned, he could see the tears in her eyes. She had put up with this for years.

"Why do you stay?" He asked. "You could get away, there are places to go, you don't have to live like this." He stretched across the table and took her hand.

"It's just not that easy John. There's more to it than this and honestly, your father is just having a bad week. Business isn't too good right now with the price of scrap being at an all-time low." Davis wondered if she knew about the drugs and if so, to what extent. She was the kind of woman to turn a blind eye and not ask any questions so maybe she was trying to convince herself it wasn't happening in her own home.

"I don't understand why you're saying that. You know that I know what he's like. Don't try to cover for his behavior." She gently caressed his hand.

"It's OK love, I'm fine. Anyway," she continued, wiping the tears from her eyes, and standing up, "how long are you here for?" He didn't want to disappoint her, but he knew his answer would.

"I'm only here until this afternoon. I have to get back; this was just a flying visit to make sure you were OK. But.... I promise I'll be back very, very soon alright?" He could see the look of dejection on her face but it didn't last long when he said he would return soon.

"OK," she replied, "now sit down and finish your breakfast." When it was time to leave Davis felt disheartened and powerless to protect his mother. But then he remembered he would be able to do something about it soon. As he walked to the end of the lane and an awaiting taxi, he could see his father standing, watching from a distance. He was accompanied by two other shady looking characters who were no doubt there for some dodgy deal. He stood and stared, defiantly.

"Not long now old man, not long now," he muttered.

CHAPTER 19

The four met at the park where Jenny and Rodders had met previously. It was a chilly autumn day and everyone was well wrapped up in an attempt to evade the biting air and cold, but no matter how well dressed they were the weather was starting to win the fight.

"Whose idea was this?" Asked Laura, "why didn't we just go to your place?" She said looking at Jenny.

"Because I thought it would be less conspicuous catching up here. Look around you, the place is full of people strolling around and at least we've got no twitching curtains or nosey parkers staring through windows. Nobody even cares we're here. Not one person has looked at us but if were seen too often at my place we could get some unwanted attention."

"One thing to note," said Davis. "The police found Bairdy's body. The MPs came by after the civvies and investigated. It was in the paper but well into the middle pages. I think they are calling it death by misadventure. Unintentional overdose will be the most likely conclusion for cause of death." Laura smiled knowing they had again gotten away with it.

"So, John," Jenny began," what's the update from your dad?"

"It's all set and he's on the hook," he replied. "He's too greedy to turn down the opportunity so when I explained that Nolan would be in touch to see if he's willing to engage again, you could almost feel the excitement running through his veins. I think if we can pull this off every one of them will get their comeuppance at the same time."

"Agreed," said Jenny, "it's time we put our heads together and came up with a cohesive strategy to close this thing out once and for all. We've managed to tie everything up neatly so far without actual 'hands on' involvement and I think that's the route we should stick to. Any objections?" The four looked at each other without speaking and Jenny knew they were all in agreement.

"So, in play we still have Nolan, Squires and Senior," Jenny said with a voice of authority which the others all liked. She was a leader in the making for sure. "Laura, the voice modulation gear is still set up at my house; do we need to make any adjustments to it if we need to link up the encrypted mobile phones? Or is it plug and play ready to go?"

"I need to juggle a few things around with I.P. addresses but other than that it's all good," replied Laura.

"Good. I need a fourth handset and I need them set up in a particular way where we can send calls and messages but the other three can only receive. Is it as simple as hiding your number on texts?"

"Yeah, it should be pretty simple with these units, a ten-minute job to set up, you tell me what you want and we can sort it whenever you have a bit of time." Laura's voice had a sense of excitement running through it. Not only was she getting some technical time in but she was happy in the knowledge that Jenny would get her payback soon and this, in Laura's eyes, was well deserved. Jenny began staring skyward and whispering to herself, making split second decisions in her head. The others knew she was formulating the beginnings of a plan and could only sit back for now and admire her method. Their input would put the meat on the bones but for now Jenny was center stage.

"John, you may need to take another visit to your parents place, will you be OK with that?"

"Yeah, no problem from me Jenny. The old man's an arschole but I can manage him in small doses from time to time," he sniggered. Jenny threw him a smile in return for his compliance. The time rolled on and after an hour or so, the plan was set.

"Right then," continued Jenny, "we need to meet back at my place on Sunday. John, I'm going to recommend a couple of days sick leave for you with the medical center on camp. Call the office tomorrow and make a rush appointment for ten o'clock. I'll have you signed off and then you need to use that time to get down to your parents' house and back again with the message and handset I'll give you for your dad, OK?" Davis nodded. "We will have this thing moving in no time at all. Do you know when Nolan is back from his course?"

"He's supposed to be back next Monday," replied John.

"Good, very good. Laura, can you head back to my house and start programming the encrypted phones? John will need to take one with him when he goes to visit his parents. Here's a key, the alarm is off so you don't need to worry about that."

"Sure, no problem at all," said Laura. "What is it you need exactly?"

Jenny explained what she wanted.

"I need the phones to act like this," she explained. "This one in my hand needs to be the master. This will send messages but the other two must only be able to receive. Is that possible?"

"Yes," stated Laura. "What else do you need?"

"I need them wiped of any existing information regarding locations or other users. I literally want these to do nothing other than receive. Leave the location services on but not just yet, it may come in handy later. Now, even though these phones are encrypted I want them to be easily accessed by someone interrogating the device, say, police forensics. You know, make it difficult for them to break into the system but not completely impenetrable."

"I can do all of that. It'll take an hour or so."

"OK then, let's break off for now. John, I'll see you in the morning. Rodders, I'll give you a lift to the bus stop and we can chat quickly about where we are heading with this and what you will need to do. Laura, I'll see you in, say fifteen minutes?" The group all mumbled in agreement and they set off in their individual directions. Jenny continued whispering to herself as she walked to her vehicle. *This could really work,* she thought to herself. It needed refining slightly and some excellent timing but it could all fit like the pieces of a jigsaw and none of them would or could be implicated anywhere down the line. It was almost perfect. The only problem she could see was the input of the targets and their reactions to what was about to unfold around them. Rodders watched her smiling to himself as she mumbled but said nothing, not wanting to interrupt her thought process. Once they were driving in the car, she spoke softly to Rodders.

"You look tired," she said. "Are you OK?"

"I'm fine," replied Rodders. He was tired but didn't want to burden Jenny with more than what she was already carrying.

"Are you onboard with everything we've spoken about today? There's a lot going on and more to come and I just want to make sure you're OK in yourself, I worry about you."

Rodders stared out of the window, the rest of the world going about its daily business as he and the group plotted the demise of their enemies. He turned to Jenny.

"Worry about me when this is over," he said, candidly.

The car came to a halt just short of the bus stop. Rodders gave Jenny a peck on the cheek and stepped out of the vehicle. His gaze was drawn to a taxi moving slowly in the traffic on the other side of the road and as Jenny pulled away he noticed a familiar face in the cab.

It was Squires.

As the two pairs of eyes met, Rodders stomach suddenly felt like a bottomless pit. There was no way he hadn't seen him and Jenny together. Squires acted instantly.

"Stop the car mate I need to get out," he yelled at the taxi driver.

"What do you meant you want to get out?" He replied, "you're booked all the way into town."

"Stop the car...NOW!" He shouted, throwing the driver a ten-pound note and turning quickly to see if Rodders was still at the bus stop. He wasn't. As soon as Rodders had seen Squires, he had set off at pace in the opposite direction, running as fast as he could. He knew he couldn't keep it up too long. He was no longer a serving soldier and although he used to enjoy fitness training, his disability meant it wasn't as easy as it used to be. The light drizzle affected his vision and he could feel his lungs burning. His breath was becoming shallow and his foot begin to sting. He looked around, still running as he did so. Squires came bounding around the corner some hundred meters behind him. Rodders knew trying to outrun him was futile so urgently scanned his surroundings to see what he had in the vicinity to help him should he be caught. He was in a built-up residential area and had considered knocking on a stranger's door but concluded that it would be unlikely for someone to open the door to a random man, out of breath wearing a hoodie claiming to be chased by a stranger. His mind was going into overdrive. *Where can I go, where can I hide?*

Squires was starting to pant himself. Although still fit, the speed at which he was running to catch up was taking its toll. He was used to marching or jogging long distances, not sprinting after people in the street; but he knew he had to catch up with Rodders. What he did with him when he had him had not yet entered his mind.

As Rodders rounded a corner, he tried to spot somewhere he could hide. The leafy suburb was lined with trees but he doubted he could climb one before being caught. He looked around for a weapon and in doing so, quickly realised that he had stopped running and was standing in the middle of the road motionless. Squires came into view and slowly came to a halt twenty feet away.

"Well, well, well.... where do you think you're going?" He hissed, slowly creeping forward. Rodders was trying hard to catch his breath. He knew if this got physical it would only be the fitter man who would walk away. Breath in through the nose and out through the mouth, he remembered, as he calculated a strategy to be the fitter man.

"That's no business of yours Squires, you murdering bastard. Did you think you and Nolan would get away with this? I'm going to let everyone know what you did."

Squires began to laugh. "What we did. What we did. What exactly did we do Rodders? You've got nothing.... NOTHING. Not one shred of evidence. Who will listen to you?" He was right. The pen drive was all he ever had and that wouldn't stand up in a court of law.

"I'll find a way of getting it out there."

Squires shook his head.

"You have to walk away from this first," he said, menacingly. Rodders glanced from side to side, searching for something to help him. As he did, Squires made his move and before he knew it, Rodders was overwhelmed by him. The two struggled and as Squires threw a punch, Rodders quickly moved to avoid it. He retaliated by grabbing his hair, which although short, he managed to get a fistful and drag Squires head down and aim a kick at his head. Squires fell and rolled over and onto his feet rapidly.

"You're moving quite fast for a one-legged gimp aren't you?" He mocked. Rodders shook it off.

"Let's do this, you fucking prick!" He screamed and ran towards him yelling. The two men clashed, each landing a light punch on the others check but neither man falling. Arms flailing, both men fought in an attempt to gain the upper hand. Suddenly Rodders felt Squires behind him, arm around his neck in a chokehold. He squeezed as hard as he could and he knew if he didn't think fast, he would black out and that would be it. He tried to grab Squires by the head but he had the advantage of seeing the counterattack coming. The only thing Rodders could do was use the ground as a weapon. Positioning his feet correctly, he tripped Squires, and as he fell backwards, he let go of his grip to try to soften the blow as his opponent came crashing down on top of him. The fall hurt Squires who was temporarily winded. Rodders rose to his feet and with both knees bent jumped onto the prone torso of his attacker. Pain seared through Squires and as he lay, trying to catch his breath, another blow came from Rodders in the form of an elbow to the face. As he stood over Squires, he knew he had to knock him out if he wanted a chance to walk away.

"You're going to pay for this and everything else you've done you piece of shit." Rodders fumed as he raised his foot and gave a swift hard stamp onto Squires' head. The whole encounter had only lasted a couple of minutes but it had left Rodders bruised and shaken. He ran back to the main road and flagged down a passing taxi to take him home. Squires was still breathing and would come around with a screaming headache but he knew Rodders was in the area and that meant that very soon Nolan would too.

Jenny was sitting at her desk when Siona knocked briskly on the door.

"Jenny are you free to take a call? I've got Private Davis on the line asking for you. He sounds quite shook up.".

"Oh dear" feigned Jenny, "put him through, I'll have a quick chat to him now." Siona closed the door gently and Jenny waited for her desk phone to ring. "Hello Private Davis, how can I help you?" He had to go through the motions.

"I'm having a bit of a rough time Jenny. My Mam is ill, I'm not sleeping and I'm having terrible nightmares."

"Alright then, maybe you should come in. How about two o'clock, is that suitable? It's the only slot I have today," she suggested.

"That's fine," he replied, "thank you so much". The next thing he heard was the voice of the receptionist booking the appointment, then the click of disconnection. He went back to his room and lay on the bed. Thoughts of his father and the way he treated his mother came into his head and this only hardened him more to what he was involved with.

Davis slipped into a fitful sleep but woke up with plenty of time to be at his appointment with Jenny. He had a shower and changed into some smart but casual civilian clothing in preparation for his meeting. Once he was satisfied with his appearance, he locked his barrack room door and headed across the camp to the main gate. As he wandered, he could hear a voice in the distance shouting at him to stop and stand still. It was Squires. He looked as though he had been dragged through a hedge backwards.

"Mavis Davis," he said in a snidey tone, "where have you been all my life? I've been looking for you everywhere."

"Erm...hello Corporal," he replied, a little shaken by his unexpected encounter. "I've been doing odd jobs while the rest of the platoon were on leave before heading off on exercise. They'll find any old shit to keep us working," he smiled nervously. He hated Squires as much as he hated Nolan and the rest of the smuggling gang. However, he was still a soldier in the Army, and he would have to bite his lip and take whatever was doled out to him, for now.

"What happened to you?" He asked the corporal, "are you OK?"

"I'm fine, I fell out of my bed after a heavy session, you know how it is," he lied.

"Anyway, enough about me, did you hear about the lads? Holy shit, four of them gone in the space of a week," Squires was being nicer than usual. *He wants something or he's grasping for information,* thought Davis.

"I read about it in the papers. Let's be honest though, Deano and Billy were on the edge before they left the army and Bairdy always had a bit of a thing on the side with blowing Charlie up his nose. I was really shocked to hear about Lewis though. He's the last person I ever thought would drink and drive. Maybe things just got on top of them all."

"What things are you talking about Mavis?" Squires' voice betrayed a hint of anger.

"You know, all the goings on when we were out of country?" Davis started to feel uncomfortable as Squires eyed him with a look of suspicion. He broke the silence.

"Anyway, the boss wants to see you," as he gestured Davis to follow him right there and then.

"I can't. I have a doctor's appointment in town," he spluttered, trying to walk in the opposite direction.

"It's not a request. You might not be part of 4 platoon anymore but you still take orders from your superiors, so move your arse and go and see him right now. Why are you going into town anyway, the medical center is where you see the head shrink isn't it?" The tone had now turned nasty as he was openly mocking the fact that Davis was struggling with mental health problems.

"I've been assigned to a civilian counsellor," said Davis, trying to keep his voice from breaking.

"Oh well there you go," replied Squires, "the army doctor's not good enough for you now. And what do you tell this 'civilian counsellor' during your little chatting sessions then?"

Davis was quick on his feet and his answer came quickly.

"Usual stuff," he answered, "why I'm a dick who can't get his shit together." He tried to lighten the situation by mocking himself for the entertainment of Squires. It worked.

"Ha," sniggered the corporal, "you're right there. Now move it and get to the boss's office right now." Davis obeyed and strode off in a semi-marching pace to arrive at Nolan's office. *If I can get out quickly maybe I can still make my appointment with Jenny,* he thought. Once he arrived at the Platoon Commander's office, he took stock of himself and knocked purposefully on the door. There was no reply but after a second gentler tap, he heard the boss's voice echo across the room.

"Come in Davis!" He boomed. Davis opened the door to find the boss looking down at some files on his desk and signing off some paperwork. He kept the young soldier standing there for what seemed like an age without acknowledgement. Once he had finished his task, he glanced up to see Davis dressed smartly in chinos and a shirt with a lightweight waterproof jacket. A snigger escaped from his mouth and he looked at Davis like something on the bottom of his boot. He didn't let it register and stood to attention waiting to see what the boss had called him in for.

"Private Davis, it's a pleasure to see you again," said Nolan sarcastically. "And pray tell me, what have you been doing with yourself whilst the real soldiers have been preparing to go on exercise?" Davis could feel emotion running through him. Nolan was a bully and used his rank and position to undermine those he didn't like, or thought were inferior to himself which was just about everyone except those inside the inner circle; the ones he had needed to help him run his smuggling enterprise.

"It's nice to see you as well, Sir," replied Davis in a soldier-like fashion. He wasn't going to let Nolan get to him, he had after all sealed his fate with Jenny and the rest of the foursome, he just didn't know it yet, but he would in good time.

"I understand you're seeing a civilian counsellor. I certainly hope you're not telling them too much now, Private. You could get into a lot of trouble if you say the wrong things to the wrong people." The threat was present in his voice. Even though he had said it slowly and in a low, calm tone, it had its intended purpose as Davis was instantly frightened. He looked at Nolan who was staring intently back at him.

"What do you mean, Sir?" He was pushing him now for him to openly say what he was implying.

"You know what I mean Davis. You may be out of the platoon but you're still up to your neck in this. I need to you to speak with your father as well. I need some of the money from the first shipment and I've also got one kilo of product I kept back just in case we needed extra funding. It seems now that we are several men down, I may have to entice others to join our enterprise and that will only be done with cold hard cash to show what can be achieved." Nolan never used words such as 'merchandise' or 'gear' when talking about opium. He thought it vulgar, like the words criminals used.

"I'll speak with him today Sir and I'll let you know what he says," Davis answered.

"Right then you can head off to your appointment. One more thing," he said stopping Davis leaving, "we will be having a live firing day down at the ranges soon and I want you to go along and help the range warden paste targets and carry out some cleaning duties," he said as he waved him out of the office. Davis nodded in response.

As he headed towards the door, he reached into his pocket to end the call which he was relaying to Jenny. Just as he removed his hand from his pocket the boss called him back.

"Come here Davis," he yelled. "Where's your phone?"

"It's in my pocket Sir, why?"

"Get it out and give it to me." Davis hestitated but did as he was ordered. Nolan picked up the phone which Davis had unlocked and went into the setting to see if the voice recorder had been running. It hadn't and once Nolan was happy, he gave him his phone back. He hadn't even thought to check the simplest function, the call register. If he had, he would have seen that the phone had been active from the time Davis had entered the room until he touched the screen to end the call moments before.

"You never know who is listening, do you Davis? Now off you go and remember, keep your mouth shut." Davis left the room and went on his way to meet Jenny. He knew that Squires must have called the boss straight after their meeting so they must be in constant communication. Maybe Squires was keeping tabs on the surviving members of the gang. After all, four men dead in a week was unusual to say the least.

A minute or so after exiting the main gate he called Jenny's number. She answered almost straight away.

"Did you get it?" He asked. There was a pause.

"YES!" She screamed, "every single word has been recorded. Well done, John. Now get yourself over here and we can have a more in-depth chat."

As he headed around the parade square towards the main gate Squires came into Nolan's office. They watched as the young soldier traipsed his way out of the camp and towards the bus stop.

"Do you think he's had any contact with Rodders?"

"I don't know, Sir," replied the corporal, "but if he has, I'll find out about it."

Davis arrived with five minutes to spare for his appointment with Jenny. She had been told by Rodders of the encounter with Squires but thought it best to tell Davis only what he needed to know to accomplish his next task. Any undue pressure could ruin the whole plan.

Once he had entered and closed the door to her office, he gave a 'Phew' and comically wiped his brow.

"That was so close," he said to Jenny who was sat listening at tentatively in her seat. "He even asked for my phone but the silly idiot didn't look at the call register. If he had, I don't know how that would have gone in all honesty." She gave him a look of appreciation for holding his nerve when he needed to most. She started to think young Davis had been seriously undermined by his superiors in the army. He had skills, he just needed guidance in how to use them.

"So, tell me John, what happens on range days? Is it just shooting? What else is involved?"

"Well," he began, "the transport will pick us up about 07:00. We will go to the ranges and yes, it's basically a whole day of shooting at targets at various distances to keep your competence up. It's a good day out actually. Usually finish by around 15:00," he replied. "However, I think Nolan might use the day to seek out prospective candidates to join the gang. He obviously won't approach the suitable ones, Squires will do the dirty work for him. Nolan likes to stay in the shadows as much as possible."

"OK, Jenny paused as she considered things. "I want you to go and see your dad. I'm going to give you a mobile phone for him to use. Tell him Nolan wants to meet. It must be on the same day as the range exercise but later in the evening. Tell him it's very important and it can only go ahead on that particular date. I'll give you an exact time later. There's one more thing you need to do when you're with Nolan and Squires," she continued. "It's going to take balls of steel and you won't like it but if you do it correctly, and I'll show you how, it will put them on the back foot and you on the same level as they are." He took a deep breath as she briefed Davis for almost an hour. Afterwards, he was a bit shaken but promised he would do his best.

"That's all we need John. If you do your best, you will be fine. I also want you to give Nolan this phone." She handed Davis two of the encrypted mobiles, each with a different colour protective case. "They've been doctored by Laura to only accept and receive calls and texts from the other two units we hold. Nolan gets the red one, you give the blue one to your dad when you see him before the meeting with Nolan." Davis inspected the encrypted mobiles.

"Are you sure this will work, Jenny?" He queried. "I mean it's a simple plan but if anyone gets a sniff of what's going on, it could all go south very quickly."

"That's the whole point John. It's so simple nobody should suspect a thing... until we want them to. Now, get up the road quickly and back down in time for range day. If you need anything let me know." Davis thought about the plan and soaked up all of the information Jenny had told him. Nolan was about to get stung.....badly.

CHAPTER 20

Range day came and the whole company stood to attention on the parade square awaiting a head count prior to boarding several large four-ton trucks. Once the company Sergeant Major was happy, the men were loaded like cattle on their way to market and the short twenty-minute journey began. Squires sat in the same transport as Davis and stared at him like a boxer does with his opponent. This troubled Davis. Why was he being so confrontational towards him? he wondered. He decided to ignore him but this didn't stop Squires attempts to make him uneasy. Once the transport had reached its destination and the troops had been organised into shooting groups, Squires made a beeline for Davis and he didn't look pleased.

"The boss wants to see you at some point in the day. You will be working at the range butts, pasting targets because you can't be trusted to carry a weapon. DO NOT LEAVE. The boss will come to you. Do you understand?" He growled.

"Yes of course, Corporal," he calmy replied. Squires, expecting some kind of cocky retort from Davis appeared agitated that it wasn't forthcoming and stormed off, incensed there hadn't been some kind of argument and the opportunity to belittle Davis in front of the other soldiers. Davis calmly spoke to the range warden and meandered off in the direction of the butts where the targets were raised and lowered to carry out the menial duty assigned to him. He thought nothing of the task. The fact he couldn't carry a weapon had no bearing on him either. His mind was fully committed to carrying out the wishes of Jenny and doing what had been asked of him. He was nervous about his encounter with the boss and no doubt Squires would also be on hand like the sycophant he had become, but he had geared himself up for the meeting and had the rest of the afternoon to get his rhetoric straight. He felt a slight buzz knowing he was putting himself on the line but at the same time felt calm in the knowledge he was doing it for the greater good of the group. He would not have to wait long before the call for him to see the Platoon Commander came.

Nolan turned up at Davis's location and waited until the young soldier ran over, saluted, and stood to attention waiting to hear what this hastily arranged meeting was all about. Nolan came right up to Davis, his face almost touching his. He didn't look happy and Davis knew he was in for a rough ride.

"I want to know what your father has done with the money from the first shipment and I want to know now," seethed the boss.

"I...I don't know, Sir," stumbled Davis. He was being honest. He knew his father had the money, but where it was, he didn't know.

"Then you had better fucking find out, hadn't you?" chimed in Squires. Davis turned his head and threw Squires a filthy before returning to the stare of Nolan.

"It's not my business, Sir," he continued. "You know I'm only privy to certain information at my dad's request. The less I know, the less I can talk about."

"I don't give a shit about you or your father, I want the money and I want it quickly," said Nolan.

"I know my dad was going to contact you, Sir, but I'm not sure when. I know he wants to set up a meeting." Davis said sheepishly.

"You listen to me," Nolan began. As soon as he started his sentence, he knew it was time to do as he was asked by Jenny. He took a deep breath and cut the boss off mid-sentence.

"SHUT UP YOU DICKHEAD!" Davis shouted at the boss. Nolan took a step back with the shock of a private soldier talking to him in such a way. He was just about to talk when he was interrupted again by Davis.

"All you ever do is whine and bully people. You're a moron," he said pointing his finger at Nolan.

"I think you're forgetting something Nolan, you don't run this outfit, my father does, and he's got enough shit on you and Squires here to have you thrown in jail for the rest of your lives." Davis could feel the power coursing through his veins. He was in charge of this conversation now and they would listen to what he had to say.

"You're a low life worm. You're not an army officer, you're a second-rate thief and drug smuggler and not worthy to wear the uniform on your back. Not only that but you, and this reptile here," he pointed to Squires, "are murderers. I know it was you who told Squires to push the Sarge into the line of fire because I was told by Bairdy before he met his maker," he lied. "You need to remember, you're only the smuggler. My dad distributes and sells your gear and that's where the money is, so don't ever threaten me again or I'll make sure he has you and knob head here strung up, chopped up and fed to the pigs by the end of the week. I don't think you fully understand who you've been dealing with all this time, do you?"

"Who do you think you're talking to?" Squires shouted. Davis looked at him, walked over and stood toe to toe.

"I've had enough of your shit as well, Squires," he said calmly. "You do so much as look at me in the wrong way from now on and I promise to god you will be in a box by the end of the day." He stared at the corporal and continued.

"I mean it," Davis said through gritted teeth, "now back the fuck off." Squires broke his stare to look at Nolan who was in a state of shock. Davis had the look of a mad man in his eyes.

"Now I have your attention gentlemen my dad would like you to have these." He handed each man an encrypted phone.

"Do not use them for anything other than its intended purpose: for my father to get in touch with you. He will tell you when and where to meet. It just so happens he wants to see you tonight, Sir," he looked at Nolan. "But whether or not you bring this prick with you will be decided by him, do you understand?" Nolan nodded. Squires was still in a state of disbelief at the swift change in the balance of power.

"One more thing both of you. When the phone rings, you answer it, day or night. Failure to do so might be detrimental to your future health." He threw up a salute to Nolan and walked back to his work area. He was shaking to the core. He had taken a huge gamble on his bluff. Nolan and Squires wandered off to their prospective positions for the live firing exercise but he knew he had not seen the last of them for the day. Even if they had acted differently, his father knew enough about the pair to have them locked up for a very long time. The drug charges alone would see them imprisoned even if the story regarding the Sarge's death was never uncovered. Davis felt strong and unbeatable. He had faced his enemy and come out the other side on top. He was still scared but he was proud of himself and could not wait to tell Jenny of his big moment. He just had to get through the day and everything should work out as planned.

Davis scanned the four-ton truck on the way back to the barracks after the shooting exercise; there was no sign of Squires. He guessed he and Nolan would be travelling back together so they could have time to chew over the events of the day and come up with a new plan which would restore the balance and give them a better footing when negotiating with Davis Senior. Davis got out his mobile phone, turned his back on the other passengers and called Jenny. She answered quickly.

"John, I've been worried about you. How did it go today?" She sounded concerned.

"I'm OK Jenny. It went well," he replied, in a hushed voice, trying to stifle his excitement. "I went for Nolan big time," he whispered. "He didn't know what to do. I didn't know if he was going to launch himself at me, have me arrested or just stand there and say nothing. He did the latter by the way. He completely crumbled Jenny, so did Squires. I'm shaking now just thinking about it." Jenny was impressed. The young man had put his neck on the line and it had paid off.

"Well done, John," beamed Jenny, "I'm so proud of you. It must have been nerve shredding. Was it?"

"To be honest it was a bit of a blur. I could hear my voice coming out of my mouth and I knew what I was saying but even I couldn't believe I was saying it to a Captain. I must have sounded convincing otherwise I wouldn't be chatting to you now. I have a feeling they might be planning a way to get back on the top spot again so be prepared for any eventuality," he said, his demeanor calmer than when the conversation began.

"You have just read my mind," replied Jenny. "I think you should head over to my office as soon as you get back. Can you do that?"

"Yes of course," he said, "it might be after five o'clock though."

"Don't worry about that," Jenny said, "we have a little bit more work to do and then we will let things take their own course. I'll see you when you get here." Jenny ended the call and Davis sat and looked at his handset for a moment. He smiled and knew Jenny was genuinely proud of him. *It's more than my father ever was,* he thought to himself.

When he arrived at Jenny's office it had just passed five. Siona had left for the day and the whole floor was in darkness except the lights from her office. When he opened the door, he was met with greetings from Rodders and Laura, both of whom had been sitting in the waiting room for his arrival. Jenny had just finished a call with another patient when she entered the small waiting area. She met Davis with a hug and then took him by the shoulders, stared into his eyes and said, "well done John. It was truly very brave what you did today, me and the others thank you for it." He smiled, embarrassed by the praise being heaped upon him and a small tear began to well in the corner of his eyes.

'Well played fella," said Rodders, slapping him gently on the back.

"Same here," Laura said, "very ballsy, I must say."

"I try," replied Davis with a smile.

"OK," began Jenny, "pleasantries over with, we have work to do." Davis could see that there were some boxes wired up to a router on the table. He didn't know what they were for and wouldn't pry until he was told by one of the others.

"John, remember I told you we still had things to do, well this is it." Apart from the boxes everything seemed the same as always.

"What do you want me to do?" He asked.

"I want you to call your father and tell him exactly what I tell you. Is that OK?"

"Sure, no problems," and after a short brief he picked up his mobile phone and rang his dad. As the call was connecting, Davis felt uncomfortable. He always did when he spoke to his father. He put him on edge, even when he was over one hundred miles away and on the end of a phone. Jenny touched his free hand and she gave him a reassuring look. He calmed as the phone was answered.

"Hello, who is this?" Davis Senior asked, abruptly.

"It's me, don't you even recognize my number?" replied Davis.

"No. Should I? What do you want?" He replied without so much as a hint of emotion in his voice. John felt embarrassed again but for different reasons this time. The others could hear the conversation and he felt unwanted and pressurized by his father. They gave him glances of consolation and he kept his emotions in check and carried on.

"I've got a message from Nolan. He wants to meet you tonight. He has some gear that was brought back from Afghan on the last tour and he wants to meet in person to talk about expanding the operation when the regiment get back out there. I think he's talking about moving quite a lot of stuff so it would be beneficial to get this over and done with as soon as possible."

"Did he say how much he will bring with him if we meet?" The old man sounded interested. Davis looked at Jenny for a number to offer his father. He knew he wouldn't do anything for less than a kilo of product, so it had to be convincing. She held up three fingers and Davis gave a thumbs up in return.

"Three kilos. That's what he told me," said Davis, biting his lip nervously, awaiting his father's response.

"What time does he want to meet?"

"He has been on a live firing exercise today so would look at meeting at the scrapyard at ten pm tonight. He says it's the only time he can do it. One more thing, he wants the money from the first shipment. The stuff you've stashed away." Davis was gaining confidence now.

"OK", replied senior. "You give him directions to the yard and I'll meet him at ten tonight." The phone went dead without a goodbye from father to son. Davis didn't care, he knew what was coming and he relished the thought of the meeting between his father and Nolan.

"Well done, John. A very convincing performance once again. You're becoming quite the actor, aren't you?" Jenny was smiling at him. He gave a shrug of the shoulders, "Maybe I'll take it up full time when I get kicked out of the army." The group had a short laugh at the comment but now was the time to get serious.

"Before we go any further John, we may have a problem," she announced, nodding to Rodders to continue with the brief.

"I saw Squires yesterday." Davis' face instantly took on a look of worry. .

"I saw he had marks on his face. Did you do that?" He asked.

"Yes, I did. He followed me and we fought in the street. I'm sure he knows nothing of our movements and he certainly knows nothing about our plans, but you need to be on your guard from now on mate. Just remember, Nolan and Squires will be trying to catch you out even more now so think hard and fast before answering any of their questions, OK? Davis knew what was expected of him and now, after what he had just been told, he knew he had to be one hundred percent on his game.

"I understand Rodders," he replied, "I won't let any of you down." Jenny gave his hand a squeeze as she indicated to the literature on the desk.

Jenny had laid out her notebook on the table and showed the group the plan that they would follow for the next few hours. This was the endgame for the gang and a conclusion to all the efforts Jenny and the team had put in to get their own brand of justice. They all huddled around the desk as Jenny began her dialogue, speaking clearly about who was going to do what, where and when.

Squires was driving whilst Nolan sat in the passenger seat of the ageing Land Rover. Both men were deep in thought over what had occurred earlier with Davis and although neither spoke, they knew each other's thoughts were both concentrated on how to get the upper hand back over Davis and his father. Nolan broke the stalemate.

"Right then Corporal, this is what you're going to do," began the Captain. Squires turned his head towards the boss who caught his glance. He indicated left and pulled the vehicle over at the side of the road.

"I'm sorry," said Squires in a commanding tone knowing that the relationship as officer and enlisted man was now a different dynamic. "What *I'm* going to do. Who do you think you are?" He questioned Nolan. "What *I'm* going to do is remind you of something. *We* are in this together. We always have been but due to your rank I've always taken the back seat with the whole operation. That's now changed. Not only does Davis Senior hold all of the cards, but Davis knows it was us that had the Sarge killed. I don't think you mean what am *I* going to do. More like what are *we* going to do. It's time to get your hands dirty Nolan, I've done it for too long now. There's only you and me in this now and we are balls deep, over our heads in shit." Nolan couldn't argue. He'd had an easy ride so far. Squires had done almost all of the logistics side of things whilst the other members of the gang had carried out the donkey work, hiding the drugs in the tyres of the vehicles. In reality, Nolan had placed himself in the position where he could deny any accusation leveled at him. There was no trace of opium on his person. He had Squires talk to the men, he had never really engaged with them in regard to the operation. In effect he was squeaky clean. That had now been called into question with the revelation the Davis and at least one other knew about the whole set up and although none of it could be proven, both men were now a liability. Once one of the parties starts to threaten or blackmail the other, it's time to look for a new partner. Getting another distributor would be difficult but not impossible, thought Nolan and that's what he intended to do.

"OK," Nolan began, "what do you think our next move should be?" Squires thought for a moment, rubbed his temples and placed his hands on the wheel.

"Do you still have the piece you brough back from Afghan?" Squires was refencing a handgun that Nolan, or rather one of the gang's lackies had hidden on a cargo plane on their return journey home.

"Yes, I do. There are only ten rounds of ammo with it but it's in a safe place where I can get hold of it easily," replied the boss.

"Good, I've got channels where I can get hold of one as well. We need to be prepared for any eventuality. Who knows," he continued, "it might all come together and the whole situation will iron itself out. I mean I don't want to shoot anyone but where there's a couple of million at stake, I'll shoot my granny. If we can keep the shipments coming and have a decent relationship with Davis Senior then that's what I think we should aim for." Nolan agreed but in his own head he knew the whole thing had run its course. He had already decided to take the money and hide it away, resign his commission and disappear, never to be seen again. But he thought it best to keep this to himself. After all, he didn't think Squires would appreciate being cut out completely.

CHAPTER 21

Rodders strode around the office going over his lines. He would be the one to talk to Davis Senior in the guise of Nolan. Although the modulator could mask voices, each person had their own little idiosyncrasies and using Davis to call his father would be far too perilous. Once he was content his performance would be convincing, Jenny dialed his number and gave him the encrypted handset. The phone rang and was answered quickly.

"Hello?"

"Mr. Davis, this is Captain Nolan. I need to chat to you before our meeting tonight." Davis Senior was intrigued.

"Oh yeah, what about?" He replied.

"I'm sure your son has filled you in as best he could, he doesn't know all the facts for obvious reasons, but I fear we may have a problem with my colleague, Corporal Squires. I've asked you to bring the money from the first shipment with you. However, I think Squires may have other ideas about our current relationship. He may decide to act on his own initiative and if that happens then the whole operation could go downhill. I don't want that to happen. There's a lot of money at stake here and there could be a hell of a lot more in the future, so we need to take care of Squires. Do you have the erm... facilities to cater for such an incident if one occurs?" Senior thought for a moment to contemplate the consequences should immediate action be required.

"I don't think that would be a problem...*if* and only *if* it's required." He replied. Murder was a dirty business and Davis Senior tried to avoid it as much as he could.

"I think we understand each other," said Rodders "I'll see you at ten tonight." He rang off, took a deep breath and sat down. He had just sealed Squires' fate in a thirty second phone call and felt no remorse for doing so. Now it was Jenny's turn.

Squires entered his room in the barrack block and threw himself onto his bed. It had been agreed that he and Nolan would travel separately to their rendezvous that evening and he needed to shower and get his head around how events could turn out. He wasn't mentally prepared for shooting someone outside of the battlefield but if put on the spot to defend himself he would act. Or if the opportunity of walking away with a few million pounds occurred. He had spoken to his contact at the armoury and gained access to the handgun he told Nolan of earlier. It was an old army issue Browning. Not the best gun ever made but decent at close range and if it all went wrong, he knew this wouldn't be a fire fight over a wide area. He took the gun from its holster and decided to clean the movement. He laid out the magazine and rounds on the bed and made sure everything was in good working order. He was happy. The armourers on camp were meticulous in their work and should it be fired in anger, they could either dispose of it completely or make it so any round couldn't be matched to the gun itself. All for the princely sum of two thousand pounds which he had managed to save from scamming the junior soldiers at cards. Suddenly, the encrypted mobile came to life. A text, appearing to be from senior.

"Nolan, do you have a handgun? I have a shotgun but if we do Squires, we don't want it too messy." Squires stared at the words. Davis Senior must had sent the text to the wrong person. This was meant for the boss. His heart dropped to his stomach as he realized they had plans for him that evening. He slipped into a fit of rage, throwing equipment and clothing all over his room. *That low life son of a bitch*, he thought. After everything they had gone through, he was willing to team up with a man he hadn't even met and kill him for a bag of money. He calmed down and realised it was exactly what he could have easily contemplated. But now he knew their plan, he would be fully prepared for an ambush. The adrenalin began to run through his body. This was the kind of excitement he joined the army for in the first place and now he was playing out his fantasies out of uniform. He tried to see the events going down in his mind's eye and he knew he had no choice now. If he wanted the cash, he would have to dispose of both Davis Senior and Nolan. It was worth the risk for a few million quid. He could pop them both, take the money and either run or wait it out. Either way, he would take the cash from them by hook or by crook. He had also put two and two together but had omitted to tell Nolan about his findings that he had concluded that Rodders and the Sarge's wife had been talking. He bit his lip while deep in thought. *Maybe I should make a quick house call before my meeting.*

Jenny looked at the text she had just sent to Squires. She knew it would have the desired effect. The trap was set for him, it was time to turn their attention onto Nolan.

Nolan was sitting in the officer's mess bar nursing a single gin and tonic. He stared into the distance while he calculated how he could walk away from this whole affair without a blemish but still holding the cash. He considered another gin and as he rose, he felt a vibration coming from the inside pocked of his sports jacket. The phone that Davis had given him from his father lit up. A text from Davis Senior he presumed.

"Squires, I like your idea. If we do Nolan, I can get rid of the evidence. Are you sure you can run this thing without him?"

Nolan stared at the phone. His eyes transfixed on the words he was reading. He raised his head slightly to see if anyone was watching. When he was satisfied no one was, he got up from his seat to exit the messroom. As he did so he bumped with force into a fellow officer and dropped the handset. The man bent down to retrieve the phone, admiring it as he did so.

"That's a cracking piece of kit you have there, Nolan. I've not seen anything like that on the market in the UK yet. Can I ask where you got it from?" It was Captain Mills, the C.O. of the Military Police detachment on barracks. Nolan was flustered but thought quickly on his feet.

"It's an import from Korea," he blurted, "it was actually a gift from my mother." He put out his hand to take the phone from Mills who decided to inspect it a bit closer. He switched on the phone only to find that no mobile phone company information was to be seen anywhere on the screen. *It must be registered elsewhere,* thought Mills.

Mills had been around the block a few times in his career. He had been through the ranks and taken a commission at the age of fourty five. He only had a few more years left to serve until retirement but that didn't slow him down. He was a dogged investigator having been seconded to the Special Investigations Branch for over five years. There wasn't a lot Mills hadn't seen, and he knew Nolan was up to something. He had come to his attention a while back when a young medic, suspected of shooting himself to get out of Afghanistan, had mentioned the name. Mills had eyed Nolan with suspicion ever since. He guessed the phone was an encrypted device and you only have one of those if you're up to something. He would keep a close eye on Captain Nolan.

Nolan rushed to his room in the mess. Once behind closed doors, he went to the toilet and threw up. The text had been sent to him by accident. Davis Senior and Squires were planning on his demise and now he knew about it. He didn't need to attend the meeting, he could just as easily walk away now and stay alive, but greed and the lure of the money was too much. He went to his locker and retrieved the handgun stashed in a box at the bottom. The Glock was almost new. He had stolen it from a house a suspected terrorist was being harbored in and asked Squires to get it back into the UK for him. As Squires had done, he took the gun to pieces, cleaned it, and rearranged everything on the bed to look for damage. He loaded the magazine with the ten rounds he had also acquired and slipped the hip holster through his belt before putting on a long waterproof jacket to hide it from view. He made up his mind. He would go to the meeting, kill Squires and Davis Senior and take the money.

Rodders was sitting listening to Laura and Jenny talk about the plan when a thought rushed into his head. "Jenny?" He asked, "given the choice of a different outcome, would you still want Nolan out of the picture altogether or if I offered you an alternative would you consider it?" Jenny raised her head from the notebook she and Laura had been poring over.

"I'm not too sure what you mean Rodders, but I'm all ears," she replied.

"What if Nolan survives but is found with all of the evidence on him to put him away for life? Does the thought of him rotting in jail give you more pleasure than him being dead?" Jenny thought for a while.

"Yes, I think it does but how do we go about that?" She asked

"I need to make a call to the barracks. It's a bit late but I might just catch who I'm after."

Mills had returned to the office to send one last email after his visit to the officer's mess. As he was about to turn off the office lights the phone on his desk rang out with a shrill. He considered ignoring it but being the perfectionist he was, he knew he couldn't. He picked up the handset which connected immediately.

"Mills?" he spoke clearly into the handset.

"Captain Mills, I have some information for you regarding an incident which will happen tonight at ten o'clock at the location I will give you in a moment."

"Who is this?" Mills demanded, not expecting an honest answer.

"Who I am doesn't matter. What matters is the drug deal which will take place tonight involving two soldiers based at your barracks. Corporal Squires and Captain Nolan, both of four platoon will be present."

"And how did you come by this information?" Enquired Mills.

"Again, how I got the information does not concern you. All you need to do is act upon it. Can you do that, yes or no?" Mills scratched his chin. He could mobilise a group of MPs at the drop of a hat, and as military personnel were involved, he didn't need a warrant.

"OK," he said, "Tell me what I need to know." Rodders proceeded to give Mills the location of the scrapyard.

"One more thing Captain Mills. I have a strong belief that all present at the meeting are armed." Rodders closed the call, disconnected the voice modulator, and placed all of the equipment into a bag. The four sat quietly around the desk wondering if they had missed any small details.

"What if Nolan gets shot?" Asked Davis.

"Then he gets shot," replied Jenny. "It's a win, win situation for us. They will still all be discovered for what they are. What we *now* have to do is get your story straight. If they interview you regarding your father, they will undoubtedly come to me for a character reference, me being your councilor," she stated. "There is absolutely no evidence to link any of us to the happenings of the last few weeks. Any interview with you will only be to ask if Nolan ever mentioned your father in regard to his dealings and vice versa." Davis understood but wasn't worried. He had become quite adept in recent times at acting and lying when required, so if interviewed he would put on his hang dog face and convince his interviewer of his innocence. They all agreed if anyone could pull it off it was him.

"What do we do with the equipment?" Asked Laura.

"I've got that all sorted out," replied Rodders. He delved into his backpack and brought out a medical sharps bin, the kind that doctors dispose of used needles in.

"We break up all the evidence, put it into here and my contact at the medical center will place it in with the other medical waste. This is all taken away on a Friday morning and taken to a specialist incinerator to dispose of. Sorted." It was simple but effective.

"All we need to do now is go home and watch the news," said Jenny. "I'll keep hold of the phone just in case we need to change the plan slightly, but I doubt we will. Rodders, do you want to do the honors and break up the expensive stuff?" She asked, indicating to the voice modulator and its associated bits and bobs.

"With pleasure," he replied.

Jenny's phone began to vibrate and she thought it may be a text from one of her girlfriends, asking to meet up for drinks at the weekend. She swiped at the screen to discover the app for her doorbell camera and the other surveillance equipment in the house had sprung to life. Someone was at her door, back to the camera wearing a hoodie pulled tight around his head. Whoever it was knew there was a camera in the bell. It was after all an off the shelf unit. The doorbell rang twice more and was followed by a bang with a fist. Suddenly, after perusing the street to check nobody was present, the caller kicked the door open, splintering the frame. Jenny gasped.

"What's wrong?" Asked Rodders.

"Someone is breaking into my house!" She screamed. They all gathered around the phone to watch the action unfold.

"I'm calling the police," she said frantically.

"Hold on Jenny, have you got all of the cameras set to record and the audio on?" Asked Laura.

"Yes, why?"

"Let's see who it is first, we might be able to get some footage and some leverage if it's who we think it is." The intruder entered into the hallway and scanned the area and then the lounge. Happy in the thought there were no cameras, he removed the hood from his head.

"Jesus, it's Squires," fumed Rodders knowing it was him as soon as Jenny had shown the hooded figure on her phone screen. Squires was unaware of the tiny recording devices hidden around the property and his features were crystal clear on Jenny's phone screen, all the while being recorded in glorious HD. In his hand he brandished what looked like a short piece of metal. He flung his arm downwards with speed and the weapon extended. It was a police issue baton and he had it for one reason only. Jenny put her hands to her mouth in dismay as she watched this animal sneak around her living room and then kitchen. He lifted up pieces of mail with his gloved hands and replaced them with great precision, attempting to keep the crime scene as clean as possible. He started his way upstairs, climbing silently in case anyone was in the bedroom. He noticed a light, not realizing it had been switched on remotely just moments earlier by Jenny.

She didn't want him in her bedroom, that was sacrosanct, and she asked Rodders to end it there and then and call the police.

"We can't," he explained. "If we call the police and he is caught, the whole plan ends right here and now. It will turn to rat shit instantly. What we need is to let him know he has been seen."

"How?" She asked.

"Watch." Rodders took the phone and activated a setting on the app. He connected the phone to the Bluetooth speakers in the house and then switched on all of the lights at once.

"Squires!" yelled Rodders, "what do you think you're doing?" Squires froze momentarily.

"We've got you on camera son, there's nowhere for you to run to now, you scumbag." Squires spun around sharply, not knowing where the voice was coming from but recognizing Rodders' voice instantly. He scanned the walls and stared directly into one of the tiny cameras he had discovered. He knew now that his options were limited to one. He had to go through with the meeting before the police caught up with him. He moved his face as close to the lens as he could.

"I'm coming for you Rodders and the bitch who lives here as well," he spat. "Call the cops, they'll never catch me." The words were full of hate and as he stared into the camera, he made a slicing motion with his fingers against his throat. Rodders and Jenny decided not to reply via the speakers. Instead, they would sit back, safe in the knowledge their plan was working. Squires took one last look around the house, kicking over furniture and smashing ornaments before leaving the property and running away as fast as he could. He knew now what he had to do to survive. There was no turning back from this. He had to go to the meeting and disappear soon afterwards. It was that, or life in a prison cell.

Rodders turned to Jenny with a grin on his face.

"Now, if this doesn't go as planned tonight, we've got leverage. Either way, he's up shit creek without a paddle."

Nolan had left early for the meeting. It would take about one and a half hours to get there which would give him time to get his plan correct in his head. He knew where he would stand in relation to the others to get the best angles to hit his targets, unfortunately Squires also had this tactic and training so Nolan knew he would have to be the first one taken out. Davis Senior was a different matter. He was a criminal so there would be a very strong chance he would have access to weapons, but what kind was the question Nolan did not have the answer to. It could be anything from shotguns to semi-automatic rifles. He decided to change his mind and shoot Davis Senior first. Squires would only be armed with a sidearm and probably an old one at that. It would be no contest against his Glock, he just needed to get off the first shot.

As he drove, he began to have doubts about the whole arrangement. His entire life had been a catalogue of risks from stealing Land Rovers to seeing action in Afghanistan, but this was different. It was like a shoot-out in a spaghetti western. The three antagonists facing off against each other waiting for the first one to draw. *I'm a half decent shot with a handgun,* he thought, as he continued to play events as he saw them over and over. Then his thoughts drifted to him sitting on a beach sipping cocktails without a care in the world. His future, with millions of pounds at hand. He smiled, "I can do this. I can do this," he chanted over and over to himself. His bravado brought him a sense of calm and at that point he was focused on nothing else but getting his hands on the money and getting as far away as possible.

Davis Senior trudged towards the huge agricultural building which sat over one hundred meters from his house. There were two entrances, north and south and each led to a door at their prospective ends. The cryptic call from Nolan earlier detailing how Squires was going to double cross him, made Davis Senior trust him that bit more. Once Squires was dead, he could patch up his relationship with Nolan and they could carry on with their previous arrangement. Bringing the money with him was a show of willingness to move forward with their operation. The hold all was large and heavy. It contained just over three million in pounds and euros. Large, untraceable notes were the choice of the criminal and it all fitted neatly into one bag. He placed the bag next to the south door in the shadows, so as not to let Squires see his potential bounty. He looked around at the agricultural equipment in the large steel framed shed and decided he would stand adjacent to a huge JCB tractor which he could hide behind if the situation became dangerous. He looked at his watch. It had just turned nine thirty and the night was pitch black. He would dim the lights in the shed, the others had no idea of the layout of the building so it gave him an advantage. He took his shotgun, loaded it, and placed it up against the tyre of the huge machine with several spare cartridges. He would wait for them to arrive and in the meantime would take in the night air and smoke a hand rolled cigarette.

Squires was driving erratically to his destination. After being identified at the break in earlier, he needed to get the money and disappear tonight and forever or Rodders would turn over the evidence to the police. He was angry and frustrated after discovering the others were going to double cross him and walk away with the money. *It's my money,* he thought. He had done all of the hard work. Nolan had done nothing. In fact, he only got his cut because he kept his mouth shut and that was his whole input, apart from ordering killings and getting other people to carry out his dirty work. Even if he could walk away from this, he would still kill Nolan. He was a thorn in his side and the only way to alleviate that was to get rid of him altogether. He could live on the money for the rest of his life. He could control the whole gambling thing, or at least he tried to convince himself of that. He would do what needed to be done, leave no trace of his actions and run. He had visions of himself driving fast sports cars and sitting on white sand beaches, and as he drove, he could almost feel the heat and humidity on his face and the taste of the rum filled cocktails on his tongue. He yearned for it and since the smuggling gig had begun it was his intention to do that with the money he made from the operation. All he had to do was get through tonight. One night and it would all be over. They would never catch him, and he would get away scott free. How he would move the money hadn't even entered his mind so blurred he was by the thought of life by the sea and endless women at his beck and call. He approached the site of Davis Senior's scrapyard and saw another car sitting outside the doorway. It was Nolan's.

Mills had gathered a team of four MP's and briefed them prior to setting off. He would need to really put his foot on the accelerator to make up any lost ground but was sure he could make it in time. The plan would be to approach the shed, place personnel in key positions and once any commotion was heard they would enter, guns drawn and make arrests. It was hastily arranged and didn't meet army protocol, at least not fully, but time was not on their side, and this had only been arranged off the back of an anonymous phone call a couple of hours before.

Mills had a notion that Nolan was corrupt to the core. He was one of life's chancers, a person who used rank and privilege to get him to higher places, with no regard for how or who he had to walk over on his journey. It hadn't really helped him get a promotion. He wasn't a good soldier. He was competent at best and would never go above the rank of Major, if he ever even reached that position. Mills believed the stories that circulated about him but couldn't prove anything until the opportunity landed in his lap. He didn't know who made the call that evening or if he would ever follow it up, but he was glad they did. If the tip was true and he caught Nolan on a drug charge, it would be the highlight of an already stellar career. He was in the zone now and heading for the showdown with excitement.

CHAPTER 22

As Nolan left his car, he perused the area and took in his surroundings. He slid the Glock from its holster, pulled back the action and saw he had a round in the chamber. He double checked the safety, placed the gun back on his hip, stood by his vehicle and let his eyes become accustomed to the darkness. He unzipped his jacket to offer easy access to his weapon and strode towards the shed. He stood by the doorway trying to conceal himself, when he heard the sound of another vehicle approaching by the same route he had done earlier. As he squinted in an attempt to see a bit more clearly, he recognized the car, it was Squires. While he observed his movements, he could see he was checking his weapon and following the same meticulous steps he had done before holstering the firearm. Nolan would want to get an advantage over his opponents so rather than wait for Squires to enter together he quietly opened the door and slid inside the shed. At the other end of the large building, Davis Senior silently watched as Nolan, thinking he was alone, scrutinized the layout of the area. Once content with his findings, he took up a position where he thought he would be able to see everyone openly yet still offering some kind of protection when events unfolded as he knew they would.

Squires walked slowly to the entrance of the shed. He guessed Nolan was already inside otherwise he would have met him outside to talk before entering as a pair. He inhaled deeply and waited for a moment, watching his icy breath rise and disappear into the night sky. Then he opened the door slightly making sure it was clear on the other side before committing to his entrance. Once inside, he could see Nolan in the dimly lit building, standing alone about ten or so meters from the doorway. He considered walking over but snapped back when he remembered why he was there. He didn't want to get too close to his target so walked away in the opposite direction to roughly the same distance. He could still see Nolan and hitting him from this distance in low light would be difficult but could be achieved. This, he thought would be exactly the same position Nolan was in. The playing field was evenly matched, but where was Davis Senior?

At the other end of the shed Davis Senior came out of the shadows and into the haziness of the shed lights. He had a very large hold all over his shoulder and once he took up his position, he shouted over to both men.

"Good evening gents. Which one of you is Captain Nolan?"

"That's me," answered Nolan, raising his left hand into the air so he could be easily identified by Mr. Davis. He kept his right hand, his shooting hand, free down by his right hip, ready to move quickly if need be.

"Are you armed Nolan?" Asked Davis Senior. Nolan wasn't sure what to say or do.

He thought quickly and lied, "no, I'm not armed."

"Then please move forward towards me," shouted Davis Senior, still thinking that Nolan could be a valuable asset and ally in his operation.

"Why not both of us?" Shouted Squires.

"It's nothing personal Mr. Squires," replied senior, "this is only to confirm what I have with me in the bag and no other reason." Happy with the reasoning behind the decision, Squires didn't reply and stood silently as Nolan made his approach.

"That's far enough Mr. Nolan," said Davis Senior, some five meters or so from the bag. He knelt down, unzipped the large hold all and tipped it slightly so Nolan could view its contents more clearly. Senior shone a torch into the bag to show the money to Nolan. There appeared to be hundreds of rolls of money and Nolan could see some were fifty-pound notes and others he assumed were euros.

"How much is there?" Asked Nolan.

"Just over three million in mixed currency," replied Davis Senior. "You can take this once you've completed your end of the bargain," his tone hushed. He zipped up the bag, slid it along the floor as he walked backwards towards the door and placed it outside. Once the door was closed, he resumed his position as Nolan walked back to his. *What end of the bargain,* thought Nolan? As the three men stood, Nolan and Squires at one end, separated by twenty meters and Senior at the other the building went quiet.

"How much was in the bag?" Said Squires to Nolan. He didn't reply.

"NOLAN, how much is in the bag?" He asked again. Nolan stood looking forward without replying. His head was awash with thoughts of what he should do and when he should make his move. He saw things in slow motion in his head and decided that if he didn't make a move soon, one of the others would. Squires was staring intently at Nolan now wondering what was going through his head. He started to very slowly inch away towards the safety of some large farming equipment to his right. He had moved almost four or five meters before Nolan noticed and snapped his head in Squires direction. The two men's eyes met and both knew this was the moment their lives were about to change. Suddenly, using their peripheral vision, the soldiers watched as Davis Senior ran swiftly towards a huge JCB tractor positioned next to him. Then, instinctively, both Nolan and Squires ran for cover to areas they had previously sought out as possible safe refuge in the event of gunplay.

Mills was driving faster now. It was already ten past ten and he was still two miles from his destination. He was followed by two other cars containing five armed MPs with whom he was in constant radio communication. Mills would enter the scrapyard grounds first. He would kill the lights on his car and travel slowly until he could go no further. The others would hold back until a short reconnaissance was carried out, then orders would be given for the MPs to take up positions around the building. He knew Nolan was up to no good but how deeply he didn't know. He would prefer to take him in unharmed but if the anonymous call was correct and he was armed he would have no hesitation to take him down with a well-aimed shot. If he felt threatened, he would make the decision to kill him if necessary. Mills was never a 'gung-ho' soldier. He believed in swift justice being served for those who rightly deserved it.

Squires lay prone on the ground of the dusty shed, listening for movement around his position. When he heard nothing, he decided it was time to go on the offence and raised his head to look for Nolan. *That sneaky double-crossing bastard will be the first to get plugged,* he thought. He could see Nolan's shoulder just poking out from behind a very large tractor wheel. The small round from his handgun wouldn't penetrate the rubber so he would have to wait until he stepped out from behind his cover to get a better shot in his direction. Suddenly a shaft of light emanated from Davis Senior's position at the other end of the shed. Two more men sneaked into the building and took up positions near and around him. How naive could both soldiers have been? Squires slunk into a shadow and began to rethink his tactics. Suddenly a loud bang from a shotgun pierced the silence as Nolan ran from his location to Squires. He hit the ground and skidded along the dirt covered floor. Once he stopped, he looked at Squires expecting to see a gun in his face, the result was quite the opposite.

"Holy shit," exclaimed the corporal, "why didn't we think of this scenario? We should have known a low life drug dealer would have muscle to back him up." He turned to see Nolan was pointing his gun at his stomach.

"In all honesty I wasn't expecting this to happen after reading the text I got from Davis Senior which I'm sure was meant for you," he said angrily.

"What text?" Asked Squires, playing a game of cat and mouse to see if Nolan would reveal his intentions before Squires was forced into doing so.

"The one where he told you to do away with me and run the show yourself. Ring any bells yet?"

"What are you talking about? I've never spoken to the man in my life." Replied Squires.

"I beg to differ," stated Nolan, "I've got the evidence in my pocket showing your conversation with him. You and him, planning my demise and taking the money for yourselves." Nolan's gun was now pointing at his opponent's head.

"Boss," said Squires, a tone of honesty and dismay in his voice, "I've got no idea what you're talking about. All I know is I received a text saying something similar and I thought *you* were planning on knocking *me* off".

Both men looked at each other with confusion and removed the encrypted phones from their pockets. Once they read the messages sent to them, they realised they had been duped by another party. Davis Senior wasn't clever enough to orchestrate such a duplicitous plan, so who could it be? Another shot rang out from a different spot, no doubt from one of Davis Senior's henchmen.

"We need to get our shit together here and quickly," whispered Nolan.

"What's the plan?" Asked Squires as the boss drew up a simple but effective attack.

"Let's not take anything for granted," he began. "We don't know the capabilities of Senior's men. Let's just say they do have some kind of military training. I doubt they've had time to plan and are relying on brute force and extra firepower to overcome us. All we need to do is take one of them out and were on an even keel. Let's go for this chap on the right and lay down some suppressing fire and I'll take up a better position for the kill. Agreed?"

"Agreed," replied Squires as they formulated a straightforward offensive plan. Trying to stay in the shadows, both men used the heavy equipment around them to silently move over to the side of the building where they could see their first target. Squires picked up a small but weighty piece of wooden kindling and threw it in the direction of their enemy. As it hit the windscreen of a small excavator their adversary made the simple mistake of revealing his whereabouts. Nolan took aim and purposely landed his first round behind the man's location and as he took one step backward to see where it had landed, he exposed his entire frame to Nolan. He fired off two shots in quick succession and the man dropped to the floor. The groans were loud but both soldiers knew from experience this would cease very quickly. Twenty or so seconds later the heavy breathing ended, and the man's body lay lifeless on the ground.

"Right then, I've now come to the conclusion these guys know nothing," said Nolan returning to Squires and pointing out the man's simple mistake.

"I agree, they're definitely counting on numbers instead of skills here," replied Squires. "If you go back where you were, I'll go down my side and we can pincer them without too much effort."

"OK, stay safe and keep your head down," Nolan said, genuinely thinking about his Corporal's welfare.

Both men began crawling soundlessly along the shed floor, stopping periodically to soak up the surroundings and calculate which equipment would be beneficial as cover when the heavy shooting started. Squires could see the shadow of his foe but due to the lighting could not place him in an exact position. He knew he would have to somehow draw him out. He could see Nolan, and after gaining his attention, sent a series of hand signals to indicate his intentions. Upon receipt, Nolan gave the thumbs up, and the plan was put into motion. With the advantage of excellent army training behind them, both men worked effortlessly as a team to hunt down their prey. The remaining henchman was breathing so hard Nolan could hear him in the distance and quickly homed into his location. He was carrying, like the others, a twin over and under shotgun but wore no other tactical equipment of any kind. Nolan was only twenty meters from him now and was primed to take a shot when Davis Senior shouted loudly, addressing both men by name.

"Nolan, Squires!" He blared, his voice echoing throughout the cavernous building. "I know you were coming here to kill me; I was tipped off but I'm willing to do a deal."

"What kind of deal?" Shouted Squires before Nolan could reply.

"We put this behind us and carry on as we were in the first place. A fifty-fifty split." The maths didn't add up for either man. They still had their men to pay, if and when they actually recruited more, and this meant the cut needed to be greater.

"OK, agreed," replied Squires. The boss could see the corporal from his location and threw over a look of anger. He mouthed the words "what the fuck?" silently but Squires simply put his finger to his lips and replied with a quiet "Sshhhhh."

"If we come out, how do we know you won't shoot?" Asked Nolan.

"You have my word," replied senior, undoubtedly lying, thought the boss. It was a stalemate. All parties now knew each other's location which made the situation more precarious.

"We all need to come into open view and place our weapons on the ground as a show of trust," said Squires. The boss now looked totally dismayed at his Corporal's decision. He was throwing away any advantage they had and for what? A second-rate deal that didn't benefit either of them. What was Squires thinking?

Mills car swung into the driveway of the scrapyard and he could see the huge steel building some fifty meters ahead of him. He recognized one of the vehicles as Nolan's but not the other. He concluded that it must belong to Squires and the meeting had already begun. He stopped the car short of his destination and made his way to the vehicle containing the other MPs.

"I'm going to head over to the shed door. You men wait until you get my signal, I'll flash you with my torch and then surround the shed as best you can, I don't think there will be more than two doors and two roller shutters, so it won't be too difficult to secure."

"Yes, Sir," replied a young Lance Corporal as they group began to exit their car. Mills walked slowly down the gravel track and could hear shouting, although he couldn't decipher words or whose voices they were. He drew his sidearm and checked to see if the chamber was loaded. It was and with that confirmation he continued his approach.

In the shed Squires was the first to show himself. He raised his hands, his weapon in his right hand clearly visible to the others. As he began to walk into open space he was followed with a slight delay by Nolan. As they walked Davis Senior, and his companion revealed their exact location and began to maneuver themselves into plain sight. Both men held their shotguns facing the ground. As the men came within ten meters of each other, all four simultaneously bent one knee and placed their weapons on the ground and stood up. All of them were now vulnerable. If one man made a grab for a weapon, the others would see it and could make it back to a safe haven if need be. Senior and his muscle lifted up their jackets to show they had no more concealed weapons and as they did Nolan followed suit. As he opened his coat, he began to turn around but as he did, he exposed another pistol tucked into his trousers. He pulled the revolver from its position and without hesitation fired two shots into Davis Senior and another two into his accomplice. Both men dropped instantly, neither dead but both seriously injured. He then aimed at Squires and indicated with the gun to leave his weapon on the floor and move towards the injured men. He did as requested, and as they moved closer, they could see the henchman was in his death throes, but Senior was still breathing.

He looked up at Nolan and Squires smiling, "I was going to do the same thing," he uttered. As his breathing became labored the blood began to pool under his body. As Nolan stood and watched he raised the pistol and shot another round into Senior's head. His skull opened like a smashed coconut, matter spilling onto the floor in all directions and onto the clothes of both men left standing. Nolan would have preferred a cleaner outcome but it was done now. He stared at the body and turned to Squires and pointed the gun at his head.

"I don't know who set us up and to be honest I don't really care now," he said. "All I know is in a situation like this there can be no loose ends and unfortunately young chap, that's exactly what you are."

"Hold on boss," said Squires nervously, "let's just take a minute to think about this. There's millions in cash just outside of those doors. We can take it, split it, and start a new venture. We've got the contacts and we could make millions more. Plus, if the cops get involved, we can make up some story and I could back you up. It doesn't have to be like this. We've been through a lot you and me, surely that counts for something?"

"You're right," replied Nolan. Squires let out a deep breath of relief. "But it doesn't," continued Nolan, and with that he squeezed the trigger and fired his weapon. The bullet hit Squires in the middle of his forehead. The small entry wound would be no comparison to the exit wound at the back. The whole rear end of the skull separated from the rest and his head appeared to deflate, like a punctured ball. His body crumpled beneath him and he died instantly.

Mills had been outside the door when he heard the shooting. Without being noticed in the melee, he had entered the building just as Nolan had delivered the final shot to Squires. He was shocked to the core. The sheer brutality of the killing appalled him, and he was a seasoned career soldier who had seen almost everything, or so he thought. As Nolan went to walk away toward the far door and make off with the money, Mills spoke up loudly.

"NOLAN!" he screamed, "that's far enough. Stop where you are, or I *will* shoot you." Nolan recognized the voice and stopped, his back to the officer. He stood, dejected, so close to completing his objective and now having to deal with yet another obstruction, albeit a world-weary military policeman.

"You can't get away son," continued Mills, aiming directly at Nolan's torso. "Please," he pleaded, "don't make me do this, don't make me shoot you, it's not worth it, whatever *it* is."

Nolan knew there was no way out. He knew the older man wouldn't go on an operation on his own and guessed the building was surrounded by now. He would spend the rest of his life behind bars like a caged animal. He contemplated his predicament for a moment and spun around so quickly to face Mills it almost caught him off guard. His weapon was already in a firing position when he faced the policeman but Mills was ready and when Nolan completed his turn, he fired twice into his chest. He didn't fall and Mills advanced quickly, firing another time into the man's torso. He stumbled backwards with blood spurting from his mouth and his body landing on his backside and falling prone to the surface. The gun fell from his open hand and as Mills picked it up with his handkerchief, he cocked the chamber to see both that and the magazine were empty. He kneeled down next to the dying man and took his hand.

"I need to tell you something," Nolan whispered. "Sergeant Edwards... I'm so sorry... the money... it was there... the mon...". His last breath drained from his body and his head tilted to the side and blood trickled in all directions. An MP entered the building from the end Senior had placed the money outside in the bags.

"Is there anyone outside corporal?" Asked Mills.

"No Sir, nobody at this end." Mills went to the door and shone his torch on the ground, not sure of what to look for. There were footprints all over the area and some marks that suggested one or maybe two large items had been dragged away from the area but there was no hold all to be seen. The money was gone.

CHAPTER 23

The leaves whisked around the park on a light breeze and the now ever-present chill became even colder. Laura was the first to arrive at the group's familiar spot and sat with her coffee, both hands wrapped around the cardboard container in a vain attempt to keep them warm. A month had passed since the shootings and once the press coverage had broken the news of the military smuggling ring, the four friends had decided it was safe to meet and catch up.

"How is everyone?" Laura opened. They all looked at each other waiting for someone to answer. The pregnant pause grew longer until Jenny spoke up.

"Jesus peeps, c'mon it's not as if we're strangers here, is it?" The laughter came at long last as the ice was broken.

"Well," began Rodders, "I'm OK. It's been a thought-provoking few weeks but I'm really good."

"What's good about it then?" Asked Laura, interested to see what he had been up to.

"The girl from the Med Center, Debbie, who helped us put our appointments together, well, I've been seeing her a bit more seriously since we ended our, shall we call it 'project.' It's all good so far."

"Loved up, eh?" Chimed in Davis. Rodders took a moment to think about it.

"I wouldn't say loved up, but I reckon I could be in a few months. I mean I've known her for years and we used to date but I'm enjoying getting to know her better now I can see the possibility of something long term. Stopped drinking as well. Actually..." He scolded himself. "... not stopped but cut down drastically and you know what, I feel so much better for it but guess what?"

"What?" They all cried.

"I've got a job," he said, proudly.

"Doing what?" asked Jenny.

"Trainee paramedic with the ambulance service, start next month. I'm chuffed to bits. I've really landed on my foot." A momentary pause came before they erupted at his intentional gaff.

"Landed on my foot," repeated Davis giggling, "at least you've still got your sense of humour." Rodders winked at him jokingly.

"Right then John, what have you been up to?" Asked Laura.

"Me?" Davis pointed to himself. "Oh, nothing you know.... well actually I've got loads to tell. I was interviewed by the MP's."

"We knew that was coming though, didn't we?" said Rodders.

"We did but I wasn't expecting it to be so intense. That Mills bloke had me answering questions from morning to noon time, but it worked out fine. I know they spoke to you as well, didn't they Jenny?" She nodded in reply. "I could prove where I was by showing I had appointments with my counsellor and character references from her as well, so it didn't go any further. I told them about my relationship with my father and how I joined to get away and Captain Mills seemed happy with the outcome. Even my notes from the Major on camp who I was seeing before I saw Jenny backed up my story."

"And how is your Mum?" Asked Laura.

"Ah, she's fine. Getting on with life you know. Strangely, and I've only just discovered this, the yard and the land didn't belong to my Dad, it belonged to my Mum. Her father left it to her, and it seems my Dad married into money. She was too scared of him to throw him out so put up with the abuse and beatings for years. She's going to rent it out as she doesn't want to live there anymore, too many bad memories. Who can blame her? They found nothing at the property, no drugs or money. They did find some hooky cars and vans but nothing more than that."

"So, what happened to the money, if there ever was any money at all?" Queried Jenny.

"No idea. If there was, it was never found. Who knows, he probably spent it and bluffed Nolan and Squires into thinking he had it. I don't think we will ever know the truth."

"So, what about the future mate, have you thought about what you're going to do?" Asked Rodders.

"I'm not too sure to be honest. I don't think I'll stay in the army though. I've pretty much had a belly full of all the bullshit and you know, it's just lost its appeal for me. I mean, I needed to get away from home and now I don't. I've got a few months left before I need to make up my mind, so I'll have a good hard think about where I want to be."

"Why not try telecoms?" Injected Laura. "I could put in a word for you when we next recruit."

"Wow. That would be great, thanks," he gushed.

"What about you Laura? What's changed since we spoke last?" Rodders smiled at her.

"What can I tell you? Life goes on, doesn't it? Work and homelife carry on and so do I. The good thing is it's getting easier to live with, you know, Tony not being here and deep down inside I feel good about myself." She reflected for a moment before continuing.

"I feel vindicated, I feel like justice has been done and I've got no regrets about anything we did. I would do it all over again in a heartbeat." A tear came into her eye.

"I'm just glad we did this together. I don't know where my life would have gone had it not been for you three. I don't even know if I would still be here, I felt that low. You guys gave me something to fight for and I'll always love you for that." She hung her head down until Jenny took her hand a gave a light squeeze as she Jenny wiped away a tear from her eyes with her other hand.

"Look at me," she sobbed, "getting all sentimental." She took a deep breath.

"Listen guys," she began, "I know we've all been through a lot, and I know we all had an axe to grind but I couldn't have done any of this without you all. Justice has been served, greed overtook them and now they're gone." She stared into the distance. "I know Dave wasn't the man I though he was, and his involvement shook me up more than anything, but he didn't need to die, neither did Tony," she said facing Laura, "although in different circumstances. I think what I'm trying to say is I feel no guilt about what we've done. We simply played on their weaknesses and they destroyed themselves and each other." They all nodded and agreed what Jenny was saying was true. "In the short time we've been together I've grown to love you all and I know we will be friends forever, but I think we all need a short break to take stock of our lives and our futures. Let's say I call you all up in...ooh.... six months and we get together properly for a slap-up meal and a good old session. Deal?" They all nodded in agreement. As they stood and hugged each other, Jenny felt a sense of loss. Although they would see each other in a few months she knew she would miss them all. She watched as Laura left, followed shortly after by Rodders until there was only her and Davis left behind.

"I'm going to miss you, young man," she confessed. "I'm so glad it worked out for you. You have a golden opportunity to start all over again now John, don't waste it. You're young and just starting out in the world and you have so much potential." She cupped his face in her hands. "Please be careful out there, OK?" He stared into her eyes.

"I will Jenny. Scouts honor." After a reassuring smile, he turned and walked away.

Jenny removed a small photograph of Dave from her purse and stared at it. She rubbed a piece of lint from the image, put it to her lips and kissed it before turning and heading in the direction of home.

EIGHTEEN MONTHS LATER

The woman sat on the beach, a large parasol casting a shadow and a towel spread out over the hot sand. She had always liked the Canary Islands with their contrasting landscapes, from volcanic rock to lush green pastures and it seemed like the perfect place to retire to when things calmed down. The hot sun and cool breeze were the polar opposite to the life she had led in the UK with rain battering down almost constantly; freezing cold days and nights in winter. *This*, she thought, *is where I want to be forever.* She had plenty of money in the bank and would never need to work again; the bags of cash saw to that. Suddenly her mobile phone rang. She had been expecting the call and recognized the number instantly.

"Hello Julio, how are you? "The voice on the other end spoke back in broken, but understandable English.

"Yes, that's correct," she replied to his questions, "yes...yes, a two-bedroom apartment. It's for my son, he's coming out here to live permanently."

"And his full name, Madame?" Asked the caller.

"Of course, of course, it's John Davis... John Andrew Davis."